## NO TALK, ALL ACTION

Dave was almost alongside Frank Ivey when Red Cates half came around and drawled, "Hear your boss lit a shuck. You'll have to get a new sucker to pay for your drunks now, booze-head."

Dave regarded him, said quietly, "I'd go careful, Red."

Red glanced over at Ivey. "Sounds like Shipley, doesn't he?"

"No," Dave said gently. "He just talked."

"So do you."

Dave hit him. With his open palm he batted Cates across the mouth, and then stood there, watching the surprise and fury wash into Cates' face.

"I don't even like to talk," Dave murmured.

# RAMROD
## LUKE SHORT

BANTAM BOOKS · TORONTO · NEW YORK · LONDON

*This low-priced Bantam Book
has been completely reset in a type face
designed for easy reading, and was printed
from new plates. It contains the complete
text of the original hard-cover edition.*
NOT ONE WORD HAS BEEN OMITTED.

RAMROD
*A Bantam Book / published by arrangement with
Macmillan Publishing Co., Inc.*

*PRINTING HISTORY*
*Macmillan edition published 1943
3rd edition through 1944
Bantam edition / February 1977*

ISBN 0–553–02984–3

*Published simultaneously in the United States and Canada*

*Bantam Books are published by Bantam Books, Inc. Its trade-
mark, consisting of the words "Bantam Books" and the por-
trayal of a bantam, is registered in the United States Patent
Office and in other countries. Marca Registrada. Bantam
Books, Inc., 666 Fifth Avenue, New York, New York 10019.*

PRINTED IN THE UNITED STATES OF AMERICA

# RAMROD

# CHAPTER I

DAVE NASH reined up and let the buggy pass ahead of him on the narrow road entering the switchbacks that finally let down into Signal's street. He noted indifferently that the lamp in Bondurant's store window below was the only light in town against the early dusk.

Riding behind the buggy in the thin acrid dust kicked up by the loafing team he wondered briefly if the man and the girl in the buggy knew there was no turning back now. He thought Connie Dickason knew it, and he had a fleeting admiration for the silence she had kept.

Walt Shipley put the buggy into the downgrade, and after that Dave thought nothing, only watched. There would be signs, if a man could read them, and he picked up the first one when the buggy leveled off abruptly at the head of Signal's main street. Two horses branded D Bar were tethered at the rack outside the blacksmith shop, the first building on the street. They shut off any retreat this way. That was enough; and Dave saw Connie Dickason turn her head and look obliquely at him, and he met her glance briefly, his sober face expressionless. She had seen too.

The buggy pulled up at the stone block in front of the hotel and Walt Shipley stepped down. He looked about him in the dusk almost covertly, his glance raking the line of empty chairs on the hotel's veranda. Watching him, Dave thought, from a deep wisdom of

these things, *That's not the way it'll come,* and he
moved up, still mounted, and put a hand out to hold
the head-stall of the near horse.

Shipley, in his unaccustomed black suit that made
his movements self-conscious, handed Connie out of
the buggy and looked over at Dave. In his dark, reckless face was an uncertainty, and his eyes sought
Dave's.

"Put 'em up at Lilly's," he said.

Dave nodded, and still Shipley looked at him, and
Dave knew he was going to say something more and
was trying to find words that would be casual enough.

"You'll be around, won't you?"

"Sure," Dave said. "Sure."

His glance shuttled again to Connie Dickason, and
met hers briefly, and she looked away. *She knows,*
Dave thought. *From the time Walt picked her up today, she's known it was wrong. And she thinks I'll
help.* She was very small and very straight standing
there beside the block, and Dave raised a finger to his
hat brim, and led the team away.

He passed Bondurant's store now, and ahead of him
the lights of the Special saloon lay dimly across the row
of saddle horses ranked at the rail. He saw another
horse from D Bar, but none from Bell, and he speculated narrowly on that as he passed the saloon. Frank
Ivey was waiting to tip his hand, as a man does who
never brags.

The pattern was familiar, and as Dave pulled his
team into the dark runway of Joe Lilly's livery barn he
had a brief, gray moment of premonition. There was
nothing keeping him here except three weeks' wages
as an ordinary puncher and a kind of odd loyalty to a
man who had helped him. He could turn this team
over to Joe Lilly without a word and ride through the
runway and out the alley to the cross street and make
camp in the Federals tonight. He could put it behind
him that easily.

Instead he pulled up the team beside the feed corral
and dismounted, a tall, lean man in shabby range
clothes with a young face more taciturn than its years
warranted. There was a soberness about the straight

mouth that was unbending, and there was a suggestion of weathered gauntness in his freshly shaven face. He lifted off his saddle and turned his horse into the corral, and by that time Joe Lilly had come through the runway.

"Your boss come in, after all," Joe observed.

The deep-set eyes, curiously green and unreadable, looked at Lilly for an uncomfortable moment. "After all what?" Dave said quietly.

Joe didn't look at him. He said, "Nothin'," and went on to the team, and Dave turned into the runway.

"Say," Joe called, and Dave stopped and turned. "You owe me a week's feed bill."

"I haven't been paid yet."

"That's all right," Joe said. He seemed sorry he had mentioned it, and Dave went on through the runway.

The street was almost dark now, and the smell of pine pitch from the Federals bulking blackly across the Bench to the west seemed to steal along the street, mingling with the odor of hot dust and the faint ammoniac reek of the stable.

Dave paused, and fashioned a cigarette, aware suddenly of the remoteness of this place, of the strangeness of these people, and he turned up the street.

He saw Jim Crew, the sheriff, leave his dark box of an office opposite the saloon and cut across the road, angling toward him, and he slackened his pace.

Jim Crew was fifty, and not tall, and dry as an autumn leaf. There was a wintry chill in his gray eyes that the darkness hid now. He was also a friendless man, and for that reason Dave liked him.

Crew came up beside him and said, "Hi, boy," and looked up the street first before he faced Dave, who said "Hello." Neither of them spoke for a few moments, and then Crew said, "How do you feel now?" in a friendly voice.

"It took about a week, but I'm all right."

"That was a bat," Crew observed, without censure.

"I'll buy you a drink," Dave said. He saw Crew's head turn to look at him again, and he said, "No, I'm all right. A drunk like that once in a lifetime is enough. I just want to buy you a drink."

"I'd like one," Crew said.

Dave fell in beside him now, and they walked toward the Special in silence. He was thinking of the seven nights that Jim Crew had hauled him, stupid with liquor, from the Special to the small jail behind his office. Crew had never reproved him, never locked him in, only watched him, Dave remembered, with a deep and sober pity. Crew had sensed, without ever speaking of it, his need for oblivion that was almost necessary for life. On the eighth day Crew had come into his cell and roused him and said, "Can you ride?"

At Dave's nod, Crew tilted his head toward the door. "Circle 66 needs a hand. You better go out there. I told Shipley about you. Rest up for a couple of days." He had not once asked a question, and for that Dave was grateful. That was three weeks ago.

They turned in at the Special now, where a big poker game was going on at one of the rear tables. The bar to the left was deserted, with the bartender watching the game. They bellied up to the bar and Burch Nellis, seeing them, came over, wiping his hands on his dirty apron.

At sight of Dave, Burch looked at Crew as if to say, "Are we going through that again?" and Crew said, "All right, Burch. Whiskey." He was a slight man in a baggy black suit, and yet he had never spoken without making a man feel his authority, as Nellis felt it now.

Dave bought a couple of cigars, and he and Crew stood side by side with their drinks. Bald Burch Nellis put his plump elbows on the back bar and regarded Dave with his soft sly eyes. "You look some better."

"I feel better."

"I bet you do," Burch said agreeably. He grinned faintly and went back to observe the game.

Dave watched Crew in the back-bar mirror, noting the older man's restlessness, and he knew it was the prospect of this trouble shaping up that made him so. For trouble would naturally bring memories to Jim Crew. His was a name that, a decade ago, had been known briefly to every man in the West. He had rammed law down the throats of a dozen railroad and mining towns, and tales of his cold courage still lingered in men's minds. He was older now, burned out and tired and taciturn, and content with the oblivion of this remote sheriff's office, and yet this trouble had the power to disturb him now. Dave saw it and wondered when he would speak.

It came on the second drink, when Jim Crew looked up and surprised Dave watching him in the mirror.

Crew grimaced, his chill eyes holding a fleeting humor for only a moment. "Why'd he bring Connie with him?"

"I wondered, too."

"Can you get her out of town?"

Dave shook his head. "No. She wouldn't go."

Crew looked down at his drink, and he said softly, bitterly, "This is a stinking job." He raised his glance again. "You stay out of it."

"I work for him," Dave said.

"Three weeks. What do you owe a fool like that? Your life?"

"Maybe."

Crew sighed and said nothing.

Dave asked, "Ivey in town?"

"He don't play it that way," Crew said wearily. "Frank never bothered to scare a man."

Crew drank his whiskey then and put the glass down. "There's no chance of moving Connie out of town, you think?"

"Ask her."

Crew shook his head and said good-by and moved out into the street.

It was building up, Dave thought idly. It was the old, old pattern of pride, and a man could never leave it. If you worked for a man you fought for him, too, no matter if you thought he was a fool and didn't believe in him. Strangely, he was dead to the passion behind all this. He put a coin on the bar and went out into the night, and headed upstreet again.

At Bondurant's corner store he went in, but instead of turning toward the hardware side, he sought the other, where the household and dress goods lay ranked on counters and back shelves.

Martin Bondurant came toward him, his eyes polite

and curious, and, because he sold clothes and had never found that they made the man, he spoke courteously to this shabbily dressed puncher. "What can I do for you, sir?"

"I work for Walt Shipley, and I haven't drawn my wages. Is my credit good?"

"Certainly." Bondurant inclined his head.

"I want enough silk for a lady's dress," Dave said calmly.

Bondurant went behind the counter and pulled several bolts of goods down. Dave picked a blue silk that he did not know was moire, and watched Bondurant measure it. He accepted the wrapped package with a faint, pleased smile on his straight lips, and did not even look at the receipt Bondurant gave him.

On the street again, he retraced his steps, passing the Special and the livery and the weed-grown vacant lot beyond. It was full dark now, and he was almost at the end of Signal's business section, which covered an exact two blocks almost at the head of Signal Canyon.

There was a lone building ahead of him with a lamp burning by a window in the rear. Dave slowed his pace now and halted at the front door, which was flush with the boardwalk. He yanked the bellpull and heard its jangle in the rear. Idly now, he looked at the woman's hat on its lone stand in the window below the letters crossing the upper panes: Dresses & Millinery Made To Order.

Presently he saw the light approaching from a passageway in the rear of the small front room, and then it became steady, as if a lamp had been set on a table, and then the door opened.

"Evening, Rose," Dave said, and took off his Stetson.

"Dave Nash!" the girl exclaimed softly, pleased. Then she laughed, softly too, and said, "Come in."

Dave stepped inside and Rose Leland closed the door behind him. She turned to face him then, and smiled in friendly welcome. She was a girl of medium height, full bosomed, with pale hair so thick it was almost untidy. She was wearing an apron now over her house dress, and her sleeves were half rolled. Her mouth was full, friendly, and there was a humor in her brown eyes now as she regarded Dave, hands on hips.

"This is the female part of my house, Dave. Come on back where we can sit down." She went ahead of him, lifting the lamp from the table. Dave glanced briefly around the room, which had always made him uncomfortable. It smelled of dress goods, and was littered with remnants of them. Besides a long cutting table and a sewing machine, there were a couple of dressmaker's dummies, some chairs, a stack of hatboxes and nothing else in the room.

At the far end of the passageway, on one side of which lay a tiny bedroom, was the kitchen-living room, and this room was the house. It reminded Dave of a hundred ranch kitchens he had known—the big wood stove sharing the back wall with the sink and the pump, the big dining table with its scattering of chairs, the worn sofa and table against the opposite wall. Only the dark rug underfoot and the bright curtains at the windows were different.

Rose put the lamp on the dining table, and Dave saw he had interrupted her supper.

"Have you eaten, Dave?" she asked.

When Dave lied and said he had, Rose went over to the cupboard, saying, "Not so much you can't hold another cup of coffee."

She poured the coffee at the stove and set it on the table, and Dave sat down. Rose sank into her chair across from him and looked levelly at him. "How's the new job?"

"Better than the one I had drinking the Special dry," Dave answered.

Rose smiled faintly. "You didn't do a bad job of that."

"Where's Bill?" Dave asked. He poured cream from a can into his coffee and stirred it, watching Rose.

She shrugged. "You know Bill. He'll hang around town for a week drinking and playing poker and camping in my lap with some friend, and all of a sudden he's gone."

"Fiddle-footed," Dave murmured.

Rose looked thoughtfully at Dave. "Where'd he pick you up, Dave? He never said."

"I bought him a drink at the Special one morning.

We both had the same idea about taking care of some whiskey, so we stuck together."

"The only difference being," Rose said slowly, "that Bill Schell likes to drink and you don't."

"Not much," Dave agreed.

"You weren't having any fun," Rose said. "You worried me."

"No," Dave said tonelessly. He was silent a moment, looking around the room. "I remember Bill and I almost lived in this room for a week, Rose. Why didn't you throw us out?"

"Where would you have spent your time?"

"The Special. Anywhere. We wouldn't have been camping on you, anyway."

Rose smiled faintly. "But I liked it. You see, I have seven brothers, Dave. I like them—and I miss them. Men like you and Bill Schell hit town and you want a drink and a woman's company. Well, I like men, and I like them around. I like to feed them and I like their talk." She laughed shortly. "They make me forget that for weeks on end all I do is talk to women about dresses and hats. That's a fair exchange, isn't it?"

"Fair enough," Dave agreed. He reached for the package he had laid on the table and pushed it toward Rose, who looked inquiringly at him. "A present to a very good friend," he said.

Rose unwrapped the package. When she saw the thick silk, like some rich metal under the lamplight, she gave a wordless exclamation of delight and slowly lifted her gaze to Dave. "It's lovely, Dave—lovely!"

Dave felt the swift stab of memory that was like a pain, and Rose went on, "I've seen it at Bondurant's, and I wanted it so badly I dreamed about it." The rapture in her face abruptly vanished, and her eyes widened like a child's who has just remembered something unwanted. "But I can't take it."

The faint pleasure in Dave's green eyes died too, and Rose saw it. She leaned back in her chair and sighed.

"It's sweet of you, Dave, but I can't. Signal is just too small, and I've a reputation of sorts to keep." She smiled wryly. "Already, Martin Bondurant has told his wife about the expensive silk some puncher bought. When I come out with a dress of the same silk, what will she say? And tell?"

"I never thought of that," Dave said in a troubled voice.

Rose laughed then. "Bless you, I know you didn't. It would take a woman to think of it."

Dave grinned at her and shook his head, and they were silent a moment. Rose fingered the silk wistfully, her eyes upon it and yet not seeing it.

She said quietly, without looking at him, "You're a good man, Dave. Because you are, may I say something?"

Dave looked closely at her and nodded.

Rose said, "You're miserable. I would like to help you if I could."

Dave was silent, and his face grew hard under the weight of his thoughts, and when Rose saw it she shook her head swiftly. "I'm sorry. I didn't mean to pry."

Dave's eyes, soft and bitterly musing, focused on her now and regarded her a brief moment, and his straight mouth softened imperceptibly. "You're right, Rose. But it's all right now."

Rose smiled and looked at the silk again, stroking it. Then Dave began to speak, and she looked up at him as he said in a low voice, "There's no reason why you shouldn't know," and he looked gravely at her. "I lost my wife years ago, Rose. We had a son. He was six last month." His voice turned hard now, with an edge of stubbornness that was the measure of the task of telling this. "I was buyin' cattle in a small way, and I had to travel most of the time, so I left him with some people in town. While I was gone, their house burned. He was in it, sleeping, and they both died too, tryin' to get him out."

Rose didn't say anything. There was pity and understanding and a deep sadness in her eyes. She sat motionless, watching Dave. He reached in his shirt pocket and drew out his sack of tobacco and fashioned a cigarette and put it in his mouth. He fumbled for matches, which he could not find, and Rose came to her feet and crossed to the stove and brought back the big box of kitchen matches and laid them beside him.

Dave looked up at her, standing beside him. "That's why I wanted to thank you, Rose. The liquor wouldn't kill it, and Bill Schell's talk couldn't wipe it out. I think it was you, putting up with us, laughing and taking Bill's teasing and his talk and not asking me questions that did it. It's all right now."

Rose smiled sadly and went back to her chair. "I think, Dave, if you don't mind, I'd like the silk," she said softly. "Thank you for telling me."

Dave's glance raised to the clock atop the cupboard, and he noted the time with brief, somber attentiveness. Afterward he drank his coffee, listening pleasurably to Rose's talk. It took him back, this friendly low-pitched voice of Rose's, to a time that was dead for him, to the first months after his marriage with Ruth. He had managed a loan from the bank and had got his land and had built his shack, and Ruth was carrying his child. He would come in only when darkness drove him, bone-weary and wolf hungry, and when supper was finished he would sit thus, watching her, half-listening to her chatter of what she had done that day. At the time it was only pleasant, a man rightfully in his home; since Ruth's death, however, he had shut those memories from his mind with an iron will. And tonight, listening to Rose, he let himself remember, and strangely found no pain.

Presently he looked at the clock, and this time he rose. He stood, tall and lonely again, his brief pleasure ended, and Rose could see it.

She picked up the lamp and led the way to the street door and unbolted it.

Before she opened it, though, she turned to him and studied him searchingly. She said then, "You know the talk around town tonight, Dave?"

"Frank Ivey?"

Rose nodded and said, "I didn't want you to be surprised," and opened the door.

Dave said good night and went out, and Rose stood

in the door a minute, watching him until the night swallowed him up.

In the darkness now Dave halted, his attention not on the night. He was thinking of this girl, and the way she had told him of what lay ahead. Jim Crew, who had seen more death than a dozen ordinary men, could not have been more casual. There had been no pleading for carefulness, no fright, only a warning and a confidence unexpressed. She knew a man did what he had to do, and whether or not she liked it did not weigh with her.

He moved on again toward the scattered lights of the store and hotel and saloon, and now he felt a wary calmness. The stage was due in an hour, and beyond that time he did not speculate. He passed the livery stable and saw Crew in the darkened doorway of his office across the street watching the night, waiting for the men to fall into place, for the minutes to be spent.

In front of the Special he saw another figure come out of the darkness by the doorway, head turned in his direction, looking toward the sound of his footsteps.

It was Walt Shipley, and when he saw Dave he exhaled his breath sharply.

"Where you been?" he asked irritably. "I thought you'd gone."

"No," Dave said quietly.

Shipley looked over his shoulder up the street and then said restlessly, "Let's have a drink."

They went into the Special, where the poker game was still in progress. Walt got a bottle and glasses from Burch Nellis and led the way to one of the front tables. The players watched him covertly, saying nothing, and he knew they were watching. Seating himself, he thumbed his stiff new Stetson off his forehead and his glance restlessly roved the room. Dave, sitting slacked in his chair, watched him and thought bleakly, *He's spooking already*. Nothing in Walt Shipley's face gave him away, Dave thought, but it was there. Shipley was a dark man, perhaps in his late twenties, with restless, bold black eyes in his long face. He had a drive about him that would not let him rest, and it had reached into his very soul and turned into ambition. He was generous and impulsive, Dave had learned in the three weeks he had worked for him; he had a temper that flared like powder and died as quickly, but the bedrock of his nature Dave had never seen. He thought Connie Dickason, the girl Walt was going to marry, had seen it and become uneasy. They would both see it tonight, anyway.

Shipley shuttled his bold glance to Dave and said, "He's not here, is he?"

"No," Dave said.

"He won't be, either," Walt said brashly.

Dave didn't answer, and Walt stared unswervingly at him. "You think he will?"

"Yes."

Walt flushed a little and said, "I saw those two horses from D Bar. One is Red Cates', Connie said. Red won't move without Frank, and I haven't seen a Bell horse in town."

"That's right," Dave said pleasantly.

Walt said, suddenly bitter, "You seem pretty damn sure he'll be here."

Dave shrugged slowly. "I've seen Frank Ivey."

Walt said, "Ah-h-h," softly, contemptuously, and poured himself another drink. Dave's drink stood untouched and Walt, spying it, looked at Dave with frank curiosity. "Tell me," he said, "are you afraid of booze now?"

Dave looked at him and then at the drink, and then picked up the whiskey and drank it. He had forgotten it was there.

Walt laughed then, his lips breaking swiftly, his teeth white and even. "That's an answer."

He leaned back now, his face altering into soberness, and regarded Dave carefully. "You know, you're a queer one, Nash," he said slowly. "Damned if you aren't. Don't anything ever excite you?"

"No," Dave said.

"Can't you talk?"

Dave grinned faintly. "Not very good."

"Well, you're lucky," Walt said, his tone suddenly wry, and he did not need to explain himself. Long

since, Dave had learned that Walt Shipley placed no
value on words; he spoke off the top of his mind, and
much of his life had been spent backing those words up.
He was backing them tonight, but he was no longer sure
of himself. That doubt was eating at him steadily, driving him to a new restlessness. He poured himself another drink and tilted the bottle inquiringly toward
Dave, who shook his head in refusal. Shipley took his
drink and coughed once from the rawness of it, and
then said, without looking at Dave, "Connie's over at
the hotel. She wants to see you."

Dave was silent a moment, hiding his surprise. Connie Dickason had never spoken with him, other than to
pass the time of day. He had been just one of the three
hands working for Circle 66, the object of more than
passing curiosity for a few days, because of the circumstances under which he had been hired. A deep caution
stirred in Dave. "Why?" he asked.

"She's got a notion I'll need help." His sardonic
glance shuttled to Dave. "Don't scare her, but go see
her, will you?"

Dave rose reluctantly and went out. His pace toward
the hotel was slow, and once, beyond Bondurant's store,
he halted. This was not a woman's quarrel, and she
should not even be in town, and he did not want to talk
to her. The pattern of this was as old as life, and nothing she could say would change it.

However, he went on, an odd resentment stirring
within him. The hotel lobby, with its dozen deep leather
chairs, was deserted; from the hotel saloon next door,
joined to the hotel by a connecting door, came the slow
murmur of voices.

Dave went to the desk and looked at the register and
went upstairs. At the head of the stairwell he knocked
on a door marked A, knowing it was the parlor and
bedroom suite which a cattleman invariably took for
his womenfolks while he was about town.

There was a short wait, and then the door was
opened by Connie Dickason. She stepped aside and said
quietly, "Come in, Dave."

Dave took off his Stetson and tramped into the room.
His black, short hair, only shades darker than the deep

brown of his face, was awry and somehow gave him, with his shabby calico shirt and levis, the appearance of a shiftless, taciturn puncher.

"Sit down, please," Connie Dickason said; and Dave sank into an upholstered chair by the table where the lamp stood. Connie Dickason sat down in a rocking chair facing him, and Dave watched her guardedly. He had, without wholly knowing it, a deep respect for this girl. It stemmed from her appearance; she was small, ramrod straight, and she had the unconscious pride of her size that Dave usually associated with a small man. If this pride bordered on arrogance, a man forgot it when he looked at her. She was truly beautiful, but the perfection of it was redeemed by flaws that made her the more charming. Her straight nose, for instance, was married by a few faint freckles that conjured up a picture of a tomboy. Her eyes were a green-blue that was really neither color, and her hair was as black and shiny as an Indians, with a wildly unruly curl. Dave had seen her wear the same dress four days running, so he knew she cared nothing about clothes, and yet she wore them like a princess, and D Bar, her father's outfit, was prosperous and freehanded. It was these small things and something else—a genuine sweetness in her speech, a character in her every movement, and a kind of shyness in her rare smile—that formed Dave's respect. And this very respect bred a caution now as he watched her lean forward in her chair and, manlike, put her elbows on her knees and lace her fingers together.

"Let's get a lot of lumber out of the way, shall we, Dave?" she began. "First, you look like a bum and you were drunk like a saloon rowdy, and you're indifferent to what anyone thinks of you—but you're not a bum. I know that, so you don't have to pretend."

Dave crossed his legs uneasily, and a fleeting humor touched his face and he said nothing.

"You're the only one that's stuck by Walt. Did you know Leach and Harvey quit Circle 66 today? Walt didn't send them anywhere, like he told you. They quit."

Dave nodded, unsurprised.

"You're the only hand left. Why didn't you leave?"

"He helped me when I needed it."

Connie nodded imperceptibly. "That's what I wanted to know." She rose and walked slowly to the window that looked out on the veranda roof and the dark street. She stood there a moment, and then turned to Dave. "You've got to help me, Dave."

Dave didn't speak.

"Walt thinks Frank Ivey was bluffing when he said he would never let Walt take that stage tonight. Do you?"

"No."

"What are you going to do?"

Dave shook his head slowly. "Nothing."

"You've got to."

Dave's voice was almost irritable. "You don't understand it. Walt says he's going to bring sheep into a country. He says it in a saloon to a bunch of tough cattlemen. He tells them the day he's going out to buy the sheep and he dares any one of them to stop him, and Frank Ivey says he will." He paused, watching Connie. "The day comes to go out. He either goes or he doesn't go. There's nothing any man can do about that. The wrong is already done."

"What wrong? Sheep?"

"No." His voice became dry now and he still watched Connie. "If I wanted to bring sheep into a country I would bring them in. I would not dare a man to stop me. Neither," he added bluntly, "would you."

"No," Connie said softly. She came back to the table and regarded him, her eyes thoughtful. "What will happen? How many will there be?"

"I saw a couple of D Bar horses downstreet. That means your Dad has given his men the sign?"

"No," Connie said immediately. "That's Red Cates and Will Owen. They'll stay clear." She hesitated. "I told Dad if a D Bar man got in this trouble tonight, I would never set foot in his house again."

"Then Frank Ivey," Dave said.

"Alone?"

Dave nodded and came to his feet, and Connie walked around the table to him. She stood close to him, looking up into his eyes. "Will you back Walt up?"

"I work for him," Dave said simply.

He saw the swift relief mount in her eyes, and she stepped back. "Thank you, Dave."

He nodded to her and tramped over to the door and had his hand on the knob when Connie said quietly, "Dave." He paused, and she stepped beyond the lamplight, so that her face was in darkness.

"What if Walt does—take the stage? What if he brings in sheep?"

Dave smiled narrowly. "He won't have to bring them in. If he makes the stage tonight, he'll own the Bench."

She didn't say any more and Dave turned the knob. A sound in the street, faint but distinct, came to him, and he listened. It became clearer then, and he recognized the sound. It was the stage, pulling in from West Station at the end of its long haul through the Signal Breaks to the east. It would pass the hotel and pick up fresh teams at Joe Lilly's, and then come back to the hotel for its passengers before it climbed the grade, crossed the Bench and moved on over the Federals.

Connie Dickason heard it too; she went to the window to look out and Dave stepped out into the hall, closing the door behind him. Connie Dickason, he thought idly, was a tough girl. She had cut old Ben Dickason, her father, out of this fight tonight with an ultimatum that he could not accept. She had tried to give Walt Shipley courage by her very presence. And, finally, she had made sure of his own loyalty, had extracted his promise, which would not have been necessary, that he would back up her man. A woman could not do any more for a man except fight his battles for him, Dave thought, and he admired her.

Going down the short stairs then, he knew that, whether he liked it or not, his own fate lay irrevocably for the next few minutes at the mercy of Walt Shipley's unstable temper, and he accepted it tranquilly.

For young Walt Shipley was hungry, and he couldn't wait. He'd got Connie Dickason, so he'd have D Bar some day. But his own small spread edging into the rich grass of Signal Bench was not enough; he looked about him at the big outfits like D Bar and Frank Ivey's Bell and he schemed, and all the time he did not see that the big outfits were only tolerating him because he was small. But because he was going to marry Ben Dickason's girl he had demanded equality, and when it was refused, he had threatened to bring in sheep. It was his bid for a big chunk of the Bench, since sheep and cattle would not mix. No man who had heard him was his friend after that, and it had taken Frank Ivey to put their dislike into words. That was two weeks ago. Tonight, he must make good his brag, and Dave, like it or not, was backing him.

The lobby seemed empty as he stepped down into it, but in the far shadows at the corner window he made out the stooped figure of the hotel clerk watching the street. Other people, behind other windows, were watching too, afraid and excited and safe.

Stepping out into the gloom of the veranda then, he put his back against the wall and reached for his tobacco. A minute afterward, Walt Shipley crossed the side street and came up the hotel steps. He saw Dave in the darkness and grunted and went on in.

Dave's attention narrowed now, and he stepped up to the veranda railing and looked down the street. In the shadows of the sheriff's dark office he saw a movement, and he knew this was Jim Crew biding his time, impersonal as death. A handful of men from the Special were drifting across the road to the deep black of some cottonwoods where there was a horse trough.

His glance traveled upstreet now, and after long seconds of peering into that gloom, the shape of a man suddenly took form. He was standing at the end of the boardwalk where it petered out into the thick dust around the blacksmith shop, his shoulder against the corner of the building. His shape was blocky and implacable and somehow patient as an Indian's. Frank Ivey was a man of his word.

Dave faded back into the half-light of the veranda again, this time on the other side of the door, and finally touched a match to his cigarette.

The stage, with its fresh teams, came out from Lilly's, passed the side street and then drew up by the stepping block.

The driver, primed by Joe Lilly's gossip, glanced uneasily at the veranda and then, his foot on the brake, yelled, "Bice!"

It could have been prearranged, but Dave thought not. At the mention of his name, the clerk scurried out the door and down the steps, Walt Shipley's valise in his hand. He passed it wordlessly to the driver and scurried back up the steps and into the safety of the lobby. The whole action did not take fifteen seconds, and Dave smiled faintly around his cigarette.

There was a bare moment of silence again, broken only by the stage team's impatient jangling of their bit chains, and then the solid warning of Walt Shipley's footsteps crossing the lobby.

Dave moved a little away from the door, and Walt came out. He paused just outside the door and saw Dave and said softly, "All right," and then they both saw Jim Crew at the same time. He was angling across from his office to the hotel at a leisurely pace.

Walt watched Crew with still curiosity. He started to move, stopped, and then, his will sufficient, he went on and down the steps.

At the same time Dave's glance shuttled to the edge of the veranda upstreet.

In less than a second, Frank Ivey's blocky body moved out of the shadow toward the stage.

Walt Shipley saw him and halted, and Ivey halted too. Ivey spoke, his voice toneless. "Made up your mind, sheepman?"

Shipley stood in the middle of the broad boardwalk. By this time Jim Crew, walking slowly, was on the walk too, and he came up behind Walt and climbed the steps and turned and waited.

"I'm going," Walt said. His voice was not in its normal register; a kind of wildness made it sing.

"No," Frank Ivey said.

Dave moved away from the wall, and at the same time he flipped his cigarette away from him. It arced out onto the boardwalk and fell at Frank Ivey's feet, a plain warning of Dave's presence. Frank Ivey said, "I see you, Drunk," and he turned his head, tilting it up a little to see Dave, and a brief dim light from the lobby

touched it. It was a cold square face and might have
been blocked out of granite, and the arrogance of its
full jowls and broad, thin-lipped mouth was regal. The
gesture of looking at Dave held a magnificent contempt,
as if what Walt Shipley might do when Ivey's attention
was diverted was not worth consideration. The man,
Dave thought narrowly, did not know fear.

Placidly, almost, Ivey turned his head to regard Walt
again. His massive shoulders moved a little under his
black coat, and he did not speak. The silence ribboned
on, until it was almost unbearable, and Dave knew
swiftly that it would have to break soon.

And then Walt Shipley said, in hot anger, "Listen,
Frank! You ain't God! You can't keep a man off a
stage!"

Dave felt a slow sick shame flood over him. It was
over. Walt was not going, and those hot, angry words
held a sentence he would never escape as long as he
lived.

Frank Ivey knew it was over, too; he said calmly to
the stage driver, "Throw down his valise, Harry. He
ain't goin'."

Jim Crew turned away then and went down the walk
and out into the road. He, too, knew it was over. The
driver, as if waiting for Jim Crew to pull out, tossed
Walt's bag to the boardwalk. He hesitated for one brief
second, then kicked off his brake and whistled shrilly
to his horses, and the stage pulled away toward the
grade.

Frank Ivey turned and walked back in the direction
of the blacksmith shop, his broad back to Walt Shipley.
He had dismissed Walt from his mind.

Walt Shipley stood irresolute for a moment longer,
then mounted the steps and walked past Dave into the
lobby. He did not look to either side of him, but headed
swiftly for the stairs.

A remote sadness stirred within Dave. An ordinary
man could hide his weaknesses from his fellow men
by a decent silence, but Walt Shipley's weakness lay
naked now before all men; it would ride him until it
killed him. And it would kill him surely, Dave knew,
for Walt Shipley was a coward.

Wearily, then, Dave went into the lobby and the clerk came up behind the desk. They did not look at each other, as if the shame of watching this was somehow unspeakable.

"Twelve suit you?" the clerk said.

"Sure."

Dave took the key and went upstairs. Connie Dickason's door was closed, and Dave speculated on that. Had Walt gone to her, who was stronger than himself?

His room was on the front corner, small and hot and dark. He closed the door and did not light the lamp, but crossed to the windows and opened them, and threw his hat on the washstand.

He paced once to the other window and then lay down on the bed and slowly fashioned a cigarette and lighted it. His time was up here, he knew. He owed Walt Shipley nothing, having paid his debt tonight. And if he remained he would be buying into a quarrel he had no heart for, a quarrel that was basically senseless. For nothing is more private than ambition; a rare man could share it and fire other men with his own, but Walt Shipley was not that man.

Dave began to speculate with a faint interest as to Walt Shipley's failure and its causes and he thought he understood them. The direct cause, of course, was Shipley's tongue; he had made a wild brag he could not back up.

After tonight, this country would turn on him, as both strong men and strong dogs turn on a proved weakling. They would trump up prior claims to his grass and his water, and his few cattle would vanish, and all the time they would bait him with a patient cruelty. Some day, Walt would decide he had taken enough, and on that day he was dead. So were the men with him.

Dave put his cold cigarette on the marble-topped washstand and sat up on the edge of the bed. Tomorrow he would drift. It didn't matter where, because he was rootless and one place was like another. He'd used up his luck and he'd made his fool drunken protest to whatever gods there were, and he was as right as he ever would be.

Rising now, he walked to the window and stood looking at the night. The street below him lay almost in darkness. He had lived through his own private hell in this town and had come out of it, and in doing it he had made some friends. But Jim Crew didn't need him, and Rose would forget him. Connie Dickason had got what she wanted out of him, which he had given in payment for Walt Shipley's help. That left Walt, and he'd paid him back that debt. The slate was clean, and leaving would not be bad.

A man came out from the shadow of the veranda below, heading downstreet. Dave followed his progress with a sleepy half attention, and then he came alert. He studied the figure closely, and then knew it was Walt Shipley. He stood there a full five seconds, speculating and rejecting. Shipley wouldn't hunt up Ivey, who was probably at the Special, for a shoot-out. It would take longer than this for him to get his nerve back.

Dave turned, swept up his hat and stepped out into the corridor. On the dark street below, he walked swiftly past Bondurant's, and when he came to the Special, he moved close to the window. It was a big, many-paned window whose lower half was painted an opaque white.

Standing on tip-toe, he looked over the painted section. Ivey and Red Cates, D Bar's foreman, and Ed Burma, Ivey's foreman, were all standing at the bar, and the poker game in the rear had been resumed. Everything was serene.

Dave looked downstreet and then went on. He was almost to the entrance of the livery barn when he heard the booming racket of a horse coming toward him on the runway.

Fading back into the deep shadow of the building, he waited a moment and presently Walt Shipley, riding a livery horse, came out.

He did not turn toward the grade, which was the way home to Circle 66. He turned south, and presently, when he was in front of Rose Leland's millinery shop, he lifted his horse into a canter and vanished south into the night.

It occurred to Dave then that maybe he had missed

the measure of Shipley's determination. Perhaps Walt was going out for the sheep after all. And then Dave knew that was unlikely, and he turned back toward the hotel.

Connie Dickason, he knew then, was not going to have a husband soon.

# CHAPTER II

THE morning came cold and gray. Dave got his breakfast at a restaurant down the cross street, which held a harness shop, a lumber yard, the bank, Bondurant's big warehouse, and a barber shop before it petered out into a clutter of small shacks that stretched almost to Feather Creek and the far wall of the canyon.

Afterward, Dave picked up the team and buggy at Lilly's, hitching them himself, and drove over to the hotel. Tying the team at the hitchrail, he came up to the veranda and took a chair in the corner, and was smoking his second cigarette and watching the morning traffic of the town when Connie Dickason came out.

Dave rose. She saw him and came over to him and said good morning. He observed her, and a slow shock came to him; she was deathly white, and as she sat down in the chair next to his own he saw that her face was utterly lifeless, without any expression at all.

He was still standing some moments later when she looked up at him, and her gaze was so searching it made Dave uncomfortable.

She said finally, "Walt's gone. You know he is, don't you?"

Dave nodded. She reached in the bosom of her dress and brought out a piece of paper and handed it to him without comment.

Dave opened it and read:

*Connie, that's the kind of a beating I can't take. The*

*outfit was made over to you long ago. Take it, and luck.
Forget me. Walt.*

He folded it and handed it back to her, and she said
"Well?" and he knew suddenly that he must shock her
out of this. It seemed to him that only a thin thread of
will kept her from going to pieces, and he said roughly,
"What did you expect him to do?"

"Marry me!" Connie countered passionately, bitterly.
"Not stick a note under my door and run!"

The anger brought some color into her cheeks, but
the cold mask of her face did not change. She regarded
the street now, her eyes musing and bitter. Dave sat
down on the veranda railing, watching her guardedly,
wonderingly.

"He wasn't hard enough," Connie said finally. "I
made a lot of excuses for him last night, but this is the
only truth. He wasn't hard enough." She glanced up at
him. "Was he?"

"No."

"And I am," Connie said coldly.

Dave didn't say anything, but he felt an acute unease.
This wasn't the soft, sweet Connie Dickason that the
whole Bench loved—or was it? He recalled last night,
and how Connie had maneuvered several men, includ-
ing himself, into positions that would help Walt Shipley. She was right; she was hard.

"I'm hard enough," Connie announced grimly, "to
beat my Dad and Frank Ivey both, and I'm going to."

Dave shifted his feet, faintly embarrassed, and his
movement brought her glance around to him. "I want
you to work for me, Dave."

"Work for you?" Dave asked blankly.

"I'm through with D Bar," Connie said flatly. "I've
only wanted one thing in my life, and that was Walt
Shipley. My father, with Frank Ivey, took him from
me. All right, I can fight too. I'm going to take Circle
66, and I'll make it into an outfit they'll have to respect.
I want you to run it."

"No," Dave said immediately.

"Why not?"

"You're not thinkin' straight," Dave murmured.
"Ben Dickason and Frank Ivey didn't take Walt away

from you. They're fightin' sheep, like any cattleman.''

"Frank Ivey has asked me to marry him once a month for two years. Dad wanted me to marry him. And if Dad wasn't against my marrying Walt, why didn't he help him long ago?'' Her eyes were blazing with anger, but her voice was soft and controlled.

"After last night, you think he was wrong about Walt?''

"I don't think that matters. What does is that any man I choose will be broken by my father and Frank Ivey. They're big enough and they'll find a reason like they found sheep a reason to break Walt. They hope that some day then I'll turn to Frank and marry him.''

Dave was silent, no longer surprised at her cold passionless anger, and Connie went on. "I won't let them do it. I've got some money left me by my mother—enough to pay a woman to stay with me and buy some cattle and hire a crew.'' Her voice altered, taking on an edge. "When I get through with them, they won't be able to break anybody.''

The sound of a rider in the street made them both glance in that direction. A big man on a big dun pulled up at the tie rail. It was D Bar's foreman, Red Cates, and he touched the brim of his Stetson with a finger, and said, "You want me to drive you out, Connie?''

The word had got around then, Dave thought, but Connie's pleasant voice did not betray any knowledge of it. "I'll drive out alone, Red. Thanks.' '

Red Cates' glance shifted briefly to Dave. He had a long, heavy-boned face, with a great beak of a nose bisecting it, and there was the faintest of thin, sly smiles on his face as he nodded and pulled his dun around and started back for the Special.

Dave surprised Connie watching Red, a hard amusement in her eyes. "Red, too,'' she murmured. "Red especially.'' She straightened up suddenly and said briskly, "What about it, Dave?''

"No,'' Dave said quietly. "If I can draw my wages from you today, I'm drifting.''

"Why?''

"It's not my fight.'' Dave shook his head. "You want a man that don't give a damn.''

Connie looked searchingly at him. "And you do? I don't believe it, because I watched last night from the lobby." She stood up, and Dave rose too. "It's too bad, because we'd make a pair. You tell Mr. Bartholomew at the bank I said to give you your wages." She put out her hand, which, when Dave took it, seemed small and warm and dwarfed in his own. "If you change your mind, come back. As long as I have 66 you'll have work—but not if you give a damn."

She went into the hotel, and Dave watched her straight proud walk. *She's an Injun, and she's headed for trouble,* he thought, and, oddly, he admired her. She had taken her beating without flinching, but she was going to fight back. Walt Shipley had been only the deciding factor in her decision, and the logical coldness with which she planned revenge was the measure of her spirit.

Dave went down the steps to the corner. He saw Jim Crew crossing the street to the Special, and he waved and Crew waved back. Turning down the cross street toward the bank, he looked at the town with that feeling close to nostalgia which a man feels for a place that has witnessed a turn in his life. Signal was a drab little cow town, and yet it was more than that. He thought of Connie's offer, turning it over once more in his mind. No, it wasn't for him. Some obscure, unexpressed code of ethics had never let him admire a man who fought without passion behind him. And Signal Bench, after helping him, had let him alone. Even Frank Ivey's cold epithet last night could be forgotten; a man up against three other men did not have to choose his words.

At the bank Dave received his pay, and came back and crossed the street to Bondurant's store and settled his bill for the dress goods.

Again he was on the main street, and now he remembered Jim Crew, to whom he would say good-by. He turned into the Special and saw several men at the bar, among them Red Cates and Frank Ivey and Ivey's foreman, Ed Burma. Jim Crew stood at the bend of the bar at its far end hunched over a drink. Burch Nellis was busy behind the bar, and when he looked up Dave nodded to him and Burch said "Howdy."

Dave passed a couple of men at the head of the bar and was almost alongside Frank Ivey when Red Cates, next to Ivey, half came around and drawled, "Hear your boss lit a shuck."

Dave halted and laid his slow gaze on Red Cates. Frank Ivey looked over his shoulder at him, his bold dark eyes arrogant and amused.

"Did he?" Dave asked.

Cates looked at Ivey and grinned and glanced back at Dave. "You'll have to get a new sucker to pay for your drinks now, booze-head."

Dave regarded him mildly, said quietly, "I'd go careful, Red."

Red glanced over at Ivey and grinned. "Sounds like Shipley, don't he?"

"No," Dave said gently. "He just talked."

"So do you."

Dave hit him. With his open palm he batted Cates across the mouth, and then stood there, watching the surprise and fury wash into Cates' face.

"I don't even like to talk," Dave murmured.

For a still second, Red Cates stood rooted, his hand rising to his face in reflex action, and then he lunged at Dave in blind rage. They met with an impact that shook the room, and Dave slashed savagely at Red's midriff. Red's impetus carried them both back, and then Dave wheeled to one side and Red, still going, fell to his hands and knees on the floor.

He came up, cursing, and Dave, hands at his sides, watched him coolly. Red came in slugging then, swinging great, rounding wild blows. Dave stepped inside his swing and hit Red once in the face, and then Red's fist hit him in the neck. Red opened his hand and gripped Dave's neck and spun him around and away from him. The chair tripped Dave and he went over backward into the table and upset it. A cascade of cards and chips showered down over him, and he scrambled to his feet, and this time he went in. It was a cold, savage stalking, and Red hit him twice in the head, and Dave took the blows, and when he was close enough he slashed Red in the face with a turning, driven fist. Red's head went back and Dave hit him again in the face, and again, and then Red's knees folded. He wrapped his arms around Dave's waist and hugged him to keep from falling, breathing in great sobs of air.

Dave brought up his knee savagely in Red's chest, and still Red hung on, and now Dave buried a hand in Red's copper-colored hair and pried his head back and then drove a wicked, down-driving smash into Red's face. He felt the shock of the blow across his knuckles and he felt Red's nose mash under his hand, and then Red's hold loosened. Dave stepped back, and Red, with nothing propping him up, dropped on his face. The sound of his head rapping the floor was a dull heavy sound, and a man back at the bar cried out involuntarily.

Red did not move, and Dave stood watching him, feet planted wide apart, breathing deeply. It was apparent to every man in that room that Red Cates, from the moment he lunged at Dave, had never had a chance, and that knowledge held them mute.

Dave's wintry glance lifted to Frank Ivey, and they looked at each other a long moment.

Frank said, "A man would never do that to me."

"Or me," Dave said.

Ivey pushed away from the bar and came over to stand above Red. His blocky body was motionless, save for the foot with which he tried to toe Red over and failed. His gaze, bold and speculative, rose to Dave now, and his square stubborn face, brown and smooth and underlaid with heavy muscle, altered faintly into a curiosity.

"You joined up with the wrong outfit," he murmured. "That's a pity."

"Why?"

"Because it's too late now. You're drifting."

"Am I?"

"Yes," Ivey said calmly. "We decided that. No man who ever worked for an outfit that talked sheep is hired here. We told Leach and Harvey. So now you go too."

"When I'm ready."

Ivey shook his head. "Remember," he said mildly,

and turned to two of the men at the bar and demanded help in a quiet, imperative voice.

Dave picked up his Stetson and put it on and tramped out of the bar. Stopping on the boardwalk just beyond the door, he laid his glance along the street and gingerly felt his knuckles. He heard a man come out of the saloon behind him, and also heard the footsteps cease, and he looked back over his shoulder to find Jim Crew, shoulder against the door jamb, watching him. Crew's chill gaze held a feeling Dave remembered. He had seen it before, when Jim Crew had put him to bed those nights, and it was pity. It angered Dave now and deepened a growing obstinacy within him.

"That's one way to make a man take out a home-stead here," Dave murmured.

"But there's lots of country other places," Crew observed.

"You too?"

"Oh, no," Crew said quietly. The look of pity was still there. "It would just save trouble," he murmured.

"Who for?"

"Both of us."

Dave said, "Well, you get paid," and turned, but not toward the livery stable. The buggy he had brought up to the hotel was still there, and he headed for it.

Approaching the veranda he saw Connie Dickason coming down the steps, and when she saw him something in his bearing made her pause. She stood on the second step, and Dave came up to her and stopped and said, "That job still open?"

Connie nodded.

"You got a foreman," Dave said.

# CHAPTER III

Dave took the grade road out of Signal, and presently, a mile or so beyond, he left it and headed out across the flats toward the Federals. Later in the morning, when he had achieved the foothills, he stopped to blow his horse and looked back at the Bench. Its rich carpet of grass, the edges ragged where the black foothills timber knifed into it, stretched deep to the south. Over against the foothills, in the direction of Frank Ivey's Bell, a tall dust-devil reeled slowly into the foothills, and was broken. Ben Dickason's D Bar lay out of sight behind a tawny ridge that jutted deep into the Bench as far as American Creek, and lay between him and Bell; and over the ridge too, but far to the east, was Circle 66. This north end of the Bench was poor graze; from here a man could see why, for the grass lost its color even under the morning's gray sky and the land broke more sharply into mottled rocky upthrusts. This was the country of the small outfits like Circle 66, but there was this difference between them; a man could reach out here for miles, and get only a hardscrabble range. Circle 66, at the far end of the Bench, would reach out into the real grass that these ten-cow outfits would never have.

Dave put his horse into a walk again, and presently rounded a shoulder of bald rock and approached a shack and corrals beyond.

He found a nameless homesteader out by the pole

shed, declined the offer to light, and asked, "Seen Bill Schell?"

"He was by a week ago," the homesteader said. "Try Swatzel. He's got a girl Bill cottons to, I hear."

Deeper into the foothills, at a shack even more dilapidated than the first, Dave talked to a pretty girl who said, "I ain't seen him and don't want to," and went back into the house.

Dave kept on toward the Federals, and now he thought of the strangeness of his errand. This morning he had been ready to ride out of Signal to the east. A few spoken words, a brief violence, and his life was altered. Thinking of those words, he wondered at himself. He did not endow Red Cates' words with any meaning; the man was a bully, and had taken a bully's beating. But Frank Ivey's words were different. They ate at a man, and nagged at his pride, so that if he heeded them he could never rid himself of them. He could have laughed at Ivey's words and ridden out of Signal, and no man, save perhaps Jim Crew, would have remembered they were spoken. Yet they had touched him at a time when his pride was sore inside him. For he had considered himself a beaten man in these past weeks, and the discovery that he was not beaten, and that there was a new hope in him, was too new for him to accept Ivey's arrogance. He had acted with the unthinking anger of a man newly discovering freedom, and he was not sorry.

In midafternoon he was in the vaulting black timber of the Federals on a trail he was not familiar with. It would lead, however, as all trails in the Federals eventually led, to Relief. This was a settlement of five buildings buried in a clearing up close to the pass and off the stage road. It had started out as a summer meat camp for the Indians across the Federals, and once a stage load of travelers caught in an early blizzard in the pass had spent a week there and named it. A horse trader had put up a place afterwards and was hanged a year later after both the Indians and the Bench outfits discovered he was stealing from one and selling to the other with equal impartiality. Now it was the clearinghouse for all the business the Bench did not want to transact in the open, a furtive place where a man could buy a meal and a drink and a bed, and, if he was going through, a horse without an accompanying bill of sale. It was the sort of place, Dave knew, that Bill Schell would hit once a month in that restless, fiddle-footed way of his.

He came up on it in late afternoon. The gloom of the tall pines suddenly lessened, and then Dave saw the clearing ahead. A wagon road led past a log shack and a tangle of corrals whose poles were caved in and useless. Beyond it and across the road was a grayed two-story clapboard building that had never been painted, save for the faded letters of the legend Hotel across its false front. There was a log lean-to next to it which was the bar, and then the wagon road passed between a couple of good-sized barns and vanished south into timber again.

As Dave rode past the shack he saw a man who had been sitting on the hotel porch rise and go in.

He dismounted at the hotel and climbed the steps and went inside. The tiny lobby, holding a couple of broken-backed chairs and the desk in the corner under the stairs, was deserted.

Dave saw the door leading into the lean-to bar, and he tramped over to it, his footsteps echoing hollowly on the floor. Poking his head inside, he observed the man who had just stepped in now at the bar reading a newspaper. The room measured about twelve by fourteen, and held only the short bar and a big round table for cards.

The man, who was bald, looked up now from his paper and nodded, and Dave came up to the bar and said, "I'm lookin' for Bill Schell. Seen him?"

The bartender shook his head, and Dave regarded him carefully. He wore a vest over a collarless striped shirt that was a rich dirty gray at the cuffs and neckband. His face was thin and sallow, and he had a kind of bland gall in his eyes that was a barrier to a man trying to read his thoughts.

He said lazily, "Nope," in punctuation and went back to his paper.

Dave said mildly, "I'll have a look around."

"Go ahead," the bartender said indifferently, not even glancing up from his paper.

Dave was sure now that the man was lying, for what reason he did not know. He was sure, because the paper he was reading was much-read and soiled. It had probably been here a week, and yet the man seemed engrossed in it.

"Maybe you better come along," Dave suggested.

The man looked up swiftly, a bright anger passing in his eyes. "Maybe I better not, too."

Dave stood there undecided. Suddenly, the faint sound of shouted laughter came to him from deep in the hotel somewhere, and he smiled. That could only be Bill Schell. He turned back into the lobby, and heard a movement behind him as the bartender ducked out from behind the bar.

Dave, heading for the rear of the building, passed through the dining room and opened the door into the kitchen. He saw a big laughing Indian woman stoking the stove. Across the room, sitting in a chair back-tilted against the wall, was Bill Schell, hat shoved far back on his head, and he was grinning.

When he saw Dave the grin faded and for a moment he stared at him, his eyes startled. Then his chair came solidly to the floor, and he grinned again swiftly.

"Old Teetotal Nash," he drawled, brushing his hat back. "How are you, kid?"

He came out of the chair with a lazy grace and delightedly shook hands with Dave. His levis were patched and faded and he was wearing a blue wash-bleached shirt whose left arm was a faded khaki color. Some ranch woman had taken pity on his raggedness, using the only materials she had at hand to fix his sleeve. He was a slim young man, not tall, with a gay, handsome face burned a near black by the sun. His dark eyes looked past Dave now, and suddenly he burst into laughter. Dave turned to see the bartender, a shotgun slacked in his left hand, standing just outside the door.

"Georgie, this is a friend of mine, Dave Nash. He's all right."

George gave a taciturn nod and faded back into the

dining room. Bill regarded Dave closely, memory of the
week they had spent in Signal bringing a grin to his
face, and he said, "You're off the reservation, kid."

Dave said, "Let's go outside," nodding toward the
back door. A sudden interest flickered in Bill's dark
eyes and he led the way out onto the sagging back
porch. Dave sat down on the top step and Bill stood
beside him, looking down at him. There was an open-
ness about Bill Schell that few people could resist.
Now, for instance, his eyes showed a real affection for
Dave and he did not trouble to hide his feelings.

He said, "You son of a gun, what did you want to go
to work for? I've missed you."

He sat down now alongside Dave, who took out his
sack of tobacco and proffered it to Bill, who accepted it.

Bill rolled a smoke and gave the sack back, and
Dave took out a paper. He said, "You on the dodge,
Bill?" and looking at him, added, "I've got to know."

Bill laughed again. "George? No. It's nothin' much.
I kissed a fellow's girl is all, and George thought you
might be him."

Bill lighted both their cigarettes and then Dave asked
quietly, "How'd you like a job, Bill?"

Bill's cheerfulness faded from his face, and he
groaned. "You come up here for that? I still got some
money. What do I want to work for?"

"There's a fight in it."

Bill's interest quickened. "Yeah?"

"Connie Dickason," Dave said mildly, "is out to beat
Ben—and Frank Ivey."

Bill's expression was one of puzzlement, and Dave
told him what had happened in Signal. He told of Walt
Shipley's ignominious flight, and Connie's bitter decision to seek revenge.

Bill listened with a rapt attention, and when Dave
was finished, he looked off across the yard at the stack
of wood by a far shed. "What else?" he said.

"That's all."

"You ain't fightin' for pay," Bill said calmly. "Me,
I'd do it if I had the notion, but not you."

"No," Dave agreed, and he told of the fight with Red
Cates in the saloon, and of Frank Ivey's calm warning.

When he had finished he glanced over at Bill and found him grinning.

Bill said dryly, "You got a notion Ivey can't run you out, and you're stickin'. Is that it?"

Dave nodded and Bill was silent, turning this over in his mind. Dave had said all he was going to say, and yet he wanted Bill Schell, for he knew the man's breed. He was shiftless and unreliable and cheerful, and more than half Indian in his thinking and his ways, but he was not afraid of God or man. His loyalty, Dave knew, couldn't be bought with money; but if something fired his imagination he would be as faithful as a dog. He knew the country like he knew his name, and beyond that he knew its politics and its shabby secrets. He was a born rebel with a hatred of towns and houses and men with too much power, a throwback to a freer time before money was everything.

Bill said suddenly, "Connie send you after me?"

"No."

Bill looked at him thoughtfully. "Then you're a shrewd man, friend Dave."

Dave, puzzled, said nothing and Bill smiled thinly. "Frank don't like me. I worry him. I have too much fun. I don't like him either. He makes too big tracks."

"Maybe he does," Dave agreed.

"Let's take him apart and see," Bill said, just as quietly.

"At my own time and under my orders, Bill," Dave said. "That's the way it's got to be. If it isn't, don't take the job."

Bill grinned and said, "That's the way it'll be, kid," and Dave knew this was Bill's promise. They smoked in silence for a moment, and then Dave said, "We'll need a couple more hands, Bill."

Bill laughed. "Hell, I know fifty men who'd work for nothin' just for a crack at Ivey."

"That's the kind I want. But they'll have to pass with Jim Crew."

Bill looked searchingly at him. "What's Crew got to do with it?"

"Crew," Dave said slowly, "is our blue chip. And we won't buy him with cheap gun hands siding us."

"But you want 'em tough?"

"Just so they get past Crew," Dave repeated.

Bill thought a moment and said, "How soon?"

"As soon as you can get them. And spread the word we'll be buyin' cows here at Relief in two days."

Bill nodded and rose and said, "I'll see you, kid," and vanished around the corner of the hotel. Dave got up and walked to the corner and saw Bill heading toward the corral, his thin whistle cheerful in the deepening dusk.

He had just made, Dave knew, the first move in a sequence whose end he could not see. The pattern was old, and he did not like it. You hired a hard-case crew because you were fighting a hard-case crew, and if you could channel that violence with an iron will, you won in the end.

He watched until Bill rode off in the dusk, and he knew now it was too late to turn back.

# CHAPTER IV

Connie drove into D Bar in midafternoon, and her buggy team, clattering across the bridge that spanned the creek running behind the house, brought young Link Thoms to the corner of the stone bunkhouse. Seeing Connie with the Mexican woman she had hired sitting beside her, Link cut across to the wagon shed and was waiting for them when Connie pulled up.

"Link, put Josefa's trunk in the buckboard," she ordered. "Where's Dad?"

"He's around somewhere," Link said. He was still in his teens, a slim, pleasant-faced young man who was D Bar's horse wrangler and who worshiped Connie with a blind and unreasoning loyalty. He helped Connie down and glanced curiously at the Mexican woman.

"Have a fresh team and the buckboard ready in an hour, will you, Link?" Connie said.

She didn't wait for Link's answer, but motioned for the Mexican woman to come with her, and started off toward the house.

The big house was a pleasant place, made so by Connie's mother, whom she barely remembered. It was of stone and log, and a gallery ran across the face of the stone two-story center section. Big cottonwoods overspread it. Connie's mother had left her mark on D Bar in two ways; she had made Ben Dickason put the bunkhouse and corrals and barns a comfortable distance from the house, and she had planted an orchard behind it that stretched down to the creek.

Connie went in the front door and straight up the stairs to her room, which looked out on the corrals and barns. It was a big room filled with big dark furniture and Connie waited until the Mexican woman came into the room, puffing from her climb up the stairs.

Connie pointed to a door in the far wall. "There's a big trunk in there. Get it out. You'll find my clothes in that wardrobe, and start packing them."

*"Sí señorita,"* Josefa said.

"You might just as well start calling me Connie," Connie said briskly. "Not Miss Connie, just plain Connie."

*"Sí señorita,"* Josefa said and then, remembering, "Connie."

Connie smiled and walked over to the window. She had been almost sharp with Josefa, and it was a true gauge of her impatience to be out of here. Since last night, after Walt had shoved the note under her door, when in the still hours she lay awake thinking of the future, she had known she was going to do this. She had thought it would take great courage, but she found it took very little. It was as if she had somehow shrugged out of her own skin, and found that she was new, with none of the old ties and the old worries and the old fears. Even the loss of Walt did not mean much to her, except as a symbol of the point at which she had revolted. She was grateful to Walt, but she had not loved him, she knew now; she had promised to marry him because he would take her out of here, would give her surcease from the unending pressure that her father and Frank Ivey brought to bear on her. It had been a fool's escape, too, because Walt was a weakling, but Connie was wise enough to know that she was not the first woman who had grabbed a man in desperation without knowing him. The difference in her case was that she had found out soon enough, and, in finding out, had found herself. She could look at that deep-grained antagonism that lay between her and her father almost with humor now. He had beat her in one way, but in doing it he had unlocked her prison.

She cleaned the wardrobe of her clothes, piling them on the bed; and she hummed to herself, something she had not done in months. A quiet knowledge of strength made her want to sing.

At the dresser, she pulled out the drawers and began emptying them. Glancing out the window, she suddenly halted and watched. Off by the bunkhouse, she saw Red Cates' dun horse. There were three hands grouped around the bunkhouse door, and she wondered if her father was inside with Red. Red's beating would startle him, she knew, as it had startled her back in Signal. Dave Nash had not told her; it had been left to Jim Crew to inform her laconically that D Bar's foreman had taken an expert, wicked beating at Dave Nash's hands. She guessed then why Dave Nash had so suddenly changed his mind, so suddenly understood, without having to be told, what kind of crew she wanted, what kind of wages she was going to pay, and what for. It gave her a small glow of malice when she thought of it. She was deep in the packing of her things when, a half hour later, she heard the abrupt knock on her door and straightened up over the trunk.

"Come in, Pop."

Ben Dickason stalked into the room, a cold cigar in his mouth. At sight of the Mexican woman and the room in turmoil he halted and slowly took the cigar from his mouth. "What's this?" he asked blankly.

Connie was her father's daughter, for Ben was small, gone a little stout now, and he had an unconscious aggressiveness about his every movement. He had a roan mustache that he never bothered to trim, so that it was worn too full and gave him a faintly comic air that went not at all with his sharp blue eyes. His hair, of an indeterminate chestnut color, cropped close to his head, was combed once a day; ten minutes afterward, in his nervous energy, he contrived to muss it so thoroughly that it stood up like burr. His clothes carried out his general appearance; they were untidy and black and expensive, and half the time he wore a collar without a tie. He was wearing Congress gaiters, which constituted his riding boots too. Altogether, now, he had the appearance of a grizzled terrier who was seeing something he didn't understand, as he looked about the room.

"Going somewhere?"

"I'm moving out on you, Pop," Connie said quietly, and she went about her packing.

Ben Dickason moved over to the bed, felt of the goods in one of her dresses, and then said mildly, "Where?"

"Circle 66. I'm its mistress now."

Ben looked swiftly at her. "You mean you married him?"

"Oh, no," Connie said gently. "He couldn't stick it out. He'd made over the place to me when I promised to marry him. He just left it to me."

Ben started to say something and saw the Mexican woman. "You, Fatty, get out," he said curtly, nodding toward the door.

Connie said, "Go down to the kitchen and ask Anna for my laundry, Josefa," to the woman, who silently left the room.

Ben sat down on the bed then and said, "Now what is this?"

"Just what I said."

"You want a house of your own, is that it?"

"I want a ranch of my own—and I've got it."

"A ranch," Ben said blankly. "What do you call this?"

"Good old Pop," Connie said dryly. "If you want to get hit on the head with it, all right. I'm leaving you. I'm going to run the Circle 66. I'm taking the money Mother left me—I saw Bartholomew today about it, and he said you couldn't keep it from me, and I'm stocking Circle 66, and then I'm moving in on Bench grass, all of it I can hold."

Ben sighed, and said, "Now, what are you sore about?"

"My whole life," Connie said flatly.

"I'm old. You have to be plain."

"I will be," Connie said placidly. "You just keep on asking questions."

She went about her packing again, and Ben regarded her worriedly. "Are you hurt about that boy throwin' you over?" Ben asked.

Connie straightened up and laughed. It was real laughter, too, and Ben didn't like it.

"You have such a thoughtful way of putting it," Connie said finally. "He didn't throw me over. He just took a look at you and Frank Ivey and decided he didn't love me enough to die for me. I can't really blame him."

"Now Connie," Ben protested, "what kind of talk is that?"

Connie looked up swiftly. "The truth, Pop. He gave you a wonderful excuse, with that threat to bring in sheep. He was a fool, in a sweet way, and it was all you needed. You drove him out. He couldn't face you. And now you and Frank are right back where you started, both of you making muscles in front of me, hoping I'll be impressed enough to marry Frank. I'm not; I'm just clearing out."

Ben considered this a moment while he studied his cigar. "All right, all right," he said placatingly. "So you're going to run Circle 66. What will you use for grass?"

"I'll get it."

"Alone?"

"I've got a foreman, and I'll get a crew."

Ben looked interested. "Who's your foreman?"

"Dave Nash."

Surprise washed over Ben's eyes, and Connie, seeing it, smiled. "Like it?"

"So that's why he tangled with Red?"

"I doubt it," Connie said. "It was for a personal reason. But you won't run him out without a little trouble."

"So," Ben said slowly, softly, considering. "He'll get soused the day you need him most. I know his kind."

"That's a chance I'll have to take," Connie said placidly. She felt a little smug in saying this; it would do no harm for both her father and Frank Ivey to underestimate Dave Nash. "There'll be a few risks in this I can't avoid, and that's one of them."

"Quite a few," Ben observed dryly. "You think Frank and I will let you steal our grass?"

"I don't think you'll be able to do anything about it," Connie answered calmly.

"And why not?"

"Nobody's ever stood up to you. You're both too big, and you have a terrific bark." There was open malice in her tone, "I wonder if you can bite."

Ben looked searchingly at her. He was not surprised at her tongue, since she was his own daughter, but something else troubled him. "Connie," he said heavily, "you're getting into a man's business. There'll be gunplay, and men will be hurt."

"Yours," Connie said curtly. She went back to her packing again.

Ben sat on the edge of the bed watching her, and presently he lighted his cigar. Connie came over and shooed him off her dresses, and he moved back toward the head of the bed, leaning on the headboard. She worked swiftly, steadily, and Ben watched her with his shrewd, musing gaze. He had broken too many horses in his day to believe there was only one way to do it, and he considered Connie now. She was headstrong, but she wasn't a fool. And she was playing a game now that had no rules. That was supposed to be a feminine talent, he'd heard, but he doubted if it applied in this case. If Connie could be licked before she started, she'd quit, since she wasn't a fool. Ben thought all this, and knew darkly why he was thinking it. He didn't want to lose Connie. She had fought him every step of the way since she was ten, sometimes stealthily and sometimes openly, but his life would be over if he lost her.

He cleared his throat then and Connie looked up. He had been silent so long she had almost forgotten him.

"Connie," he said slowly, "I'm not going to let you do this."

"You can't stop me."

Ben made a gesture of impatience with his cigar. "I don't mean that. I'll not try to stop you—only I think it doesn't have to happen."

Connie paused in her work. "Now what?"

"What would satisfy you?"

Connie thought a moment. She folded her arms across her breast and paced once to the door and turned and came back to the bed. "If you and Frank pull back to American Creek."

Ben's jaws clamped down tightly on his cigar and he felt a quick stirring of anger. It passed unnoticed, for he was a good gambler. "That's a pound and a half of flesh," he said bitterly.

"Closer to two," Connie countered.

Ben sighed. "Well, you'll get the D Bar when I'm dead, so I suppose I might as well give you a third of it while I'm alive. As for Frank"—he shrugged and spread his hands—"he's been asking you to accept even his name. I don't think he'll object."

"I do," Connie said. "I'm counting on it."

Ben rose and said casually, "Who's over at 66?"

"Nash might be there by now."

"Tell you what," Ben said. "I'll send a man to bring him over to Frank's tomorrow. I'll let Frank know we're coming, too. We'll talk it over at Bell and I think we'll agree." He smiled faintly. "You can stay one more night, can't you, Connie?"

Connie thought a moment, and Ben could almost read her thoughts. She was thinking that he was trying to neutralize her by kindness, and if he knew Connie she would agree to stay, only if to bait him and Frank further and prove she was immune to kindness. Well, that was all right; he only needed one night.

"I'll stay tonight," Connie said.

"Good," Ben said. "We'll ride over together, tomorrow." When he went out of the room, there was the faintest of smiles playing under his roan mustache.

# CHAPTER V

DAVE reached Circle 66 in midmorning. The rain which had threatened yesterday still held off under a gray sky, and a chill ground wind off the Federals stirred the deep grass as he came across the flats, skirted the Ridge and forded American Creek. Circle 66 lay five miles beyond, and presently its windmill poked above a rise. He climbed it and looked back over his shoulder, and the whole rich tawny floor of the Bench lay before him. He hardly blamed Walt Shipley for his ambition, then; a man could not look at this golden grass without wanting it.

The house itself lay at the foot of the bald slope of a hill to the North. It had the air of a working ranch—a long log shack built low to the ground, a big log barn, slab sheds and pole corrals. Not a tree graced the place; it was built for utility, and Dave wondered idly how Connie Dickason would change it.

Pulling into the yard he saw a horse standing hipshot by the veranda, and its rider seated beside it. Bill Schell, apparently, had done his job quickly, if this was one of the newly hired crew.

Dave rode up to the veranda, and the man rose. At first sight, he seemed merely a boy, with a kind of gangling awkwardness about him. Dave's glance shuttled to his horse then and he saw the big D Bar branded on the hip.

He reined up and Link Thoms grinned. "Howdy. You Dave Nash?"

"That's right," Dave said, in a neutral voice.

"Connie Dickason said you was to come with me," Link said. He came over and pulled a folded piece of paper from his shirt pocket. It was a note from Connie ordering him to accompany the bearer.

Dave put it in his pocket and said, "I'm ready," and the kid mounted.

The direction he took angling north drew an immediate question from Dave. "Where we bound for?"

"Bell."

Dave looked at him sharply, but young Link Thoms' face was innocent of guile. The note was in Connie's handwriting all right, but Dave felt a faint uneasiness. He was remembering Frank Ivey's warning, and he smiled faintly. Maybe Connie knew what she was doing; but if she didn't, he wondered what his welcome would be. There was only one way to find out, and he settled back into patience.

They crossed American Creek and afterward moved over the ridge which ran like an upthrust rocky spine from the Federals slantwise with the Bench as far as the creek. From its height, Dave could see the distant tangle of timber far to the east that marked, by a precipitous drop down into the badlands, the edge of the Bench. At the foot of the ridge's north slope lay one of Bell's line camps, a big shack built long and narrow, bunkhouse style, a couple of sheds and a big holding corral. In winter, when the snows forced the stock down from the Federals onto the flats, a part of Bell's crew worked out from here instead of the home ranch.

They passed it, heading north, deep into Bell's range. All morning, fat cattle and their Bell-branded calves were seldom out of sight. Link Thoms, with the garrulous innocence of a hand who does not understand his employer's politics, talked cattle and horses and of the coming roundup two months away.

They passed a shouldering upthrust of dun colored rock, and were suddenly in a deep boxed valley that climbed gently straight in through the fringe of foothills toward the Federals.

Presently they came in sight of Bell, nestled snugly at the head of the valley, timber rising straight behind it to the swift vault of the mountains.

As they approached the house Dave observed it carefully with a faint twinge of memory. His mind traveled back to the spot he and Ruth had built in; a box canyon like this, green as a park, not so big as this and not so fine. There was probably grass on the roof of his shack now, and neighbors had helped themselves to the windows, for Dave had left it after Ruth's death. It had been easier, after that, to work with a lot of men, exchanging his independence for their company, because the heartbreaking labor of making something for himself alone had not been worth the struggle. It was better to be a steady top hand saddled with responsibilities, with his sole privilege a ride into town on a Sunday to see the boy and play with him.

Dave moved restlessly in the saddle and put these thoughts away. Bell, he saw with a practical eye, was a well-run outfit. Its low log house, sprawled in an L among some straggling pines, was the kind of a womanless place that a man would build for men. Bunkhouse and cookshack made up the biggest part of the building; the main house was only the base of the L, and it contained the office, in front of which three horses were tethered now. The barns were big, the corrals solid, and someone, as if furthering the impression of efficiency, was clanging at an anvil down in the blacksmith shop.

Dave rode up to the other horses, and Link, saying, "So long Nash," drifted down to the corrals.

Dave tied his horse with the others at the rail nailed between two pines, and Connie came out of the office. She was wearing a riding habit of a gray color, and the full skirt made her seem almost diminutive.

"Any luck?" she asked in a low voice.

"Bill said he'd get them," Dave answered.

Connie gave him a swift smile of thanks and turned into the office again, and Dave followed her.

Ben Dickason, sitting in a worn leather chair, nodded

and said, "Hello, Nash," in a completely neutral tone. Frank Ivey, his back planted solidly against the back wall, said nothing.

Connie sank into the wired barrel chair in front of the littered roll-top desk and crossed her legs.

"Let's hear it," she said to her father.

Dave put his shoulder against the wall beside the door and tried to get the feel of this. He felt Frank Ivey's bold, searching gaze on him, and he shifted his own glance to meet it. There was something tough and unforgiving in Frank Ivey; he leaned against the wall, blocky in his waist overalls and sweat-stained calico shirt, his big arms folded across his chest. His curly dark hair, close fitting as a cap, reminded Dave oddly of the curly hair on the forehead of a whiteface bull. Dave felt instinctively that Ivey and Ben Dickason were making a last play to hold Connie.

"Frank," Dickason said. "Connie's got hungry all of a sudden. She wants an outfit, and she's got one."

Ivey looked at Connie, and when he did his face softened subtly. The man was in love with her, and Dave would have known it instantly even if Connie hadn't told him.

"She can have mine any time she wants it," Frank said stolidly. It was like the man to declare his love simply and bluntly in front of anyone who cared to listen; and Dave felt a stirring of admiration for him.

"Not with your strings, Frank," Connie said coldly. "Your strings are ropes."

"Now Connie, let me talk," Ben said mildly, and he looked up at Frank. "Shipley left her 66. She's taken out her mother's money and she's hiring a crew and buying stock, Frank."

*He's heard this already,* Dave thought, watching Frank Ivey's face.

Ben went on, his tone faintly sardonic now, "She claims with this crew she can take grass away from us, Frank."

The faintest of smiles played at the corners of Ivey's mouth, and he didn't comment.

"I told her," Ben went on, "that there'd be men hurt and hell raised generally, but she don't seem to care."

"You can leave the 'seem' out. I don't care," Connie said.

"We get down to cases now," Ben said, leaning forward. He lifted his glance idly to Dave and then dropped it again. "Connie says she won't cut loose her dogs if we meet her proposition, Frank. I'm willin', and I come to ask you if you are."

"Go ahead and ask," Frank drawled.

"She wants all the grass on her side of American Creek."

Dave glanced swiftly at Connie, who did not move. She was watching Frank Ivey, and there was a faint flush to her cheeks. A sudden admiration for Connie's courage came to Dave then; she wouldn't fail for lack of boldness. The range on their side of American Creek, if added to what she already held, would make her Circle 66 rank just a little smaller than D Bar and Bell.

"Does she?" Frank murmured. "And what if we don't give it to her?"

"I'll take it," Connie said, with a superb arrogance.

Frank Ivey smiled, but he was angry too. The very gall of it rankled him, as it would have rankled any man. He shuttled his glance to Dave. "What are you gettin' out of this?"

"Wages."

"And booze?"

"All I can drink," Dave murmured.

Frank's gaze again settled on Connie. "I don't get it, Connie," he said slowly. "First you hook up with a big-mouth sheepman, and now with a drunk. Usin' land that we let him take and he gave to you, you aim to fight us. Why? Why?"

"I don't like bullies," Connie said calmly. "What's your answer, Frank?"

"I just think you're crazy," Ivey murmured.

Connie stood up then and said, "And you, Dad?"

"I've backed Frank up so long it's a habit," Ben said. "I can't change at my age."

"All right," Connie said briskly. "Free grass is for the outfit that can take it and hold it. I'm going to make my try." She glanced at Dave and said, "We're through," and stepped outside. Dave was half turned when Ben Dickason's voice, quiet and imperative, said, "Nash."

Dave halted in the doorway, his big frame almost filling it.

Ben said, "You don't look like a fool to me. Didn't Frank tell you you're through here?"

"Somethin' like that," Dave agreed.

Ben eyed him shrewdly. "If you think Connie's big enough—or will be big enough—to keep you here, you're wrong. Shipley went, Leach and Harvey went. You better go."

Dave smiled faintly. "I've seen Ivey's tracks and your tracks, Ben. They don't look big enough to scare me."

Ben, however, was too confident to be baited. He nodded politely, and asked curiously, "What's your game here?"

Dave's glance shuttled to Ivey, who was watching him with a quiet arrogance, and he said, "Why, somethin' Shipley said got me curious."

"What was that?" Ben murmured.

"He said Ivey wasn't God. Ivey says he is. I want to see who's right." He laid a level, insolent glance upon Ivey for a brief moment and saw the slow stirring of anger in the man, and then he tramped out.

Untying his horse, he stepped into the saddle and pulled up alongside Connie. When they were out of earshot of the house, Connie glanced over at him and smiled wryly.

"It was worth trying, wasn't it?"

"Whose idea was it?"

Something in his voice made the smile fade from Connie's face. "That we talk with Frank? Dad's. Why?"

Dave thought a moment before he answered: "Ivey knew your proposition before your father told him. How'd he know?"

Connie, still watching him, said: "Dad could have sent him word last night. I told him yesterday."

"That's it," Dave said. "They've pulled us both off 66." He reined up, looked briefly at Connie's horse, and said sharply, "Get down, Connie, and trade horses with me," and slipped out of the saddle.

Connie didn't hesitate a moment. She dismounted and uncinched her side-saddle, and by that time Dave had the saddle off his own horse. He put it on Connie's horse, which was far fresher than his own, while Connie stood watching him, mute dismay in her face. "What do you think they've done, Dave?"

"Nothing, if Bill's there. If he isn't, anything."

Connie shook her head. "I'll learn," she said in a low hard voice. "That's Lesson One. Don't trust anybody, not even your father."

Dave said quietly, "Lesson One, Connie, is don't make a brag unless you can back it up." He stepped into the saddle and touched spurs to Connie's horse and headed out of the canyon. The first distant drum of thunder from up in the Federals came to him now, and he thought of Frank Ivey and Ben Dickason, who had doubtless watched the exchange of horses and smiled over it.

Connie had made her first mistake, and he wondered how serious it was. He knew now that the burden of this fight, its planning and its execution, would lie with him. Connie had the will to fight, but the way of it was foreign to her.

He settled down to steady riding, crowding Connie's chestnut as hard as he dared. In late afternoon, as he was crossing the ridge, the first big sparse drops of rain fell. By the time he had put his slicker on, the rain began, a drenching downpour that soon slacked off into a drizzle which might last days.

Night came early, when he was still a couple of miles from 66. He was shivering a little from the cold, and a vast impatience was riding him. Presently a faint sound came to him and he reined up, listening. It came again —the sound of a gunshot. While he listened he heard two more shots, far apart, and he tried to read something into their spacing, and could not. Lifting his horse into a lope then, he rode on, and when he came upon the ranch it was cautiously, from the hill to the north.

Everything was dark and silent below him. Suddenly, from the house, the sound of a rifle shot slapped sharply through the drizzling night. Immediately there was a wink of orange from beside the wagon shed, and then the answering crack. On the heel of it, five guns opened up from the house, and he could hear their slugs booming into the wagon shed.

It couldn't be Bill Schell in the house, unless he had exceeded his orders and hired more men than he was authorized to, so it must be Bill in the shed. Which meant that either Ben Dickason or Frank Ivey or both had sent a crew over in his absence to take over Circle 66. It was neat and effective and cunning, he reflected somberly. Connie couldn't run an outfit without shelter for her crew, or corrals, wagons, feed, and all the hundred things needed to keep a ranch working. They had been too smart to drive off her stock and leave themselves open to a bald charge of rustling. This way, they simply claimed grass and a shack—and hamstrung the outfit.

Dave pulled back over the brow of the hill and made a wide circle which brought him up behind to the barn. He dismounted here and moved over so that the shed lay between him and the house, and then tramped toward it.

A voice challenged him abruptly out of the darkness, "Sing out!"

"Dave Nash!" He bumped into a wagon which had been shoved out of the shed and walked around it.

He heard Bill Schell's soft swearing, and then he tramped into the shed, which was open on the side toward the barn. Someone struck a match, and the faint light from a lantern bloomed. Bill Schell and three men who were strangers to Dave knelt behind the cordwood which had been stacked against the shed's rear wall out of the weather.

Bill Schell came slowly to his feet, rifle in hand. He was soaked to the skin, and his lips were almost blue with cold, his boots caked with mud, which was smeared over his shirt and levis.

Bill grinned swiftly, but his eyes were questioning. "Who was asleep, Kid?"

"I was," Dave answered.

Bill turned to the three men. The closest looked half Indian; his taciturn dark face scarred deep on one cheek. He too was soaked, and had a torn slicker thrown over his shoulders for warmth.

"Meet your crew," Bill said dryly. "This is Bailey—no last name. This"—he indicated a slight, tough-faced puncher who seemed to be the possessor of the only slicker, because he was dry—"is Tom Peebles." He pointed to the third man and laughed. "Curley Fanstock. He ain't happy even when he's dry." Curley, of course, was bald and middle-aged, and he had the appearance of a steady hand.

They all looked at him, and they did not smile, and Dave felt a slow despair mingled with wrath. He said softly, "Welcome to a nice warm bunkhouse and hot grub, boys."

Curley grinned at that, and Dave said to Bill, "What happened?"

"Nothin'. We just rode up at dark and all hell broke loose from the house. My horse is lyin' out there gutshot. I got pitched thirty feet and skidded forty more on my face. We forted up here, and they started to saw this thing off on our heads. That's about all."

A sudden fusillade from the house made Bill Schell drop swiftly to his knees, and Dave followed.

The slugs ripped through the thin slabs, and some of them pounded solidly into the stacked wood. The firing ceased as abruptly as it began.

Dave peeled out of his slicker and threw it to Bill, and said, "Let's have a look, Bill."

He tramped out into the night, Bill at his heels. When they reached the corner of the barn, Dave halted, feeling the rain cold on his shoulders.

Bill hauled up beside him, and for a moment they didn't speak. Bill said then, "You can't ask 'em to brace that crew, kid. Not on an empty belly, anyway."

"No," Dave said. He was trying to throttle his anger and think. Even the weather seemed to be playing into Frank Ivey's hands. Chilled and hungry and tired men, pulled cold into an ambush and without even the prospect of shelter, would quit on him, and he wouldn't blame them.

Bill swore briefly, passionately. "Give 'em a toehold, Dave. That scar Bailey wears come from Frank Ivey's boot. Tom Peebles got pushed off American Creek and his shack burned on him. Curley Fanstock was a top hand at Bell for ten years until the morning a horse throwed him and broke his leg. Ivey paid him off that afternoon. They'll nail Ivey's hide——"

Bill ceased talking as Dave laid a hand on his arm. They both listened. They heard the soft splash of a horse walking, and the sound of its labored breathing. A scattering of shots came from the house, and then it was quiet again, and again they heard the horse, closer now. They both faded against the wall of the barn, and now the horse was in front of them.

Dave said softly, "Connie?"

"Dave," Connie answered.

They walked in the direction of her voice and they heard her dismount, and then she was a small figure before them. Dave put his hand out to steady her and she shook it off. She too had no slicker, and she was soaked as the wettest of them.

"Who's in the house?"

"Bell, I reckon," Bill said laconically. "Your crew," he added bitterly, "is holed up behind a pile of wood in the wagon shed."

"It's my fault," Connie said glumly. "I fell for their stupid trick, and I even pulled Dave in with me." She paused, and Dave heard her sigh deeply. "Well, it was a good idea while it lasted. I guess I can't finance an army to throw them out of here, though."

"You won't have to," Dave said quietly. . . . "Bill, go pull the boys out of there. Get your horses. You got one?"

"Curley brought his string."

"Bring them around here."

Bill faded off into the night, and Dave felt Connie's hand on his arm. "What is it, Dave?"

"Wait," Dave said.

Presently, the crew appeared, leading their horses, and pulled up in front of him.

David said quietly, "You boys figure a five-mile ride is too much to pay for a crack at Ivey?"

There was a moment of silence, and then Bill Schell said, "Not me. Twenty ain't."

"There's a Bell line camp over the ridge," Dave said. "It's a tight stone shack bigger than ours. It's got grub and, likely, beds." He paused, and then said with a quiet exultation, "Come to think of it, it might make a good headquarters ranch for 66, seeing as we're movin' up to American Creek."

Curley Fanstock said, "Ah," with a quiet satisfaction, and Dave knew then these men were his.

The ride over to the ridge was a dismal hour of chill misery, and Dave rode alongside Connie. She did not speak once, and Dave knew then, if he had ever doubted it, that she had stamina enough.

They passed the crown of the ridge, the hooves of their horses sinking deeply into the soupy clay of the top, and slanted down the slippery trail on the far side. Once on the flats, they were in plain sight of the Bell line camp; lamplight dimly framed a window, and it looked warm and cheerful through the steady straight-down drizzle. They approached within several hundred yards before Dave reined up.

"Bill, you're the drifter, and they know you. Ride up like you were on the grub line. Keep 'em inside and we'll do the rest." He turned to Connie. "You keep the horses, Connie."

He dismounted, and the others with him, all except Bill and Connie. They walked ahead until they were close to the shack, and then Bill, whistling thinly, pulled ahead of them. As he approached a man appeared in the doorway, and Bill called, "Hello the house. I can lick anybody inside for a meal and bed."

"Bill Schell! Ain't you got sense enough to get out of the rain?" the man at the door called. "Come in here."

Bill unsaddled, threw his saddle under the shed and turned his horse into the corral, as he would normally do, all the while carrying on an exchange of name-calling with the man at the door.

He disappeared inside, and Dave waited a moment, and then tramped on toward the house. Curley and Bailey, without having to be told, headed for the rear door and the end window.

Dave pulled his gun then and stepped silently through the door. There were three men here, and they were all seated on one bench, their backs to the door, talking with Bill Schell, who was standing in front of the warm stove. A partition separated this big room, which was the bunkhouse and cookshack combined, from the kitchen. There was food cooking, and the smell of a mulligan lay thick in the room.

Bill looked up and saw Dave, and he asked idly of the man closest to him, "How many you boys are here, Jess?"

"Just us."

Bill grinned and said to Dave, "They're all here."

The three Bell hands turned almost as one, and looked straight into Dave's gun, held hip-high. At the same moment Bill Schell pulled his gun, and stepped back against the wall.

One of the Bell hands came slowly to his feet, and Bill drawled, "Meet Ed Burma, Dave. He's Ivey's tough ramrod."

Dave recognized the short, blocky foreman, who was regarding him with a hard-eyed caution.

Bill said sharply, "Stand up, you two." The other two Bell hands came to their feet, and Bill indicated the tallest man, an unwashed, stupid-looking puncher whose bony, taciturn face was expressionless. "Virg Lea," Bill murmured. "Try to hang him and he'd chew through the rope. And Jess Moore. He likes to play Injun." Moore was slighter than Bill, and at Bill's words he turned and spat precisely at Bill's feet, and Bill only grinned. "It's a hell of a night out, boys," Bill drawled. "Go try it."

Ed Burma turned his head toward Bill and murmured, "You damn saddle-tramp. I'll remember this."

"I hope so," Bill said cheerfully. "You might even remember it better if you walked."

"No," Dave said quietly. "Put your guns on the table and ride out of here. Tell Frank Ivey we don't mind the trade. Tell him it's for keeps, too."

The three men surlily laid their guns on the table and filed over to their slickers hanging on the wall. Bailey drifted in from the kitchen with a lighted lantern, a sheltering gunny sack held over it, and stepped out the door on his way to the corral. Connie came in then, and she walked past the Bell hands without so much as a glance at them.

Under Dave's gun, with Curley holding the lantern and Bailey posted by the corral gate, the three Bell hands saddled up and mounted.

As Burma rode past Dave he looked down at him and said quietly, "You can't get away with it, Mister. We'll be back."

"Any time," Dave invited, and watched the three of them ride off into the night.

He tramped back into the bunkhouse and found Connie ladling out Bell's stew onto tin plates and Bill pouring coffee into tin cups. Wordlessly, all of them sat down and ate, and Dave knew then that he could keep this crew. With a full belly and warm fire, they would forget the misery of the day, and it would come to them that it was too late to back out now. They were in it together.

Afterwards, Dave rigged a bed for Connie in the tiny kitchen and hung a curtain in the partition doorway, while the rest of the crew rolled up in Bell's blankets. Finished, Dave surveyed the bed, and then his glance lifted to Connie. She was standing with her back to the warm range drying out her clothes. She looked small and indomitable, and she caught Dave's glance and smiled.

"It's not a bad trade. I can rig up one of the sheds for Josefa and me."

Dave nodded and turned to go, and Connie said quietly, "I was a fool today, Dave. It almost cost us everything."

"That's the way you learn."

Connie said, "Dave, I want to ask a question. We have five men. Dad has six and Ivey has eight or so. What happens?"

Dave took a last look about the kitchen, and when he glanced at Connie he saw her watching him questioningly. "What happens?" he repeated idly. "Well, it will be mostly Jim Crew, Connie."

When she shook her head, not understanding, Dave put his shoulder against the wall and regarded her gravely. "Jim Crew," he murmured, "is worth a dozen of Frank Ivey's hands, Connie. More than that, he's sheriff. The first time any of us make a wrong move, Crew will move against us, and the outfit he moves against will be licked."

Connie was silent, listening intently, and Dave went on, "We'll play our hand straight, Connie, and all the time we'll try to pull Frank and Ben into a wrong move. Once we do that, Jim Crew is ours, and Ivey's beat."

"But this is a wrong move," Connie pointed out. "This camp isn't ours."

Dave came erect, smiling faintly. "It will be. Wait and see. Good night, Connie."

# CHAPTER VI

FRANK IVEY ate a leisurely breakfast after the rest of the crew had finished. He had waited purposely until they had scattered for work this morning, because he wanted to think this out alone. Last night he had been roused by the trio that had been kicked out of the Ridge line camp by Dave Nash and Connie, and he had dispatched a man immediately to D Bar with the news. Right now, he was a little sorry he had sent word to Ben; it looked too much as if he were asking for advice or help, neither of which he wanted. He had done it on impulse, since it was D Bar's crew who had occupied Circle 66; but this morning he wondered if that was important.

Now, in the cold light of a sunny day, he reviewed what had happened. Obviously, Connie and Nash both thought it was Bell who had moved in on them, and they had retaliated on Bell. Which was all right with him. The first move against 66 had been Ben Dickason's idea, and, because it was a good one, Frank regretted it had not been his own. But the brunt of the fight, as had been proved last night, would fall on Bell, however, and Frank wanted it that way.

He rose and stepped over the bench, put on an ancient and curl-brimmed Stetson, paused to pick a toothpick from the glass in the center of the long table, yelled, "All done," to the cook, and strolled out into the

fresh morning. The earth was a blazing, washed brightness after the rain.

One glance at the corral told him the boys were
stalling, and he smiled faintly. The indignity suffered by
Bell last night was smarting, and they were waiting for
orders from him. That, he reflected, was the way to
keep a crew—proud, jealous, on edge, and quick to
revenge a slight. In this instance, though, there was no
hurry.

He tramped down to the corral—a solid, burly man
with a light, careful walk, his toothpick jutting out of
one corner of his wide mouth. His vest, old and button-
less, was split at the back by some forgotten exertion;
he looked comfortable and was completely at ease in
the work clothes that no way differed from those worn
by his men.

Ed Burma broke away from the corral and came out
to meet him out of earshot of the crew. This, too, was
ritual; they would discuss the day's work a moment,
then Ed would go back and give the orders, and Frank
would go on about his business. Today, Ed's unshaven
face was a little tight as he nodded good morning, and
there was an air of expectancy in his glance.

Frank saw the crew watching them, pretending not
to, and he said idly, "Mornin', Ed. My gray come in
with the bunch?"

Ed turned and yelled to one of the crew, "Frank's
gray in there?"

The man looked over the horses inside and called,
"Yeah."

"Saddle him up," Ed directed, and when he turned to
Frank there was a gleam of anticipation in his eye.

"Not so fast," Frank murmured. "You gettin' in a
hurry, Ed?"

"You're damn right."

"Well, don't. Send Jack over to 66 to see what happened there. Tell Virg to have the boys at the ford in
the middle of the morning, where I can pick 'em up on
my way back from town. You, you're goin' to Relief."

The disappointment in Ed's face was so keen it made
Frank smile. "She's buyin' beef, and the only outfits

that'll sell to her are on the other slope. I want to know how much stuff she's buyin' and who from, and what she' payin', and where it's goin'."

"All right," Ed said, and he asked, almost sulkily, "You goin' to leave her there at the Ridge?"

"Just long enough to find out where I stand."

Ed hesitated a moment and then said, "Did I tell you Curley Fanstock is workin' for her now?"

"You did. Him and Bill Schell." Frank's heavy face was bland and hard and musing as he murmured, "A" in good time, Ed. All in good time."

He went on to the corral and got his horse, mounted, and rode off toward the mouth of the valley. It was a beautiful day, such as a man saw in midsummer only after a drenching rain. Frank turned his thoughts to last night, and, reviewing what had happened, he saw nothing to merit alarm. Connie was crowded off 66, and furthermore, she would stay off, for Walt Shipley had merely slipped in there and thrown up a shack, with no jot of title to the land.

Thinking of Connie, then, he was mildly troubled. It was natural, he supposed, for a woman to be hurt when the man she was to marry was revealed as a coward. And when people were hurt they struck out blindly. That explained this sudden stubborn rage of Connie's; it was her way of striking out. This thought satisfied him completely, because he knew no man alive was as stubborn as he was—or woman either for that matter. He'd have Connie some day, if only through wearing down her resistance. Besides, he admired her spirit. He didn't want a meek, demure wife; he wanted a woman with fire and a mind of her own, and Connie had both. It never occurred to him that she might, in the end, refuse to marry him. He was the best man he knew, and that's what any woman wanted.

He dropped down into Signal in midmorning, the sun warm on his back. The street was mired in a soupy mud churned up by the morning's traffic of wagons, and its rank earth smell was pleasant.

Passing the hotel, Frank glanced at it, and he thought immediately of Walt Shipley. He'd put him away without any trouble at all, he reflected contentedly, and

Nash was up next. He hadn't figured how, yet, but it would come.

Reining up in front of Jim Crew's office, he dismounted. Such as it was, these three cramped buildings in a row opposite the Special constituted Signal County's courthouse. The sheriff's office and jail occupied the corner building that used to be Armistead's saddle shop; the clerk's office and files occupied the one adjoining, and the Land Commissioner's office the last. These were the only buildings on that side of the street, and abutted the canyon slope.

Frank stepped into Jim Crew's office and found it empty. On the narrow boardwalk again, he considered the rest of his business here. He had already stepped out into the mud, intending to cross the street, when he paused. He'd almost forgotten what he came for.

He stepped back up on the sidewalk and went past the clerk's office and turned into the Land Commissioner's office. It was a big room, three-quarters empty, furnished with a desk, a brass spittoon, a chair, and a table loaded with curling maps. The shirt-sleeved clerk sat with his feet on the desk top, his swivel chair tilted far back, and he was studying some correspondence.

Frank tramped in, kicking the mud off his boots at the door, and said, "Mornin', Hildegarde."

The clerk came to his feet and said, "How are you, Frank?" He was an elderly man, and there was a deference in his tone that Frank did not miss.

Frank said with heavy jocularity, "Get out your maps, Hildegarde. I'm about to become a landowner."

Hildegarde laughed. "You ain't gettin' religion, are you, Frank? I thought you figured the homestead law was a pretty sorry mess."

"I do, except when I need it," Frank said truly.

Hildegarde, chuckling, moved over to the table and rummaged around the maps.

"I got a line camp a mile east of the road that crosses the Ridge. Gimme a look at it."

Hildegarde looked closely at him, was about to speak, and then did not. He spread out the map, checked the range and township number, and stood aside.

Frank leaned both hands on it, a blunt finger tracing

the road to the ridge, then moving over and stopping. "Right there," Frank said. "I'm goin' to homestead that section."

"I don't reckon you are," Hildegarde said slowly.

Frank looked up, puzzlement in his broad face. "No?"

"You can see it outlined there in black ink," Hildegarde said. "It was filed on this morning."

Frank slowly came erect, his bold eyes on Hildegarde. "Who filed on it?"

"Fella name of Nash. Dave Nash."

A swift rage boiled up in Frank's eyes. "Why, damn you, Hildegarde, that's my land!"

"You filed on it?"

"I've got a line camp on it."

Hildegarde shook his head and said slyly, "That's too bad, Frank. That there was public domain. All you had to do was file and prove up, and it was yours. But you always figured it was a piece of foolishness."

"That's my land," Frank reiterated flatly. "Nobody takes it from me."

"You try and keep it and you'll have a U.S. Marshal to answer to," Hildegarde said smugly.

Frank looked down at the map again, but it had curled up. He gave it a savage bat with his hand and started past Hildegarde. Suddenly he hauled up and said angrily, "Let me see that again."

Hildegarde patiently picked it up and spread it out, and Frank leaned over it. This time his finger traveled over the ridge and he read the contours that marked the low elevations of the east side of the Bench. "This section here," he said, jabbing his finger on it. "I want to file on it." It was the location of Walt Shipley's Circle 66, and Frank looked up at the clerk. Hildegarde was shaking his head.

"No can do," Hildegarde said. "I ain't marked it yet this morning, but I got a file on that, too, at the same time. Fella name of Schell."

Frank turned without a word and stalked out. At the door, he halted and called back, "To prove up on a homestead, you've got to live on it, don't you?"

"Yes sir," Hildegarde said. "You got to——"

But Frank was gone. He went down to his horse, mounted, jerked his horse around so savagely that it reared and almost threw him, and then took the grade out of town.

Rose Leland got up from the table close to her window and went outside and watched Frank until she was sure he had taken the grade. Then she came back inside and slowly closed the door and leaned against it. Dave hadn't told her this would happen, but she had known it would. She knew it even as Dave and Bill, over breakfast coffee in her kitchen, had told of what had happened on the Bench, and of their plans to file this morning as soon as the Land Office was open.

And here it was. Rose walked slowly across the room and stopped suddenly in front of the wire dressmaker's dummy on which the blue silk Dave had given her was draped. Sight of that seemed to make up her mind, and she got her hat. Hastily, she let down her hair, which she had pinned up off the back of her neck, tidied it, and put on her hat. Her dress was not a street dress, but at the moment she did not care.

Locking the shop behind her, she picked her way across the muddy street and turned up it. She saw Jim Crew leave the Land Office, walk to his corner and turn into his own office.

Rose slowed her pace now. Faced with the immediate results of her decision, she was hesitant. But it was only for a moment; she kept thinking of that silk on the dressmaker's dummy in her shop, and knew that she was going to pay her debt.

Jim Crew was seated in the wired barrel chair in his small office, that still held the good smell of leather from the old saddle shop. His chill eyes were gazing absently at the yellowed reward dodgers on the wall behind the desk, and when he shuttled his glance to her there was a moment when he did not recognize her. Then he came to his feet swiftly, and said gently, "Hello, lady," and smiled his faint, distant smile.

Rose sat down in the chair beside his desk. "You just came from the Land Office, Jim?"

Crew nodded, and said in his dry voice, "I've been tryin' to make sense out of it."

Rose told him then of what had passed on the Bench, and as she talked Crew's gaze seemed to turn inward and the corners of his straight mouth thinned imperceptibly. When Rose was finished, Crew didn't say anything for a moment. Then she heard him sigh.

"What are you afraid of?" he asked quietly.

"Frank Ivey. Not because I'm a woman, either."

"No," Crew agreed.

Rose waited for him to say more, and he did not, and Rose said, "Dave and Bill Schell are headed for Relief to buy cattle. They won't be there."

Crew nodded, and murmured, as if to himself, "Hell hath no fury," and ceased talking, leaving his quotation unfinished.

"That's not quite right," Rose said.

"No, Connie turned on the wrong man. But she's turned—and God help her." He rose now and asked idly, "What do you think Frank will do?"

"I don't know. I know one thing, though. Dave was wrong when he said Frank would stop short of pulling a marshal in here. He'll get that line camp back if he has to fight two armies."

Crew really smiled then, and it was a fond, sad smile. "You know more about a man than he does about himself, Rose."

"I had seven brothers," Rose said, with a faint, dry humor.

Crew went over to the nail where his hat was hanging. "You know so much, Rose, what do you know about Dave Nash?"

"Nothing that would help you."

"Are his hands clean?" Jim asked quietly.

"Yes. I'd be willing to bet," Rose answered slowly, and, looking searchingly at Crew she asked, "Why, Jim?"

Crew took down his soft Stetson and turned it in his hand. "Bill Schell," he said idly, "is trouble. I like him, mind you, but he's trouble. Curley Fanstock lives to get even with Frank Ivey. Bailey is Injun. I wouldn't kick a dead Injun in the face let alone a live one. Who else did he hire?"

"Tom Peebles."

"He's a beauty," Jim murmured. "Every mouthful of beef he's eaten in four years is Bell beef. That," he finished, "is what is called a hardcase crew, Rose. Every man in it would shoot Frank Ivey in the back."

"Dave won't let them."

"He better not," Crew said gently. "That's what I mean."

Rose came to her feet now, and Jim Crew still watched her, his pale eyes curious.

"You like him, don't you, Rose," he said, and it was not a question, but a statement of fact.

Rose nodded. "So do you."

"Yeah," Jim Crew said slowly, and his eyes were sharp once more. "Trouble is, most of the men I've liked in my lifetime are dead."

Rose knew what he meant, and did not answer. She stepped out and waited for Jim to close the door and walk up with her to the livery, where he kept his horse. And while she was waiting she saw Burch Nellis, in apron and shirt sleeves, standing in the doorway of the Special.

Jim Crew, seeing him too, observed dryly, "Burch don't miss much, does he?"

"I don't care," Rose answered truthfully.

# CHAPTER VII

CONNIE, with the help of Curley Fanstock, had the shed cleaned of its gear by midmorning. She stood in the doorway surveying the room, noting the wide cracks in the floor planking and its gentle tilt downhill. This room, with its single small window, was to be her room, and she would probably share it with Josefa too. When she thought of her own room at D Bar she had to smile a little, but it was only for a moment. She turned to Curley, who was standing in the sun, wiping his bald head with a not-too-clean neckerchief.

"Go see if the water's hot, Curley."

"You aim to wash this place?" Curley asked skeptically.

"I suppose," Connie answered wearily. "At least I can scald a few spiders."

As Curley cut across toward the bunkhouse, he glanced out across the sun-drenched flats toward the Federals. He halted abruptly then, and squinted his eyes for a moment, and afterwards called over his shoulder, "Callers, ma'am."

Connie turned now and looked out. Presently she saw the outline of several horsemen traveling in a bunch toward them.

Curley made a move toward the house, and Connie said peremptorily, "No gun, Curley. That won't do any good."

"You goin' to let 'em take it back?"

"They can't," Connie said. "It's filed on by this time. Just go about your business."

Curley grunted and stayed where he was. Connie rolled the sleeves of her work dress down and automatically smoothed her skirt before she thought of what she was doing. It made her a little angry then to think she had even unconsciously tried to make herself look nice for Frank Ivey. For it would be Frank, she knew, and for a moment she was not quite sure of her position. Bailey and Tom Peebles had ridden over to gather up what Circle 66 horses they could find, serenely confident of Dave Nash's wisdom, and she was alone, except for Curley. Dave had pointed out, and both Connie and Bill agreed with him, that any move against them after the land had been filed on would draw legal action. That meant, of course, that Jim Crew would side with them against Ivey.

As the riders drew closer, Connie moved out in front of the shack and Curley drifted up to put his shoulder against its corner.

It was Frank, all right, with four of his crew. He rode at the head of them, blocky and solid in the saddle. They reined up some yards from Connie, and Frank dismounted, as did the others. He looked about him before he glanced at Connie and touched his hat.

"Where's Dave Nash, Connie?" he asked.

"Riding. How do you like my new place?" Connie countered. She didn't trouble to hide the malice in her voice, but Frank seemed not to notice it.

"I didn't know I'd sold it," he answered.

"It's not exactly an even trade, but it has its points," Connie said.

A noise up the ridge behind the house made Connie turn, then. She saw three horsemen, Bell hands, putting their horses carefully down the slope, which was still slippery from last night's rain, and she turned to Frank again. "Call them in. Curley and I are alone."

"That's a new way to hold a place you've stolen," Frank said dryly.

"It doesn't have to be held. We let the law do that."

"So I heard."

Connie suppressed a start. Somehow, she hadn't been

prepared for this; she had been looking forward with pleasure to seeing Frank's face when the news of the filing was broken to him.

"Then get them off," Connie said sharply. "Yourself, too."

One of the riders came around the corner of the house beside Curley and halted. Frank called, "Bring Curley over, Virg. He'll have to do."

"To hell with you," Curley said quietly.

The rider freed a foot from the stirrup, pulled his horse over and kicked Curley in the back. Curley sprawled off balance, slipped in the mud, and came up wheeling. He looked up into the barrel of big Virg Lea's gun. It had happened swiftly and silently, and now all was quiet again.

Curley slowly turned his head to look at Connie, and he said bleakly, "You want me to go about my business, ma'am?"

Frank watched the other two riders move around the end of the bunkhouse, dismount and go inside.

Connie felt a sudden panic, and she said fiercely to Frank, "Get them out of there, Frank, or so help me I'll swear out a warrant against the lot of you!"

"Sure you will," Frank said, and he lifted his voice and called, "Bring him over, I said."

Curley came of his own accord now, and halted sullenly behind Connie. The two riders came out of the bunkhouse, silently shook their heads, and moved in behind Curley.

Frank surveyed Connie with his bold, bright eyes now, and he said, "You're smart, Connie. That homestead idea was good. We can't move you off."

"Of course you can't."

"I don't reckon we'll have to," Frank said heavily. "You can't work an outfit with no crew, can you?"

"I've got one."

"You won't have," Frank murmured. He turned his hot gaze on Curley. "Curley, you're through here. Don't show up again." He looked over at brawny Virg Lea and said, "All right, boys."

Two men behind Curley grabbed his arms, and Virg

Lea sent a smashing blow into Curley's face. Curley swore passionately and struggled to get free, and Virg hit him again, twice, as hard as he could swing.

Connie, shocked into action, lunged for Virg, and Frank grabbed her arm and yanked her back.

And then Virg went to work. He slugged at Curley's face, at his chest, at his midriff, and his feet were planted wide so that he could get leverage in his blows. Curley, his arms pinned behind him, struggled furiously to free himself, turning his head to avoid the blows. His face was bleeding now, and he grunted under the impact of each new blow.

But Virg Lea went about it with a methodical savagery. He slugged Curley's belly until Curley's head came down in an unconscious jackknife, and then Virg drove uppercuts into Curley's face. Curley made a stolid, silent stand for a half minute, and then his knees buckled. The two men supporting him, however, did not let him drop, and Virg started in again.

Connie, horrified, turned to Frank. "Make them stop! Make them stop!"

Frank only smiled thinly, and Connie turned away, burying her face in her hands. The sound of Virg's fists smacking the bloody pulp that had been Curley's face came to her with the sickening regularity of a pendulum. That sound and Virg's grunting as he swung.

It went on and on, and Connie covered her ears and shut her eyes. Presently, she felt the earth tremble a little and whirled. They had dropped Curley; he lay on his back, his face a pulpy mass of raw flesh, his shirt torn and drenched with bright blood. Virg Lea stood over him now and kicked his face time and again. His shirt too was covered with Curley's spattered blood, and his face held a tight viciousness. And then, when he was tired, he stopped.

Connie looked up from Curley to the other men, and they would not look at her. Now that the thing was done, they moved uneasily, covertly watching Frank, the shame of it plain in their faces.

Connie moved toward Curley, and Frank hauled her roughly around by her arm. His face was cold and wicked with anger, and he said levelly, "That's what any man will get that works for you, Connie. Tell Dave Nash that."

"You devil!" Connie said bitterly. "You cruel devil, Frank Ivey!"

"Any man that works for you," Frank repeated.

He let her go then, and turned to his horse. The rest of the crew, still silent, broke and sought their horses, and they still would not look at her.

Connie came slowly over to Curley and knelt beside him. She wanted more than anything else to be sick, and she looked away from that mashed face until her queasiness left her. The Bell crew rode off, still silent. One man, Connie saw, turned to look at them briefly.

Connie got a grip on herself. She put her hand on Curley's wrist and found a faint pulse beating. She did not see how a man could live after that beating, but Curley was alive. She went into the house and got a cloth and put it over Curley's face, and then set about dragging him into the bunkhouse. It took her many minutes, with frequent rests, and her anger now was a live thing, giving her strength.

Once she had him in the bunkhouse, she maneuvered him into the bunk, and then set about cleaning him up. This was the worst; his face was cut to a soft, purple pulp, and she could not find his nose. His eyes, mercifully, were hidden in the torn flesh, and one eyebrow was gone. Some deep stubborn will within her kept her at it, with hot water and clean cloths. Finally, she had done all she could for his face. She stripped his shirt off then, and was cleaning his bruised and livid shoulders and chest when she heard a horse outside.

She rose and ran to the door, and saw Jim Crew stepping out of the saddle.

Jim's hand was on its way to his hat when it paused. He had seen the blood on Connie's clothes.

"Connie, what—" Jim ceased talking, and moved swiftly toward her. Connie stepped back into the room, and wordlessly led him over to the bunk where Curley lay.

Jim Crew looked carefully at Curley, and his face

had gone tight and smooth, and then he turned away to face Connie. "Frank?"

Connie nodded and sank down on the bench. She rose again, not tired, not anything except wildly angry, and glanced at Jim Crew.

"Two of them held him while Virg Lea beat him. They all watched."

Crew said meagerly, "A warrant will only get Virg, Connie."

Connie seemed not to hear him. She walked over to the door and stood in it, staring blindly out at the tawny flats. No, a warrant wasn't the way to beat Frank Ivey. Jim Crew's words were apologetic enough to tell her of the insufficiency of that way. Lea could be jailed or fined, but Frank would pay Lea's fine and his wages in jail, and himself go untouched on his arrogant way. This was not the act of Frank Ivey's that Dave said would force Jim Crew to move against Bell. Suddenly Connie realized that Frank Ivey knew this too. Frank Ivey was afraid of Crew. He would do anything short of provoking Crew, with his iron sense of justice, into action against him. Yet this piece of savagery could not remain unavenged, and Connie's thoughts turned then to Dave. He would know how to do it, because already he had seen the way to beat Ivey in the end.

She turned and came back to Crew, who was waiting for her answer. "No, Jim. I'll take care of this my own way."

Crew said in a discouraged voice, "Don't lose your head, Connie."

"Will you saddle a horse for me, Jim? Then will you stay with Curley until Bailey and Tom come back and take him in town? I'm going."

# CHAPTER VIII

THE cattle began to come into Relief around mid-morning. Bill Schell's word that Circle 66 was buying had sifted down the far slope to the small outfits on the edge of the reservation. The cattle came in small bunches of a dozen or so, and were driven into the corrals, so that when Dave and Bill Schell arrived at midday they had a small herd to look over.

Dave was looking for bargains, and he was not particular. The sum Connie had given him, and which now reposed in a shoe box behind George's bar, had to be stretched as far as it would go. For Dave had stubbornly assumed that he was stocking a large range.

Furthermore, he was not taking chances with what he bought. As fast as the cattle were bought, he and Bill Schell set to work. The cattle were driven into the smaller corral one at a time, roped, thrown, their old brands vented, and a Circle 66 branded on the left hip with a running iron. If Ivey or Ben Dickason had a notion of raiding the herd as soon as it hit the Bench, this precaution would help.

As afternoon wore on, they worked doggedly, helped by the small ranchers who had driven the beef up here. The big holding corral got a freehand job of patching under the hot sun, and it began to slowly fill up with bawling cattle.

In one of the lulls Bill Schell put his horse across the road to get a drink behind the hotel. Dave was resting against the inside of the corral rolling a smoke and talking with one of the Indian police, who had come up from the reservation to check on the brands. His faded shirt was plastered with sweat against his back, and his Stetson, shoved to the back of his head, revealed his sweat-matted black hair.

Bill Schell returned then and let himself in the corral, and Dave, fumbling in his shirt pocket with a poking finger, saw him and said, "Got a match, Bill?"

"I got more than that," Bill murmured, handing him a match. He nodded toward the hotel. "Ed Burma."

Dave glanced up across the road to the hotel porch and saw Ed Burma, chair tilted back against the wall, regarding the activity with motionless curiosity.

Bill murmured idly, "Now he's packin' a pistol, I wonder has he got any objections about last night."

"Don't ask him."

Bill glanced at Dave, a quiet deviltry in his eyes. "Why not? It's a fair question."

"Settling what?" Dave murmured. "He isn't Ivey, Bill."

"I don't like him snoopin'," Bill said irritably. "I don't like him even if he ain't snoopin'."

"Let it ride," Dave said flatly.

He saw Bill look at him speculatively, faintly resentful of the order, and then Bill shrugged. "Hell, you never let a man have any fun," Bill protested, and again he looked longingly at Burma.

A new bunch of cattle broke out of the timber and scattered, and Bill stepped into the saddle and put his horse across the road to head them off. Dave watched him, a faint uneasiness within him. Sooner or later he and Bill would clash, he supposed. Bill was in this to wreck Bell, fight its whole crew, and kill Frank Ivey if he could do it without hanging. His impulsiveness and his recklessness, valuable in an open fight, was a solid risk in this waiting game they were playing now. Bill didn't understand the necessity for waiting, didn't even want to, and Dave knew a showdown was inevitable.

He looked up at Burma and discovered a resentment in himself at the man's presence. Bell's watch dog, Dave thought, noting everybody's business with a bland gall that no other outfit could match. Then he forgot it, and went to work on the new bunch.

The big holding corral filled up during the afternoon, and Dave and Bill had no time to think of Bell's foreman. A small crowd of ranchers alternated now between helping with the branding and visits to the bar.

It was in late afternoon when Dave, having loosed the last cow of the most recent bunch, stepped into the saddle and pulled his horse aside to avoid the cow's angry lunge. The gate was swung open and Dave hazed the cow in with the others and then pulled his feet from the stirrup, sitting slackly in the saddle, and looked about him.

His glance caught a movement at the north edge of the timber, and held it, and then he saw Connie Dickason ride out into the clearing.

Dave said, "Bill," and nodded toward Connie and put his horse toward her. They met at the hotel steps, and Dave stepped out of the saddle and took the bridle of Connie's horse. The dried blood on Connie's dress would have told him something was wrong, even if he had not seen it on her face. A cold fury lighted in her green eyes, and Bill Schell handed her down from the saddle wordlessly.

"Have you got a room here, Dave?"

Dave saw she did not want to talk here under the curious gaze of half a dozen men on the porch, among them Ed Burma. He led the way into the lobby, took a key from the board behind the desk, and the three of them mounted the stairs.

Dave went to his room, a front one, opened the door and stepped aside, and Connie went in, Bill behind her. Dave closed the door behind him, and then said questioningly, "That's blood on your dress, Connie."

"Curley Fanstock's blood," Connie said levelly. "Two of them held him while a third beat him to a pulp."

The whole story came tumbling from her lips then, and as Dave listened to it his face turned bleak and still. Connie told it all—how Virg Lea would not stop until he himself was almost exhausted—and when she

finished, neither man spoke. Bill Schell lifted his glance
to Dave then, and it was searching and hot and wicked.

Connie went over to the bed and sat on it, and she,
too, was watching Dave. She said suddenly, "I want you
to pay Frank for that, Dave. I don't care what you do,
either." There was plain and arrogant outrage in her
voice, and Dave said nothing for a moment, watching
Connie's hands at her side, bunching the blanket.

Then he said meagerly, "If you think a minute,
you'll care," and turned slowly toward the window. He
went over to it and halted, both hands fisted in his hip
pockets, and looked blindly out at the corrals below.
His own anger was steady now, something that would
never leave him until this was avenged. He saw Ivey's
strategy behind Curley's beating. Ivey wasn't reckless;
he hadn't made the mistake of trying to drive them off
the land already filed on. His strategy was terror. Beat
a man, scare him, make it so he never liked to ride
alone, put the fear of Frank Ivey into him until he
couldn't stand it and rode away. And beyond that, of
course, was Ivey's hope that 66, infuriated by Curley's
beating, would retaliate in a way that would bring
Crew's wrath down on them. A slow rage burned in
him, and he ran his flat palm hard and slowly across his
face. The small hurt of it seemed to sober him, and he
turned his head toward Connie and found her watching him, the anger in her eyes unabated.

Bill Schell spoke two words then, very softly. "Ed
Burma." He started for the door.

Dave said, just as softly, "You go out that door, Bill,
and I ride out of here. How about it, Connie?"

"Wait, Bill," Connie said.

"He's down there!" Bill flared, his voice wild and hot.
"By God, let's send him back to Bell in a basket!"

Connie looked at Dave and said, "They did it to
Curley. Why not?"

Dave said meagerly, "Who you fightin', Connie?
Burma or Ivey?"

"Ivey."

"Then fight him, not Burma. What's Burma done?
Get some sense in that thick little head of yours."

Connie's head jerked up and the color flooded into her face, and he stared coldly at her, the expression on his lean, hard face not breaking.

Connie said defiantly, angrily, "You won't defend your own crew?"

"My way," Dave said flatly. "It'll be my way, or I ride out of here."

They looked at each other steadily and it was Connie's gaze that fell first. She said then, meaning it, "I'm sorry, Dave. I deserved that."

Dave turned to regard Bill then, and he said levelly, "Next time, Bill, I won't go to teacher. You take my orders or get out!"

A wild protest mounted in Bill Schell's face and he murmured, "Careful, Dave."

"Take my orders or get out," Dave repeated flatly, recklessly. "I want to hear you say what it'll be."

A warning, wicked anger danced in Bill's eyes, and Dave stood motionless, waiting for it to break.

Bill said thinly, "You're too tough, friend."

"Just tough enough."

Bill watched him a still moment, and then his grin, never far from the surface, broke. "All right. Quit ridin' me. I'll take your orders."

Dave turned back to Connie then. "How bad is Curley hurt?"

"I don't know. Badly, I think."

Dave picked up his hat off the bed and went over to the door. He paused there before he opened it, and spoke to Bill Schell. "I back up my men, Bill, but I do it in my own way. Leave Ed Burma alone. I'll settle for Curley."

Bill said nothing, and Dave stepped out. Both Bill and Connie stared at the closed door for a long moment, and then Connie said dully, "Where's he going, Bill?"

"I only work for him," Bill said bitterly. "I don't know."

He went out too, then, and Connie rose from the bed and went to the window. Presently, she saw Dave ride out into view from under the porch roof, and he clung to the road that went north out of the clearing toward Signal. She speculated on Dave's intention a long moment, and then gave up and came back to the bed and sat down.

She found she was still smarting under the lash of Dave's words, and she felt both humble and angry. She had made a second mistake, she knew. The first had been in pulling Dave away from 66 and leaving it to be taken. The second was in telling Dave what he should do.

The first time he had been patient, but this time he had struck back, and it hurt. She had been, she saw now, wrong in siding with Bill's suggestion to beat up Ed Burma. Dave was right in saying Burma had done nothing, should not be punished for something he had no hand in. Still, it was equally wrong to let Ivey's action go unpunished, and when you punished a man's crew, you punished him, no matter what Dave said.

She took a deep breath and looked about the room, and again her thoughts returned to Dave and what he had said to her. He had been rough and disrespectful and not wholly right, and she had taken it meekly. The realization of this troubled her a little. Frank Ivey had spoken to her just as roughly a hundred times, and it only made her mad and stubborn and hating—and yet she took it from Dave with a school girl's meekness. It puzzled her.

Down in the corrals, Bill Schell was working over a new bunch of cattle in silence. A steady anger was eating at him as he went through the motions of his work. Dave's reprimand still smarted, but when he thought of Curley he cursed silently and bitterly. His liking and his respect for Dave was something deep and unshakeable, but he knew Dave did not know how he felt about Curley, because he was new here. But Curley had been his friend, even when he worked for Bell. They had ridden together and got drunk together and hated Frank Ivey together, and now Bill had to stand by, helpless and silent. And he wasn't made that way. He could pull out, of course; nothing was making him work for Dave Nash. Yet Bill knew that wasn't the answer, and it galled him to know it. He'd seen enough of Dave Nash to know that Curley's beating would be paid back double, to know that if he stuck with Dave he would see Frank Ivey brought to his knees. It was that prospect that had made him join Dave in the first place, and it was worth holding his temper to witness. Only, there was Curley now. His mind made the full circle, and he got no satisfaction out of his brooding as he worked on in dogged silence through the afternoon.

Dusk saw the job done. Bill took a last look at the big corral jammed with bawling cattle and then rode his horse over to the horse corral by the barn and turned him in. What he needed was a drink. Maybe that would take the taste of Curley out of his mind. But first, though, there was the tally book to tote up against what cash remained in the cigar box under George's bar. He thought of the bar pleasantly crowded with his friends, and he knew he couldn't work there, so he got the lantern and lighted it and sat atop the feed box and drew out the tally book.

If he was working for Dave Nash he might as well prove to him that he had hired a steady hand who could take a tongue-lashing and still do his work. Bill wasn't much good with figures and he was finding it hard to keep his mind on this business when George came out to feed his horses.

Bill bummed a cigar from him and fired it up, and while George forked some hay out into the corral, Bill labored silently at his figures. A breed from over on the reservation wandered in and began to talk with George in a low voice as George worked.

Disturbed, Bill looked up and said irritably, "Dammit, George, shut up."

George looked over and grinned. "Pokey is tryin' to get me to sell him some liquor."

Pokey was mostly Indian, and George wasn't supposed to sell liquor to Indians, and Bill growled, "Sell him some, then, but shut up."

He went back to his figuring, now the talk was stopped. And then, behind his laborious concentration, he heard another distracting sound. Someone else had come up and paused within the barn. Bill tried again to figure, but finally, in annoyance, he turned to see who was watching him.

It was Ed Burma. He had his shoulder against the stall partition and was watching Bill with a quiet dislike. Bill felt that instant hatred of anything Bell rise within him, and added to it now was the knowledge of what had happened to Curley. Burma's very presence here was somehow a challenge.

He said, then, "I don't aim to forget last night, Bill."

"You ain't supposed to," Bill drawled. "What do you want to do about it?"

"Nothing, now," Burma said.

Bill grinned wickedly and said, "Or ever, friend."

Burma straightened up and came over and said, pleasantly enough, "How many you buyin'?"

"Why?" Bill asked.

Burma grinned faintly, missing the edge in Bill's voice. "We'll be buyin' 'em from you when 66 breaks up. I just wondered."

The bland gall of it touched Bill Schell's nerves like a whip, and his face, under its deep tan, whitened with anger. He rolled his cigar in his fingers and said thinly, "If your nose was an inch longer, Ed, I'd tie it to your belt."

The amusement in Ed Burma's eyes vanished abruptly. As foreman of Bell, he was used to a certain deference, but even from a Circle 66 hand this talk was a little rough. He looked carefully at Bill who had risen now, and saw the measure of his temper and was surprised at it.

He asked reasonably, "What's got into you, Bill?"

"You smell," Bill said flatly, wholly reckless now. "Get away from me. I don't like it."

Burma heard a movement back in the barn and he turned, and saw George and Pokey watching this. He saw George, who never carried a gun, reach over slowly and lift Pokey's gun from its holster and hold it hanging at his side.

He knew then he was about to be braced, and he made his decision swiftly.

He said, "All right, I'll get out," with a tolerant smile, and took a step toward the door.

Bill moved in front of him then, and said in a hard and wicked voice, "You ain't got two men to hold me,

Ed, like they held Curley. You won't take the chance without them, will you?"

Ed looked levelly at him, a faint flush of anger in his face. He didn't know what Bill was talking about, only he recognized the insult. He said quietly, "If I'm a mind to fight, Bill, nobody has to hold for me."

"What would it take to get you a mind to?" Bill drawled thinly.

A cold caution was on Ed Burma now. The cause of this was unknown to him, but he recognized Bill's intent, and he read the finish of this trouble accurately. It was no time for pride. He said mildly, "An awful lot, Bill."

Bill cuffed him with the flat of his palm across the face. The blow shoved him off balance, and he braced himself against the feedbox that held the lantern. His hand on the box, he looked carefully at Bill, and then at George, then back at Bill.

Slowly, he put both hands on top of the feedbox so that his movement could not be misread, and he said, "Bill, I got no fight with you about last night or anything else. Now quit it, will you?"

Bill came up to him, and his face was tight and wicked as he said, "I'm goin' to kick your face, Ed. So help me."

Ed's hands remained on the feedbox and he knew with a cold and dismal feeling of fear that if he lifted them off it, he was a dead man. "Some other time, Bill," he said quietly.

Bill was holding the cigar in his left hand. Now he took it and jammed the lighted end down on Ed's hand. Ed pulled back his hand instinctively, and in that second he knew his time was up. In the same movement he wheeled away from the feedbox, his hand streaking for his gun.

It was quick, desperate, and it had caught Bill off guard. He dropped behind the corner of the feedbox. With his gun clear and Bill out of sight, Ed wheeled and laid a shot at George, and got an answering one on the heel of his own.

And then Bill rose. Ed saw him, and tried to pull his gun around, and was too late. Bill shot.

Ed slammed against the wall of the stall, and rolled off it and fell heavily in the dust of the floor on his face. Bill came over to him and rolled him halfway over and, seeing his face, let him roll back.

He wheeled now, and looked at Pokey and George, who still held the gun. The three of them regarded one another for a brief moment, and then Bill said quietly, "Pokey, take your gun and drift. George'll have a bottle for you tonight."

The breed accepted the gun with a stolid face and headed for the back door of the barn. Already there was the sound of men running toward the barn from the saloon.

"Pokey," Bill said.

The breed paused.

"You never saw this. You weren't even around. Remember?"

The breed nodded and slipped out the back door of the barn, and again Bill looked at George. He did not have to say anything to George, nor George to him. The promise of whiskey insured Pokey's silence; of each other, they were sure.

They were both standing beside Burma when the first of the saloon crowd reached them.

Bill looked them over and did not speak. A couple of them moved toward Burma, and George observed wrly, "He got it in the face," and they stopped, not wanting to see it.

They were standing this way, mute, when Connie, breathless from her run, came up with several more men and saw Burma lying there. A small cry escaped her, and she looked swiftly up at Bill, dismay in her face.

"Ask George," Bill said quietly. He glanced over at George. "Tell her. Go ahead."

George looked around at the men, eying each of them and his glance moved to Connie.

"He jumped Bill and got in two shoots before Bill pulled on him. I saw it."

# CHAPTER IX

Night came in the timber suddenly, and with it a whole new life seemed to waken. Close to where the trail dropped into the foothills, Dave jumped a pair of deer and paused and listened to the sound of their passage, the faint jarring of the earth through the deep humus of the pines, die silently away in the night. A pair of owls called back and forth, and far off in the foothills a coyote lifted his chattering cry. He went on, then, and was presently in the foothills, where the rocks still held a little of the day's heat.

He could think of Connie's news now and know he was right. Ivey wanted nothing better than to have 66 strike back blindly in revenge for Curley's beating, for that would bring open war, with Crew behind him and his hands twice outnumbering Connie's. He thought of Jim Crew then, and again tried to read the man. Crew, he believed, did not like Ivey, but he would not let that influence him. Crew was old and he was tired, and his passions were spent. He wanted to be left alone, and he would deal his law out of the book, never surprised at the folly of man. But there must come a time when he could no longer be neutral, when he must punish someone. And once he was sure of his ground, he would be merciless as a wolf.

The lights of a homesteader shack moved slowly past him to the north, and as he leveled off onto the flats he heard the long baying of some ranch dog. He wondered again with a persistent speculation if Curley's beating would pull Crew off the fence, and again he doubted it. But in passing up the chance to even the score with Ed Burma, he was making Connie's case clean as possible. And thinking of Burma, he thought of Connie. He had been rough with her, because this was important to him. The thought of squaring accounts with Ivey by beating up his foreman was personally distasteful to him, but he did not blame Connie or Bill for their passion. It was that very fire in them both that he liked. In Connie, it was an endearing wildness that was tempered by her sweetness. She was, he thought, a strange and wilful girl that he almost understood.

He dropped down into Signal in midevening, and its afterdark somnolence seemed unchanged. Bondurant's store was still open, and there was a scattering of saddle horses in front of the Special. Jim Crew's office was dark, so he passed it and went on to Rose's. He dismounted behind her place and knocked on the door, and presently it was opened to him by Rose.

Her greeting was quiet, and when she stepped aside for him, he saw Jim Crew sitting at the dining table. At another chair sat an elderly man, a black satchel beside him, and Dave supposed this was the doctor and he looked questioningly at Rose.

"We brought Curley here," she said, and as she took Dave's hat she looked briefly into his face. "This is Doctor Parkinson. Dave Nash."

Doctor Parkinson had a round, merry face that did not like sobriety. Always, he seemed eager to smile, and he did now as he rose and shook hands with Dave.

Jim Crew nodded wearily, and he too looked searchingly at Dave.

"Curley one of your men?" Doctor Parkinson asked, and when Dave nodded, the doctor's face became genuinely grave.

"Well, there's no more I can do tonight. I'll set the nose tomorrow, since I don't dare risk it tonight."

"How bad is he?" Dave asked.

Doctor Parkinson shrugged. "He's alive. I don't believe he'll ever see again, though." He hesitated. "Was he dragged by a horse?"

"No," Dave said, and went into Rose's room. Curley was under the covers, and when Dave looked at his face a sick rage came over him. He heard the doctor and Jim Crew saying good night to Rose, heard the door shut, and he stood motionless, still looking at Curley, thinking, *I'm going to kill a man.*

Rose came in and adjusted the window, and Dave went back into the kitchen. She came out presently, and pulled the curtains behind her and passed in front of him to the stove. Suddenly, he heard her sobs, quiet, muffled as she tried to stop them.

Dave went over to her, and she turned away from him, and presently she said, "It's all right, Dave. Somebody has to cry for him, I guess."

Dave went over to the table and slacked into a chair and looked dully at the base of the lamp. "Who's this Virg Lea?" he asked presently, when Rose was silent.

"I don't know," Rose said. She came up beside him and said, "Want some coffee, Dave?"

"Sure," Dave said idly.

He waited until she had put the cup and saucer beside him and sat down at the table, and Dave glanced over at her. Her face was sad, and behind the sadness was a still quiet anger that he had never seen there before.

"They all come to you, don't they?" Dave murmured.

Rose smiled fleetingly and said nothing, and Dave rose and took a turn around the kitchen and then halted behind her chair. He put both hands on it and spoke softly to the back of her head. "I'll get him, Rose. I'd like to give him what he gave Curley, but I won't. I'll just get him."

Rose nodded once, slowly. Again Dave circled the kitchen on his restless prowl. He stopped once by the stove and looked idly into the coffeepot and then came back to the table and stood where he could see Rose's face.

"What kind of a man is Ben Dickason, Rose?" he asked slowly.

Rose hesitated a moment before she spoke. "A bullhead, Dave. That's the worst you can say of him." She watched him a moment, and then said quietly, "He's in town."

Dave's glance lifted quickly, and he was motionless a moment, and then went over to where his hat hung, took it, and stepped outside into the night.

He walked down to the Special, and looked over the opaque lower half of its windows and saw Ben Dickason sitting at one of the rear tables with Red Cates. A couple of homesteaders were at the bar talking with Burch Nellis as Dave stepped in.

He nodded to Burch and made his way back to Ben Dickason's table. Red Cates, he noticed, had a thick and very white bandage across his nose, and at sight of Dave he put both hands on the table and waited, his eyes hard and hating. Ben Dickason had been drinking; the flush on his cheeks was like a stain, but his eyes were steady and watchful and only faintly truculent as they followed Dave's progress up to the table.

Dave nodded to him and said, "Busy, Ben?"

"Not at all," Ben said in a low voice.

"I've got something to show you," Dave said. "Come along."

"I don't want to see it," Ben said slowly.

"Afraid to, Ben?" Dave murmured. "Connie wasn't."

He saw Ben's jaw thrust out a little in demurrance, and he waited, not moving. Ben looked at Red, and Red shrugged, and Ben sat a moment longer in sullen indecision before he came to his feet.

Red rose too, and Dave said quietly, "Not you," and stepped aside for Ben to pass him. He did not look at Red again, and Ben did not choose to insist on Red's presence.

Ben tramped out of the Special, Dave at his heels, and on the walk Dave fell in beside him. Ben apparently knew what he was going to see, for he cut across the vacant lot to Rose's back door without any prompting.

Dave didn't knock this time, only palmed the door open and stepped aside for Ben. Rose was at the stove, and at sight of Ben she nodded pleasantly, and Ben

said in his grave, courteous voice, "Evening, Rose."
He looked around him curiously, and then his inquiring glance settled on Dave.

"In there," Dave said, nodding toward Rose's room.

Dave made no move to go in with him, and Ben went in alone and afterwards it was very still. When he came out, after a long time, his face was sick, and he looked immediately at Rose, as if to ask if the man was alive.

Rose watched him, and so did Dave now, and Ben shuttled his glance to Dave, who was leaning against the wall. Ben reached in his pocket for a cigar, and when he had it he glanced down at it and studied it, as if he had never noticed the shape and feel of one before.

Slowly, then, he put it back in his pocket and said in a low, tired voice, "So Connie saw that?"

"She dragged him into the house and doctored him."

"Where——" Ben began, and he paused and shook his head and cleared his throat. "Where are his eyes?"

"Doc Parkinson said he didn't think he'd see again," Rose said.

Dave murmured, "He was kicked," and watched Ben accept that, saw the stirring of revulsion within him.

Ben said tiredly then, "What do you want of me, Nash?"

"Nothing. You can go back to Frank now."

Ben winced then, and protest mounted in his tired face. He went over to the sofa and sat on it, and leaned forward, his fingers laced together, and studied the pattern of the worn carpet.

"Why didn't Frank shoot him?" he asked finally, not looking up.

"He leaves the shooting to D Bar, especially if there's a woman to shoot at," Dave said.

Ben's head came up with a jerk. "A woman?"

"Connie was there while her crew was tradin' shots with yours."

Ben's face paled, and he said in a shaken voice, "Nobody told me that."

"Nobody figured you cared," Dave said mildly. "You're runnin' with Frank Ivey, now."

Slowly, Ben leaned against the back of the couch, his chin sunken against his chest. He watched Rose and Dave both now, his eyes somber and steady with the shock of what he knew.

Rose said at last, "You do care, Ben. You're not that kind of man."

Ben said quietly, "Thank you, my dear," and he turned his glance upon Dave. "What's got into Connie? Do you know?"

"She's got pride," Dave said narrowly. "You broke her man in front of her."

"So she tried to ruin me."

Rose said, "I would in her place," and she came away from the stove, crossing the room to stand in front of Ben. "You don't know a woman's heart, Ben, or you'd never have let Frank do that."

"But he was trash," Ben protested grimly.

"And what is Frank Ivey?"

Ben's protest died in his throat, and Rose went on quietly, "Trash or not, Ben, it was Connie's right to find out for herself."

Ben's chin sank to his chest again, and he slowly stroked the worn leather of the sofa. Dave knew that this decision was coming hard to Ben Dickason, as it would come to any proud and loyal man. But the deep, sighing breath of Curley Fanstock in the next room seemed to creep in here now, as if reminding Ben of his choice, prodding his decision.

Ben rose after a while, and reached for his hat and said, "I'll pull my crew off 66. Send Connie to me, will you?" and tramped toward the door. Dave knew then that he had pried Ben away from Frank.

Ben halted short of the door, and wheeled to face Dave. "I get her side of this. I don't get yours," he said slowly. "You after Connie?"

Dave pushed away from the wall and said, "You better go, Ben," and Ben, after waiting a puzzled moment, stepped outside.

Dave glanced over at Rose, then, and said, "That leaves Frank," and only afterwards did he notice the expression on Rose's face. It was one of strangeness, as if Ben Dickason's question had suggested something to

Rose that had not occurred to her before, and for a brief puzzled second she was considering it. And then the expression was gone, and Dave heard her say, "Yes, only Frank," and it came to him that he had never told Rose why he had changed his mind that morning. For that matter, he had never thought of it himself. He watched Rose go into Curley's room, and drew out his tobacco and fashioned a cigarette and asked himself the question.

Rose came out presently and found him sitting on the sofa. She went over to the cabinet and took out some linen, some silver, a cup and saucer and arranged them on the table in readiness for breakfast, and Dave watched her sure deft movements, the soft curve of her arms as she worked at this homely task. When she moved between the lamp and himself, her thick golden hair seemed to light up with a momentary glow from the lamplight.

Rose said quietly, "I'll have my dress done soon," and when Dave did not answer, she halted and looked at him. He was watching her intently, not seeing her either.

Rose raised her hand and snapped her fingers sharply, and Dave's eyes came into focus and he smiled faintly in answer to her smile, and tossed his cigarette in the saucer on the table.

"I was thinking of what Ben said," he murmured.

Rose was suddenly intent on arranging the silver, and she said, "Were you?"

"It was seeing Ivey break Walt Shipley there in front of the hotel and thinking, 'He'd never do that to me.' "

"And then he tried," Rose said, and she turned to regard him. "Is that why you stuck after Walt left?"

"That's why," Dave said. He missed the inflection of her voice as she asked the question, the undertone of happiness. He rose and got his hat and said, "I've got to see Jim."

Rose went to the door with him, and Dave said good night. Rose watched his tall shape fade into the night, heard the squeak of leather as he stepped into the saddle, and she waved.

Afterward, she shut the door and stood there, her

hand still on the knob. A faint, wise smile was on her lips then, and when she turned to cross the room, she began to hum softly. He hadn't stayed for Connie's sake, then, and Rose found herself oddly happy.

Dave rode over to Crew's office. It was dark inside, but the door was open, and Dave sat in the saddle a moment speculating. He dismounted and crossed the boardwalk and stepped inside. He saw a shape move by the desk and Jim Crew said, "I wondered if you'd come."

Crew struck a match and lighted the bracket lamp on the wall over his desk, and gestured toward the chair beside his desk. His coat was off and his arms through his shirt sleeves looked thin and deceptively frail as he tossed Dave his sack of tobacco. Dave made a cigarette and returned the sack to Crew, who was tilted back in his chair, regarding the open doorway.

"What do you do now?" Crew said.

"I came to ask you that."

Crew said bitterly, "I can arrest Virg Lea and get him time in the pen. That satisfy you?"

"No."

"I'll kick Ben off 66."

"He's off."

Crew spread his thin hands and let them drop to his knees. "You don't want to talk to me."

Dave studied the end of his cigarette. "They'll be packin' Virg Lea's body in to you some day soon."

"Naturally," Crew said dryly.

"What'll you do about that?"

"Nothin'."

The two of them exchanged an understanding look, and then Jim Crew murmured, "It's the ones they tote in afterward I'll get curious about."

"How curious?"

"Real curious," Crew drawled. "I'll earn my pay."

"I never doubted that," Dave said soberly. He came to his feet and went almost to the door and threw his cigarette out into the night and said idly, "I'm short a hand, Jim," and glanced over at Crew.

Crew smiled thinly and said, "Considering my age, that's a compliment."

Dave grinned too. "I'm not buyin' a horse. I won't look at your teeth."

Crew almost laughed then, and he shook his head slowly. "Not yet, son." He was silent a long moment, and then said carelessly, "I don't like your crew, Dave."

"I don't either."

"You better tell 'em," Crew said, "that I'm playin' this one by the book. They better believe it."

Dave nodded. Outside, two horses were coming up the street, and both Dave and Crew listened, faintly curious. The horses stopped outside the door, and Dave stepped against the wall as Crew rose and went out into the night. Dave followed him, and they both halted on the boardwalk, peering at the mounted figure beside Dave's horse.

"Somebody better give me a hand," Bill Schell said.

Dave's glance shuttled to the second horse. He saw the canvas-wrapped bundle across it, and the cold certainty of what it contained hit him like a solid blow.

Crew stepped forward and approached the bundle. "Who is it?"

"Burma," Bill said calmly.

Rage, quiet and wicked, crept through Dave then, and Bill Schell turned his head to peer at Dave, whose back was to the light. Bill's face was limned in the faint glow, and it was hard and reckless and defiant.

Bill said then, "He pulled a gun on me at George's."

"That better be so," Dave said slowly.

"Hell, I gave him two shots at me before I pulled on him!"

Nobody answered him immediately, and he turned now to look at Crew.

"Sure," Crew said softly. "You don't mind if I'm a little curious, Bill?"

"The whole west slope was there. Ask them, ask George."

"He will," Dave promised.

# CHAPTER X

CONNIE slept very late and only wakened when George's Indian woman slipped into her room with her dress. It was washed clean of blood and pressed, and the Indian woman, smiling, laid it across the bed, shyly placed a comb and brush beside it, and disappeared.

Connie lay there a moment staring at the ceiling, remembering last night, and depression settled on her like some insufferable weight. She sat up in bed and looked at the dress and thought *I've seen one man dead, and one man beaten up, and I don't guess I'm changed.* She knew differently, though.

She slipped into her fresh dress, and went over to the washstand and took down the mirror—which was set for the average tall man and useless to her—and propped it up against the window. Pausing a moment there, she looked across the road at the corral full of her cattle. They were nosing around in the last remnants of the hay forked over to them by George's man this morning. A quick hard pride came to her; these cattle were hers, the start of Circle 66.

Connie dragged a chair over to the window and sat in it, adjusting the mirror so she could see herself. She began to brush her dark curling hair then, and the pleasant, effortless business of it left her free to speculate again on last night. If Bill Schell had killed Ed Burma in self-defense, then the law was on her side.

91

Frank Ivey and her father would have to take that, or, in retaliating, they would forfeit the protection of the law. But the trouble was, Connie thought miserably, she wasn't sure Bill had killed in self-defense.

She kept remembering Bill Schell's face yesterday afternoon when she told him about Curley, and only Dave's hard flat warning had checked him. She remembered, too, all the stories of Bill Schell's wildness and his hair-trigger temper, and a nameless dread rose in her. What if Bill, in shooting Ed Burma, had committed the very act that would forfeit Jim Crew's help? Dave would never forgive Bill, nor would he forgive her.

Connie gave her hair a last pat, put the mirror back and went downstairs. This morning, it was hard to believe that a man had been killed here last night. The road, the lobby, the dining room were all empty, and she went into the dining room and sat down at the place laid for her.

While eating her lonely breakfast, she made plans for the remainder of the day. Dave would probably be up for the cattle with a couple of hands. She might as well stop at D Bar and pick up Josefa and take her over to the Ridge camp.

Slow footsteps on the porch made her look up through the doorway that let out into the lobby, and she saw Jim Crew enter. Panic seized Connie for a moment, then: "Jim Crew is here to check on Ed Burma's death. Well, why not?" she thought. It was only a routine thing, and it had to come sometime.

Jim came into the dining room and, seeing Connie, touched his hat with his thin frail hand and said, "Hello, Connie. George around?"

"I just got up. I don't know."

Jim tramped over and passed her and looked in the kitchen and turned back.

"Is it—about Ed Burma?" Connie asked.

Crew nodded briefly. "Finished breakfast?" When Connie said she had, Jim said, "Come along and let's find George."

It was spoken courteously, but Connie knew it was an order, and she got up and joined him.

Going through the lobby, Connie said, "How's Curley?"

"He's at Rose Leland's, and he's no different." He looked obliquely at her. "Your father saw him last night."

"Did he cheer?" Connie asked bitterly.

Crew was silent a moment. "No. As a matter of fact he's pullin' off 66. He'd of done that anyway—without Curley. He wants to see you, he says."

Connie said nothing, and Jim steered toward the bar. Poking his head through the doorway, Crew saw George behind the bar at work with some figures on a sheet of worn wrapping paper.

At their entrance, George looked up, no surprise in his sallow face, and said, "Mornin', folks."

Crew came up to the bar and said, "Makin' lots of money, George?" and George said, "Not enough, Jim," and smiled carefully and put the paper away. They both eyed each other warily, Connie noticed, but George's face in particular was bland and hard as a river pebble.

Crew turned so he could see both Connie and George, and then asked mildly, "What went on here last night, George?"

"What did Bill Schell tell you?"

"You answer first," Crew said dryly.

"I never heard what started it," George said quietly. "It was in the barn. I was forkin' hay out into the corral. Bill was sitting on the feedbox, figurin' in his tally book by lantern light. Burma come up and they talked. Somethin' he said made Bill mad, and Bill answered sharp. Burma shoved away from the feedbox and pulled his gun."

"First?"

"The first shot turned me around. Ed's gun was out, Bill's wasn't. Figure it out."

"Why didn't Ed kill him, then?"

"I'll never know," George said. "Bill dropped alongside the feedbox and Ed shot again, into the floor. Then Bill come up and he shot Ed."

Connie, watching him closely, knew he was lying.

She didn't know how she knew, but she did; he was lying superbly.

Jim Crew's chill blue eyes never left George's face, and George accepted the stare tranquilly. "That sounds open and shut," Crew murmured idly. "Too good, almost."

George smiled thinly. "Too good for who?"

"Bill Schell. He ain't the kind to let a man shoot at him twice before he moves."

George moved toward the end of the bar and lifted out Ed Burma's gun and shoved it across to Jim. "Everybody up here heard three shots. Two of 'em were Ed's, one was Bill's."

Crew made no move to take the gun. He said, "Who else beside you saw it?"

"Nobody." A wicked amusement was in George's eyes, but his face was bland. "Don't settle it on me, Jim. I don't pack a pistol and never have."

Crew was silent a moment, his expression utterly noncommittal. He asked then, "Who was in here?"

George turned to the back bar, picked up a small and soiled notebook and tossed it on the bar. "There's the men Nash bought stuff from. They was mostly here."

Crew pocketed the book and shoved away from the bar, and then he stopped. "Burma had a burn on his right hand. Where'd he get that?"

George said musingly, "A burn," and frowned and then said, "I don't know."

"Guess," Crew suggested gently, a faint sardonic edge to his voice.

George, however, ignored the sarcasm; his face was thoughtful. "Well, Bill was smokin' a cigar when the trouble started. It might of been on the edge of the feedbox and Ed put his hand on it."

"This was on the back of his hand."

"Well, he fell on his back. It might of been under his hand."

And then Connie knew he was lying. When she saw Ed Burma he was on his face, as if he'd been flung there by the violence of the shot. She had arrived at the barn only seconds after the first men, and she had seen nobody touch Burma. He was lying on his face, his blood pooling the dirt under his shoulder.

Jim Crew said mildly, "All right," as if he didn't believe it, and touched his hat to Connie and said, "I'll check this story, George."

He went out the open front door, and George moved over to the window and watched him until he had ridden past the hotel, heading south. George came back then, and his curious gaze was on Connie. "Ready for your horse, Miss Dickason?" he asked politely.

"Ed Burma wasn't on his back when I saw him," Connie said slowly.

"I turned him over."

"Where did the burn come from? Why does it matter?"

George regarded her with cold impudence in his eyes. "You really want to know?"

Connie hesitated a moment and then said swiftly, "No."

"I didn't think so." George looked down at his hand on the bar and said in a low voice, "Funny. I thought 66 was out to break Bell."

The reprimand brought the color into Connie's cheeks, and she murmured, "It is."

George glanced up swiftly. "You better let me alone, then. That's my story." He even grinned faintly, without humor.

Connie nodded slowly, understanding little of this, except that George was lying for her and for 66. Her hands were clean; she was innocent of any direct deception, and that was the way it was to be.

She turned then, and George said, "Just a minute." He reached under the counter and brought out a cigar box holding the money for the cattle, and opened it. "I paid out all but a hundred and ninety-two dollars. The law," he added dryly, nodding toward the road, "has got the figures in that tally book, but they'll check."

Connie looked at the box and then at George. "Keep it," she murmured. "66 knows its friends."

George looked at her a still moment, and then said with a dry courtesy, "I thank you."

Connie's horse was brought and she mounted and rode south along the road Crew had taken. But presently it forked, and she took the left turning, which sloped off toward the Bench. Afterward, she took a branching trail that turned farther south through the timber. This trail was the one used by the Bell, 66, and D Bar.

The ride was through the deep shade of the big pines, and Connie enjoyed it. As she rode on through the afternoon an inexplicable feeling of confidence and strength grew in her. It was as if she had skirted some dangerous precipice and now that she had passed it successfully, it would never frighten her again. Nobody would ever discover Bill Schell's guilt, for hadn't she seen George present irrefutable evidence of his innocence? The ethics of it did not bother her either, and she thought of them only briefly. Burma worked for Ivey, and knew his risk and should have been more wary. This was war, and since Frank Ivey gave no quarter, she would give none. She thought, then, of Dave and she knew she could hide it from him. He need never know about Bill. Since the proof of Bill's innocence would not jeopardize his relations with Crew, there was no reason why he should ever know the truth. It came to Connie then that guile had its place in this fight, and by the judicious use of it she could contribute her share to ultimate victory.

Presently, the timber began to thin out onto a short grassy flat, and then the land broke away abruptly for the foothills. Connie crossed the flats and presently was in the narrow trail that let down into Hondo canyon. It sloped down around a long shoulder of rock to the left, dropping off on the other side into a tangled mass of scrub oak that could barely cling to the steep sides of the canyon. A mile on, the trail leveled off on the canyon floor and she followed it out into the foothills and then the flats and turned south again toward D Bar.

Crossing the bridge at D Bar always sounded a warning, and Connie was curious today as to how the crew would receive her. A pair of them drifted out of the bunkhouse when they heard her horse on the bridge, and seeing her, dodged back. Only Link Thoms, who came around the corner of the cookshack as he always did, stayed to watch her.

He came toward her then, and Connie said, "Hello, Link," and the youngster grinned shyly. He held up his hand to help her down, but she did not accept it. "I won't get down, Link. Do you suppose you could bring Josefa and my trunks over?"

"Just like first time," Link said, in a slow, troubled voice, and then he blurted out, "You ain't really leavin', are you, Connie?"

"I really am this time."

Connie heard the door to the house slam and glanced over toward it. Ben Dickason, bareheaded and smoking his eternal cigar, called "C'mere, Connie."

Connie pulled her horse around and rode over to the cottonwoods, and Ben came out to meet her.

"Hello, Pop."

"Get down and come on in," Ben invited.

"No, I'm in a hurry. I'm taking Josefa this afternoon."

"You aren't in that much of a hurry," Ben said, with a mock roughness. "Get down."

"No, thank you," Connie said, her voice firm and impersonal.

Ben took the cigar from his mouth and said humbly, "I wanted to have a talk with you, Connie, about all this."

"We've had it, haven't we?"

"No," Ben said slowly. "I—well, maybe I was a little hasty the other day."

"You mean the day you put your crew on 66?" Connie asked dryly. "Yes, you were, but I'll learn."

"I pulled 'em off, Connie," Ben said earnestly.

"Of course you did," Connie replied, and laughed shortly, without humor. "Even you aren't big enough to buck the government."

"That wasn't why," Ben went on. "I—talked to Nash last night. He——"

"You mean you haven't run him out of the country yet?"

"Dammit, Connie, be decent!" Ben said explosively.

Connie smiled faintly and was silent, and Ben, flushing, went on. "I talked with Nash last night. I saw Curley."

"That was a thorough job," Connie murmured. "Your idea or Frank's?"

Ben said resentfully, "Don't get mean, youngster. You know I'd never stand for that."

"You stood for it in your partner, which is the same thing."

"That's what I'm trying to tell you," Ben said impatiently. "I won't stand for it."

Connie regarded him closely, a shrewd speculative glance in her eyes. "What'll you do, Pop?"

Ben made a violent motion with his hand. "No more of that sort of stuff! I'll tell him!"

"Maybe," Connie said dryly, "he'll think it's too late to listen."

"Why would he?"

"Bill Schell killed Ed Burma last night. In a fair fight."

Ben's jaw slacked open and he stared blindly at Connie for five full seconds. Then his glance slowly fell, and he said softly, "Oh." Connie didn't speak, and Ben shook his head slowly. "Connie, Connie," he murmured, "come back home."

"It's too late, Pop."

"But that isn't for you," Ben pled. "You're a girl, Connie."

"I always have been."

"But not like you are now. You're hard as hell, Connie."

"Why am I?" Connie countered implacably. "I had to be, or you'd have broken me. Hard things don't break so easy, Pop."

"But that's over now," Ben said, his voice humble. "Do you think I'd want you to marry Frank Ivey now?"

"He's the same man."

Ben shook his head, eying her strangely. "You never forgive a mistake, do you, Connie?"

"In my own way," Connie said thoughtfully, "which isn't coming back to you for your blessing. I'm going to do what I said I would, Pop. I'm going to make 66 something as big as D Bar and Bell. I asked for your help and understanding once. I don't need it now."

Ben tossed his cigar away and said dispiritedly, "All right, Connie."

"You notice I don't ask what your terms are if I come back? I don't even care."

"I noticed," Ben said quietly.

He looked very old and very helpless, standing there below her, and Connie steeled herself against pity. "I want all my things, Pop—clothes, books, saddles, horses, everything. I'll send over for them."

Ben said nothing, and Connie pulled her horse around and rode away. She had cut her last ties with D Bar and her father, and, strangely, she was not unhappy.

# CHAPTER XI

DAVE rode into 66 sometime after dark. Lamps were lighted in the house, and it was past suppertime. He turned his horse into the corral, and afterward got a long drink from the pipe at the horse trough. He built himself a smoke and lighted it, and his hunger was a solid ache in his stomach; and yet he perversely shrank from going up to the house.

He saw a movement at the corner of the barn, and went over there and found Tom Peebles waiting for him. He said with blunt censure, "You keep a nice guard here, Tom," and Tom wisely did not answer him. Dave said, more reasonably now, "What did you see at Bell?"

"Not much," Tom told him. "Crew left early. Frank sent a couple of men into town after that, and that's all."

"Connie back yet?"

"At the house. She brung a cook."

Dave considered what Tom had told him, and saw no clue to Frank Ivey's temper in it. Perhaps Jim Crew had warned Frank flatly to hold his peace until the circumstances of Ed's death were more clear. He said, "You and Bailey pick up the cattle at Relief tomorrow and start 'em down," and he left Tom, tramping toward the kitchen. He had ridden the edge off his temper today, scouting all the Bell cattle that were on this side of American Creek, and now he was tired and hungry and able to think once more, without anger, of Bill Schell. Perhaps if Frank Ivey hadn't moved against 66, Bill's story was straight, and Dave thought of this with a faint hope before skepticism set in. No, Bill wasn't the kind to let a man shoot twice at him before he defended himself. And if Crew found that Bill had rawhided Burma into a fight, so he could kill him, Dave knew what he was going to do. He would turn Bill over to Crew and let the law take its course. All day he had thought of it, and he did not like it, and yet he knew this was what he had to do.

There was nobody in the kitchen when Dave entered. He lighted the lamp, feeling the chimney still warm. He saw the mud scummed and dried on the floor, and when he put his boot down there was the brittle grating of broken glass underfoot. D Bar had not been gentle with the place while they had it.

He rummaged around and found some fresh biscuits and a plate of cold steaks, and after filling a cup with water, he stood at the table and wolfed the food, washing it down with the water.

His low spirits made his dark face somber and strangely hard. He heard someone coming through the dining room, and he turned, his cheeks bulging with food, to see Connie come in.

"There's a fire left for coffee, Dave," Connie said quickly.

Dave shook his head and swallowed and said, "This'll do, Connie," and drank again deeply, and went on eating, watching Connie now. Somehow, the very sight of her cheered him.

Connie smiled and said, "I like to watch a man eat like that," and went over to the bread box. She lifted out half a cake, and Dave, a biscuit still in his hand, came over and looked critically at it.

"Just one piece left," he said with a mock soberness.

Connie laughed then, and Dave smiled, too, and looked at her so thoughtfully that Connie frowned. "What's the matter?"

"I was just trying to remember," Dave said. "That's the first time I've heard you laugh, Connie."

Connie nodded soberly. "Too many ghosts, maybe."

"You're not scared of them, Connie."

"Not just one," Connie said. "A lot of them, maybe I am. There's Walt. I—don't like to think about that. And Dad, and Frank Ivey and—oh, everything people used to be and aren't any more, and things too."

Dave leaned against the table and put his cup down carefully. "Your choice, Connie, wasn't it?"

"I know," Connie agreed. "Still, it was nice once upon a time. Like being a child is nice, except you wouldn't go back to it."

"You could go back to some of it, Connie. Your father."

"Frank Ivey's partner?" Connie asked scornfully.

"Not any more," Dave said. "He's through with Ivey. He hasn't any heart for this fight. He wants to see you."

Connie said calmly, "Should I make up with him?"

"Yes."

"Tell me why."

Dave got up and went over to the sink and pumped his cup full of water and drank it, and slowly came back to the table. "Ever stop to think, Connie, that stubborn streak of yours is a present from your father?"

"I've thought of it and I don't like it."

"Then don't nurse it," Dave murmured. "He's a good man, Connie. He's old and he's lonesome and he's made a mistake that hurt him. Give him a chance to make it up to you."

Color crept into Connie's face, and she was silent, and Dave knew she was stubborn still. The hurt had reached deep, he thought, and Ben Dickason would pay her price before it ended. But there was a sweetness there and a pity that would change her in time, when the memory of all this was not so fresh.

He heard now the heavy footsteps of one of the crew in the dining room, and he turned and saw Bill Schell haul up in the door. An indefinable irritation was in him as he looked at Bill's face, sulky, and watchful and smoulderingly defiant.

Bill said, "Tom says him and Bailey are goin' up after the stuff tomorrow. What about me?"

"You stay here," Dave said quietly.

Bill looked at him with a hot suspicion. "You playin' Crew's game, Dave?"

"I'm playin' it, all right, and what is it?"

"You figure 66 is jail until he checks my story?"

"Something like that," Dave agreed.

Bill came into the room and leaned both hands on the table and said carefully, "Don't do that to me, Dave."

"Worried, Bill?" Dave prodded gently.

"You couldn't get me out of this country with a posse," Bill said flatly. "That what's eatin' you?"

"I'd thought of it."

Bill straightened up, and said thinly, "I ain't afraid of Crew or you or what Crew'll find, Dave. Just don't set me up in the corner like I was still in school."

"All right."

"I'll ride anywhere I damn please."

"And ride back."

"And ride back," Bill said flatly. He wheeled and stalked out of the room, the very set of his back reflecting a smouldering rage.

Dave followed him out as far as the dining-room doorway and watched him tramp down the porch and turn into the dark bunk room. He had a dismal moment of suspicion, which faded gradually into puzzlement. Something was wrong with Bill, and yet he wasn't going to run, Dave knew.

He heard Connie behind him, and turned to regard her somberly.

"Were you really trying to keep Bill here for Jim Crew?"

Dave nodded.

"Bill's your friend, even if he's wrong," Connie said slowly. "Why are you?"

Dave let this question run through his mind a moment, and then said slowly, "Bill made a bargain, Connie. I told him my wishes, and when he hired on he did the same as give his word. If he's broken his word, he'll pay for it, like a man pays for everything he does."

"You can be hard," Connie said quietly.

Dave looked searchingly at her. "Why, yes, Connie, when there's a time for it."

Connie said slowly, "Would you be just as hard with me, say, if I'd let you down?"

"I'd ride out," Dave said calmly. Connie didn't say anything, and Dave, looking at her, smiled faintly. "Only you never would."

A sound out in the yard now drew his attention, and he looked out into the night and listened. He dimly heard the soft rhythm of a ridden horse approaching, and he stepped back into the room and blew out the lamp in the wall bracket and came back onto the porch. Connie was behind him now, and was silent, listening too.

Dave waited in the deep black shadow of the porch until the horse was close, and then he called, "Sing out."

"It's Rose, Dave."

For a brief second, surprise kept him motionless, and then he stepped off the porch and went out to where Rose had reined in, and Connie was beside him.

Dave took the bridle of her horse and said, "Curley?"

"He died this afternoon," Rose said.

Dave said nothing, feeling nothing for a moment. And then the cold certainty of what he had planned took shape in his mind now, and he said, "Get down, Rose, and come in."

"Yes," Connie said hurriedly, as if in apology for not having invited Rose herself.

Dave led the way back to the living room and lighted the over-head lamp above the table.

Rose was wearing waist overalls, a man's faded blue shirt, and an age-softened buckskin vest that matched the color of her Stetson, which she took off now. Her hair was yellow as wheat against her darker skin, and she looked about the littered room briefly before she turned to Connie and smiled.

"It's filthy," Connie apologized swiftly. "We just got moved in this afternoon."

"It must be nice to be back," Rose said, with complete friendliness. Dave regarded the two of them curiously, struck now by their difference in so many things. It was Rose who was at ease, and Connie who was faintly uncomfortable, and it should have been the other way. Dave thought, he knew why, too; Connie had been the queen too long, going her way sublimely indifferent to both the troubles and the pleasures of a girl like Rose. And now that Connie was no longer queen, but only a girl with a small outfit, a short crew, and powerful enemies, she felt humble and unlearned in the ways of easy friendliness.

Dave said now, "Suppose Josefa could scrape up a bite for Rose?"

"I'll do it myself," Connie said, and she shook her head at Rose's protest and vanished into the dining room.

Dave said in a low voice to Rose then, "Who knows about Curley?"

"I made Doc Parkinson promise he'd give me two hours start before he let the word get out."

"Good."

Only then did he remember a chair, and he cleared one of gear for her, but she did not sit down. She threw her gloves on the table and said, "You go ahead, Dave," and glanced curiously at him.

Dave said slowly, "You know a lot about a man, don't you, Rose?"

"Well, Jim Crew is over on the other slope. He can't take care of it. It doesn't take much figuring, does it?"

"Not much," Dave agreed, and he went out. At the barn he got a lantern, lighted it and hung it on the corral pole. His chestnut, nosing vainly in the dust for the last wisps of hay, looked up as he entered, and then came over to him. Dave saddled up then and blew out the lantern, and afterwards led his horse up to the porch and tied him alongside Rose's.

Rose and Connie were in the kitchen, and the murmur of their voices made him pause in the dining room as he went back in. Their words were lost, but the careless musical cadence of the voices was pleasant to hear, and somehow lonely, and he listened a moment longer before he stepped to the door. Rose had finished eating and Connie was seated at the table across from her.

Rose caught Dave's glance as he entered, and she rose and said, "I've got to get back, Connie."

Connie came to her feet then and saw Dave standing in the door, hat in hand. She looked questioningly at him, and Dave answered, "I'll ride back a little ways with Rose, Connie."

He went out to the horses and Rose and Connie came out. Connie put out her hand and Rose took it.

"Thanks for coming, Rose," Connie said. "You're a good friend."

Rose said quietly, "Somehow, I don't feel as if my news was very bad. Curley wouldn't have had any fun living."

There was a movement from the other end of the porch, and Bill Schell, in his sock feet, came up to them out of the darkness. "What about Curley, Rose?" he asked swiftly. "I heard you."

"He died today."

Bill turned to look down at Dave, who was standing by Rose's horse. "You want me, Dave?"

"No."

Bill kept looking at him for a while, and then, without a word, he wheeled and started back for his quarters. He halted abruptly and looked back at Dave. "I don't get it," he said, his voice angry and resentful. "What do you hire a man for?"

Dave didn't answer, and presently Bill turned and went on into the darkness.

Connie said in a puzzled voice, "Why is he angry?" and Dave didn't answer her either.

Rose said, "Bill is just talking, Connie. Good night," and stepped off the porch.

Dave held her horse while she mounted, and then he came around to his own, and found Connie watching him curiously. "I'll stay at the Ridge camp, Connie. Good night."

He and Rose left the yard and were soon out on the flats, and they did not talk. Dave was thinking of Bill Schell and wondering how long he would last. Bill had been on the lonesome too long to stand restraint; he was getting edgy now, and tonight made it worse.

Rose spoke abruptly. "Were you afraid to tell her, Dave?"

"Tell her?" Dave asked in a puzzled voice.

"Connie. Where you're going."

Dave was silent a long time, and then answered almost irritably, "Maybe I was."

"That's not fair," Rose said. "She deserves to know. She's your boss."

"That's a little rough, when you put it in words," Dave said slowly.

"This whole thing is a little rough. Connie will have to know that before long."

Dave considered that and agreed, and he said wearily, "You're right, Rose, but I won't go back now."

# CHAPTER XII

IT WAS long after dark when Red Cates rode into Bell, having passed the pair of guards at the mouth of the canyon. The bunkhouse was dark, and the only light in the big house was in Frank's office.

Red rode up to the tie rail and Ivey came to the door, scratching his head with blunt fingers and yawning. "Jess?" he called.

"It's me—Red," Cates answered.

Frank grunted, "Come in," and turned back into the office, and Red stepped in, squinting against the light from the lamp on the desk.

"Ben didn't come," Frank observed, slacking into the chair at the desk and swiveling it to face Red. He grinned faintly and shook his head at sight of the bandage on Red's nose. "Man, why didn't Doc tie your whole head up?"

"It'd look worse with it off," Red said bitterly, and slacked into the deep leather chair. Frank took a cigar from his shirt pocket and bit off the end, and only then remembered Red. He threw him a cigar, and then tilted his chair back against the wall.

Red looked longingly at the cigar and said, "It hurts my nose," and put it in his pocket.

"Where's Ben?" Frank asked, putting a match to his cigar.

"He's quit on you, Frank."

Frank ceased puffing his cigar and looked over the

match flame at Red for a brief moment, and then fired his cigar.

Red went on, "Connie stopped on her way down today and spilled it about Ed. That did it."

"I'm broken-hearted," Frank said sardonically, and watched Red grin. "Why didn't he tell me himself, instead of sendin' you?"

"Ask him," Red suggested.

Frank shook his head and said with slow anger, "The hell with him. I knew it would turn out this way."

Red said nothing, and Frank contemplated the far wall for a brooding moment. Then he said, anger close to the surface, "I'm warnin' you, Red. Ben better not get in my way."

"He won't."

"I'll break him, same as I'll break Connie, if he does."

"Hell, don't blame me," Red said wearily.

"You work for an old woman," Frank said contemptuously.

Red's green eyes glinted warningly. "Quit ridin' me, Frank," he said levelly. "I only work for him. I don't think like him."

Frank put his cigar in his mouth and laced his fingers across the back of his head. He regarded Red now with a quiet, speculative intentness, and presently said, "Why?"

"Why what?"

"Why do you work for him?"

Red said wryly, "Times like this, damned if I know."

"Don't be a hammerhead, Red. I'm offering you a job," Frank said quietly.

Red's long face altered with surprise, and he regarded Frank carefully. He was about to speak once and then was silent, and presently said, "Foreman?"

Frank nodded. "Ed's job. Ed's wages."

Red's long face was thoughtful a few lingering moments, and then it broke into a faint reflective grin. "Why not?"

"You'll be expected to do more than chase a bunch of punchers, too."

Red nodded. "If I can't, I'll quit."

He and Frank rose and shook hands on it unsmilingly. Frank went back to his desk now, and Red followed him over and watched him sit down. Frank put down his cigar carefully on the edge of the desk and said, "Crew'll be back in a couple of days. I'm waitin' on him."

"Talk to anybody that saw the fight?"

Frank smiled faintly. "I don't have to. I know Bill Schell."

"Bill Schell," Red observed quietly, "is dead. He don't know it, but he is."

"No," Frank demurred. "Dave Nash is dead. I'm goin' to trade Connie, Burma for Nash."

Red eyed Frank carefully, and Frank went on. "Crew is goin' to find out that Bill killed Ed without givin' him a chance. All I want is for Crew to find that out and tell it to me. Because Bill Schell will dodge out, and I will get Nash instead. Crew won't like it, but he can't do anything about it. Because Connie started this trading dead men off, and she'll be just as wrong as I am. Crew can't do anything about it."

Red nodded. "That'll make sense to a cow-country jury, and Crew knows it."

"And Nash," Frank said slowly, "is what's proppin' Connie up. I get him and she's no good. And I'll get him without pullin' Crew down on my neck. Connie — What's the matter?"

Red's head had turned toward the door, and he said, "Somebody just rode in."

Frank went to the door and called, "That you, Jess?"

A voice out in the night called, "It's Burch Nellis, Frank. That all right?"

Frank stepped out into the night and said, "It's all right, Jess," and he waited until a rider loomed out of the night, and then said patronizingly, "Hello, Burch. You're off the reservation."

Burch Nellis dismounted, grunting, and stretched his legs and came up to Frank. "That's a long way for a man to carry a belly like mine," he observed, and shook hands.

Frank led him inside, and Red drawled with easy, half-contemptuous familiarity, "When'd you start nighthawkin', Burch?"

"Tonight, and I'll quit tonight," Burch said.

He slacked his heavy, soft body into Frank's chair and sighed, and Frank said, "Want a drink of your own poison, Burch?"

"That's handsome of you," Burch said.

Frank pulled out the bottom drawer of the desk and removed a bottle of whiskey and several glasses. He poured a drink for all of them, and Red put his shoulder against the wall and regarded Burch with a faint curiosity. Burch didn't leave the Special once a year. They drank and Frank put his glass back on the desk, and he too was watching Burch. The saloon owner, who by trade had a talent for appreciating a well-turned story, was enjoying this new importance. He took off his hat and swabbed his bald head with his coat sleeve and put his hat back on and said to Frank, "Don't know whether it makes any difference to you boys or not, but Curley Fanstock died this evening."

Frank's thick eyebrows lifted and he said slowly, "Yeah. It might make a difference to Virg."

"So I figured," Burch said. He leaned back in his chair expanding under the warmth of liquor. "Funny thing. I seen Rose Leland ride out on a livery horse, and I got to thinkin' it was a queer time for a ride. Ain't it, now?"

Frank nodded silently, and Burch looked over at Red to see if his story was being appreciated. Red, too, was attentive.

"So I waited until Doc Parkinson left her place and went back to his office, so, thinks I, 'Somethin's happened to Curley.' Well, I just went down to Rose's and walked in her place."

"Walked in?" Red echoed.

Burch smiled slyly. "Most folks have only got one door key and I figured Rose likely took her's, leavin' Doc without one." He spread his hands out. "Well, there was Curley, dead."

Frank said, "Crew's still away, isn't he?"

"Oh, sure," Burch said.

Frank took a slow turn around the room and paused before Burch's chair. "Had anything to eat, Burch?"

"No, thank you. Wouldn't care for any. I could take another drink of that liquor, though."

"Help yourself," Frank said. "Better put up here to-night."

Burch declined the offer, poured himself another drink, received Frank's thanks, and was escorted to his horse.

They watched him ride out into the night, and then Frank said, "I better tell Virg to move."

Red didn't speak immediately. When he did, his words did not seem relevant. "Who'd Rose ride out to tell, Frank?"

Frank puzzled a moment as to what he meant, and then said, "Connie likely."

"Nash, more likely," Red countered.

Frank thought of that, immediately angry, and said, "Then Virg better clear out of here now," and he started off toward the bunkhouse.

"Wait, Frank!" Red called, and walked over to him. Frank could see Red's face in the half-light from the window, and it was oddly excited.

"How bad you want Dave Nash?" he asked in a low voice.

Frank grunted. "Bad enough to get him," he said simply.

"It's right in your hand, and clean as a whistle," Red said, and when Frank did not answer, Red said, "We tell Virg about Curley now and he can beat Dave Nash out of the country, can't he?" Frank nodded and Red went on, "Suppose we don't tell Virg until daylight."

"Nash'll pick him up, follow him and get him."

"And if we steer Virg to a spot where we got a man, we get Nash."

Frank smiled slowly into the night, and Red held his silence. Frank said, "They had a shoot-out, hunh?"

"That's what," Red declared. "He's mine, Frank."

"Take him."

# CHAPTER XIII

CONNIE went back into the kitchen, and as she cleaned up the dishes and stacked them for Josefa she thought of what had passed there on the porch. As she worked, her movements became slower, and presently ceased entirely, and she stared at the sink, her thoughts sharp and curious and suddenly resentful. It was odd that Rose Leland had ridden clear out here to bring word of Curley's death, when she might have sent out someone from the livery. And something had passed out there on the porch between Dave, Bill and Rose Leland that she did not understand. And now that she thought of it, it was odd, too, that Curley had been taken to Rose's place. At the time, she had thought it Jim Crew's idea, and of course it was, but there was something beyond that. Dave was close to Rose, and she had not known it, and the discovery now was oddly sobering.

Finishing her work swiftly, she blew out the lamp in the kitchen and moved out onto the porch and down it until she came to the door of the dark bunk room.

Here she paused and called softly, "Bill."

Bill's answer was immediate. "Comin'."

In a few moments he came to the door and Connie turned and walked up the porch, so she would not disturb the others, Bill at her heels. She halted then and faced Bill and said, "Where's Dave going, Bill?"

Bill hesitated and then said evasively, "Didn't he tell you?"

113

"No."

"After Virg Lea."

Connie accepted this with faint surprise and no shock. After all, Dave had said he would take care of this in his own way, and now his own way was apparent to her. He had waited for Curley's death, which was the clear justification for this. Or was it?

"What will Jim Crew do?" she asked them.

"Nothin'."

"But no matter how much Lea deserves it, it'll be us who got him."

"No," Bill said slowly. "That don't count, Connie. Anybody that'd do what Virg done to Curley is a dead man. Crew don't care. He'd shoot Virg himself, except he's the sheriff. I wish I could."

"I see," Connie said slowly. "Good night, Bill."

She stepped off the porch and strolled toward the corral in the night, and as she walked she found a slow resentment building up inside her. Dave had told Rose of his plans to go after Lea, of course, or she would not have brought out the word of Curley's death. And he had not bothered to tell her, his employer. When Connie thought about that, her pride was touched. It wasn't that she cared if Dave knew other women, she told herself; it just galled her to think that another woman knew more of his plans for 66 than she herself did.

Men, she thought with a sudden contempt, were strange and inconsistent in many ways. Here, for example, was Dave keeping Bill Schell under vigilance in case Jim Crew turned up evidence that Bill had killed Ed Burma unfairly. And now he had ridden out to get Virg Lea, and would kill him.

In one instance it was wrong to kill a man, in the other it was right and had the sheriff's tacit sanction. It was grotesque, Connie thought resentfully.

She stopped at the horse trough and idly dipped her fingers in the cool water. Her thoughts kept returning to Jim Crew. Their whole lives, she thought resentfully, were dedicated to trying to crowd the other side into a move that would forfeit Jim Crew's help. Dave thought so, and apparently Ivey thought so, so it must be true. Connie tried to be contemptuous of Crew, then. He was an old man, aloof, almost unfriendly, and his office was a sinecure. And then she remembered her father's stories of Crew, and the respect all men accorded him, and she knew there was a reason behind it.

Then there must be some way to force Frank Ivey into the wrong, so that Crew would be with 66 irrevocably. There must be a way, and she had to find it, because that was what would win for her.

Slowly, then, it came to her. At first it was just a faint whispering of thought, and then it held on and grew, and she let her hand rest motionless in the water. The full implication of it came to her and for minutes she stood there, searching for a fault in it. She could not. It was a wild gamble, and if it worked, 66 was on top. Beyond that it was her own idea, which neither Dave nor Rose Leland nor any other outsider would share.

For perhaps ten minutes she walked back and forth in front of the horse trough, and finally looked up toward the house. She saw the dim coal of Bill Schell's cigarette up there, and she turned toward it.

When she was close to the porch, she called softly, "Bill, come with me."

The cigarette arced out into the night and Bill approached her silently, and she turned now and walked over to the wagon shed. The spring wagon was still out, and she seated herself on the tongue and was silent so long Bill shifted his feet restlessly, trying to see her in the dark. She felt a kinship to Bill now, and recklessness in his talk and his very posture was reassuring.

"Bill," she said finally, "how far can I trust Tom and Bailey?"

"Not far," Bill said dryly. "They come here for a crack at Ivey, and that's all."

"This is a crack at Ivey—one Dave must never, never know about."

"That's different. They'll be all right."

"I've got to be very sure it's me they're loyal to, not Dave."

"If you can show 'em a way to hurt Frank Ivey, you could nail 'em to them barn logs," Bill said solemnly.

And Connie, believing him, told him her plan.

# CHAPTER XIV

AT FIRST light of day Dave moved his horse back deeper into the foothills timber and shucked out of his slicker, which he had worn during the cold night vigil. He unsaddled and put his chestnut out on picket in the thin light of morning, and then knelt and tied his slicker on his saddle. Rising then, he flailed his arms across his chest a dozen times until he was warm against the chill of dawn, and afterwards built a smoke, listening idly to the shrill morning song of the birds.

His smoke tasted strong and bit into his lungs with a pleasant harshness. He shook out his match and rubbed the burnt end between his fingers, and then moved toward the shoulder of the ridge on his right.

He came up behind a tree and moved slowly around it and sank to his heels beside it, looking off at the steep timbered slope and flats beyond. The shape of the country was now plain, and he saw the far side of the canyon which marked the entrance into Bell, saw the faint V of the wagon roads meeting at its mouth to ribbon up the canyon out of sight.

He was patient now, but he was also curious. Doc Parkinson had promised Rose only a two-hour start. It seemed to him someone around Signal friendly to Frank Ivey would have brought out word of Curley's death before now. Frank Ivey was no fool, either; he would tell Virg Lea to drift, and unless Lea was senseless he could read the future. Jim Crew would pick him up and Ivey wouldn't lift a finger to help him, so there was nothing to do but get out of the country while there was still time. And he had not passed here tonight.

Dave knew there was no other way out of Bell's headquarters place except through this canyon. He sat now against the tree and finished his cigarette, and afterwards his patience was steady and he watched the country below take on shape and substance as the dawn turned into day.

The sun crawled swiftly down the slope and touched him with no warmth and finally was on the flats, and then he saw the two riders come out of the mouth of the canyon. He watched them, not moving, noting the pack horse with them, and saw that one of these men was Lea. He rolled another smoke and finished it, while the two horsemen, striking straight east, finally disappeared over the roll of the flats. Lea, then, was heading east off the Bench into the Breaks, since if he went out through the Federals there was the likelihood of meeting up with Crew, who could guess the reason for him being there. The presence of the second man puzzled him. It wouldn't be a partner or a friend, since a man who would do what Lea did to Curley was not the breed of man who made friends. Beyond that, no man would side Lea now. It was too dangerous. It might be that Frank Ivey, in acknowledgment of a debt to Lea, had supplied a companion to guarantee safe-conduct as far as the Breaks. Dave rose and went back to his horse and saddled up, his mind running carefully over this. He must watch the second man and account for him before he moved in.

In the saddle, he put his horse along the foothills toward the south until he was a safe distance away from Bell's canyon, and then cut east across the Bench. An hour later, he saw from the Ridge the three pinpoints of dark color barely distinguishable from the tawny rolling grasslands, still heading east, and he went on.

Now, however, he kept well to the south, heading for the nearest jutting of timber on the Bench's east boundary, and he traveled steadily, taking advantage of the cover he could find. He knew Lea and his companion would pause on the edge of the timber for a long look over their back trail, and he was willing to sacrifice distance for the security of the timber.

He reached it some hours later, and without pausing sought and found a cattle trail that took him northeast again. He rode steadily, sitting slack and somnolent in the saddle, and he had no taste for this chore. But it was one that had to be done, and that custom had put upon him, just as it had allowed him to tell Crew of his intentions, and allowed Ivey to disclaim the deed that made it necessary.

Sometime in the middle afternoon he came upon a trail that held to the east and he reined up short of it and dismounted to study it. There were three sets of tracks, and he memorized them each, and gave special attention to the shoe marks of the pack horse, which were over the others because he would be led through the timber.

Afterwards, Dave moved east, not crossing the trail, and came back to it now and then, always careful of his approach. He was brought up by the abrupt falling away of the land and the timber thinning out. He saw ahead of him and below through the sparse trees the beginning of the Breaks, a stretch of dun-colored and sterile clay dunes and rubble monuments.

Here he sat long in the saddle, his feet out of the stirrups, studying the shape of this country ahead. The Breaks were new to him, and yet there was a pattern in Lea's flight if a man could read it. The land drained imperceptibly to the south, and that way lay the dry country of the Mormon Sinks. Lea would avoid the settlement to the north, and head for the lonesome places to the south until he was well away from here, so Dave judged his course accordingly.

To follow Lea's trail was out of the question; the Breaks were too barren of cover, the trails too tortuous and the whole country lent itself to ambush. Too, his horse would leave a plain track in the soft clay for any man to read whose caution prompted him to circle back on his trail.

Dave found a way off the Rim a mile below where he came in sight of the Breaks, and was soon deep in its tangled stillness. Once in the early afternoon, he cut sharply east, following the rocky bed of a stream until he came upon the place where the trail crossed. The tracks were there, bearing steadily south; he crossed the trail, now, trusting to the rocks of the stream bed to hide his tracks, and again swung south.

As the sun heeled over, this bleak country around him began to take on color and cast fantastic shadows across the ravines and canyons. After the heat of the middle day had eased off somewhat, the birds began to fly again, and now Dave watched them. A hawk cruising high off in the west dipped a wing and came down to look at something far ahead of Dave and, satisfied, wheeled off incuriously. As the shadows lengthened, Dave began to see a pattern in the flight of the occasional birds to the southwest, and he judged there was water there, and put his horse in that direction. The trails of the smaller animals, as fixed in their habits as man, confirmed this presently, for they too paralleled the flight of the birds.

Dave pulled sharply west, then, wanting another look at the trail. When he found it, he dismounted and studied it, and saw immediately that one rider was missing. Kneeling there, his curiosity sharpened. The second rider might have turned back, or he might have only dropped back to scout the back trail, or he might even have lagged behind in order to approach the water from another direction and protect the first man.

Dave made a quick decision then. He put his horse on the trail and went back, watching the trail carefully. At last he came upon the spot where the second rider had parted from Lea. Dave followed his tracks long enough to make sure he was headed home, and then he again turned south, and knew that Lea was ahead of him at water, camped alone.

Now he kept to the soft clay, moving south in the beginning dusk, and presently, with nothing except instinct prompting him, he dismounted, ground-haltered his horse and set out afoot.

The land soon started to fall away, and Dave cut to the right, walking carefully. He climbed a steep slope after several minutes, and from its eminence he could see several hundred yards ahead. There he could make out the soft shape of clay dunes, but between himself and these dunes was a depression. This, Dave judged, was the water hole.

He moved more carefully now, keeping right, and when he saw the last small ridge ahead of him, he bent over and crawled up its side and took off his Stetson. He did not move, only listened, and presently he caught the unmistakable sound of a horse stamping flies.

He moved up, and looked over. The land lay in the shape of a large saucer; in the very center of the depression was an oval pool of water, its surface reflecting the bright blue of the high sky. There were two horses picketed side by side to the right of the pool, facing away from it, a bedroll and saddles at their heads.

And by the water's edge knelt a man. His hat lay beside him, and he was in the act of stripping off his shirt. The flesh of his broad back gleamed whitely in the dusk as his shirt peeled off. It was Lea.

Dave unbuttoned the flap of his holster, rising, and stepped over the lip of the ridge and walked slowly down toward the man. One of the horses turned to eye him, and he made no attempt at stealth.

He saw Lea's hand move out to drop the shirt, and then it paused, and his head came up as he listened.

Dave halted and said, "Get on your feet," and his voice was oddly loud in the dusk.

Lea swiveled his head then and the two men looked at each other, and Lea's hand let go of the shirt, and it fell soundlessly.

Dave waited, giving him time to crowd his nerve into the one desperate try they both knew he must make. The fear and the despair were in Lea's long face, and he knelt there, watchful, making no move.

Dave said, "I won't tell you again. Get on your feet."

He saw the muscles in Lea's right shoulder jerk suddenly, and Dave reached down for his gun. Lea flung himself sideways, toward Dave, and landed on his belly, grunting, and his gun swung around dragging in the gravel at the bottom of its arc, and he fired hurriedly, desperately. Dave sighted along his lifting gun and pulled too high, and again Lea shot, and now along the sight Dave saw Lea's legs, and then his back, and then his shoulders, and he fired.

The sound of his own gun was the only thing he had heard. He saw Lea's body jar, and the man fought almost to his knees, and then pitched heavily on his face, and where his neck met his shoulders the stain welled out and down into the sand.

One of the horses snorted uneasily, and then it was quiet, and Dave walked over to Lea and stood above him. He was oddly aware now of his own heart pounding, and of the still-heightened awareness of his senses, so that Lea's body, in the dusk, seemed visibly to deflate inside the relaxing muscles.

The new sound came to him distinctly; he recognized it immediately. It was the faint sound of a gun coming onto cock. Without looking Dave lunged for the horses, and he had not taken two steps before the sharp flat crack of a rifle shattered the silence. The horse ahead of him and in line with him screamed thinly and reared up, and then its hind legs seemed to cave and it came over backward. Dave tried to dodge him and could not, and ran glancing into him, and was knocked savagely to the ground so that his breath was driven from him.

He rolled and came to his knees, gagging for breath, and heard the sound of the panicked thrashing of the downed horse behind him drowned by the second shot. Now he lunged for the protection of the other horse, which was plunging wildly and throwing his head back, trying to free himself from the picket rope.

The third shot—this one calculated—caught the second horse, knocking him sideways into Dave, and again Dave went down, rolling away from the horse as it crashed down on its side. He half crawled, half dived for the shelter of the horse, and hit the ground with a violence that jarred him to his bones.

The horse lay on its side, and he flattened himself along its back, face in the dirt, and dragged great gusts of choking dust into his mouth. The horse was kicking rhythmically as the next shot jolted into it, and Dave grabbed its mane and pulled himself closer and buried his face in the dirt, trying with a sick desperation to get his breath. The warm butt plate of his gun, which he still held, bit into his palm so that it hurt, and he smelled the sweet, rank odor of the horse's mane as he sucked in great gusts of air.

The horse was still when the next shot came, and he jarred heavily under the impact. Dave moved closer against it, and all he knew or cared about then was that the dead horse was between the rifleman and himself. He lay there and got his breath, his face flat against the ground and the mane coarse and sharp in his mouth, and now the thin chill danger of his position came to him as his panic faded.

He rolled slowly over on his side, and the next shot, kicking gravel behind him, drove him flat against the warm back of the horse again. He looked carefully around and saw the bank behind him was too steep to climb without spending fatal seconds.

He would have to get out of here, he knew. If the rifleman kept him down, it would be only minutes before he maneuvered around in back of him or to the side for an open shot. Dave weighed his chance coldly and knew he must take it, and he waited patiently for the next shot. The interval needed by the rifleman to lever in a shell was all he needed. The shot came, then, tentatively under the neck of the horse, and Dave came to his knees and vaulted the horse and dove sprawling for the protection of the second downed horse, lying now near the pool yards away. He briefly saw the rifleman's hat outlined above the rim of the depression as he dove for the cover of the horse. The rifle cracked again, and too late. It was wet here, and he felt the warm blood of the horse seeping through his shirt as he lay there.

He was cornered, he knew, and the rifleman would not wait for darkness. Ivey had rigged a simple ambush, and he had walked blandly into it, and now he was cornered. Once he had accepted that, it was easier to think. He lay with his back against the horse's back and watched in both directions, and it came to him, as the minutes ribboned away and darkness lowered, that there was only one thing to do. He could not lie here and wait for the rifleman to circle him and finish this. Moving, any kind of moving, was better than that.

He felt no anger now, only a murderous and implacable urgency. He put two shells in his gun, so that all the chambers were full, and observed now that the dusk was fast deepening. He raised his foot above the back of the horse, and no shot acknowledged it. Maybe the rifleman was biding his time or was moving around the rim.

Dave did not wait longer. He gathered himself and lunged to his feet and came over the horse, and then he saw to his left the quietly stalking figure of a man on the rim, black in the dusk. He cut toward him, running, firing twice in succession. He saw the man's rifle come to his shoulder, saw the flash, and then something hit his body with stunning force and knocked him sprawling to the ground. He came to his knees quickly, running again, and he saw the man shoot again and this time he shot in answer, and the man went down out of sight beyond the rim. Dave was on the slope now, racing up it, and he knew that unless his lucky shot had killed the rifleman, he would be waiting for him to top the rise. He did not check his stride as he approached the rim, only bent his body a little. And then, his legs driving him steadily up the slope, he dove on his belly over the rim, his gun held ahead of him.

The blast of the rifle was almost in his face. He was blinded by its flash and the sting of the gravel thrown in his face by the bullet, and he landed heavily on his belly. He shot blindly then, emptying his gun with closed eyes, and he cursed doggedly and furiously. And nothing answered him. He lay still a bare second, blinking the hot, smarting tears out of his eyes, and slowly, as if seen through deep water, the shape of a man lying on his face not six feet away from him took shape in his vision.

He pushed to his knees and half achieved it, and his arm seemed to give way and he pitched forward on his face. This angered him, and he tried again, and this time he could not push himself up, and now he thought of this with a kind of startled anger. He lay there a moment, watching the man who did not move, and he saw it was Red Cates.

Now he put his attention on rising, on moving his arm, and he found that he could not. The arm of the hand that held his gun was strong; his left arm was numb and useless. He sat up now, feeling his chest and belly warm with a wet stickiness, and he put his hand inside his shirt. Now the ache was here, slow at first as he felt his shoulder. There was a steady seep of blood there that startled him, and the ache was increasing to a hot and searing throb in his whole shoulder.

He rose now, and stood unsteadily, feet planted wide, and felt the flow of the blood down his side and his leg, and he was suddenly furiously thirsty. He went over to Red and looked down at him a moment, and then turned away and went down the slope toward the pool. Oddly, he was having trouble making his knees take his weight at each step. When he got to the pool, he knelt and drank and, his body tilted forward now, felt the flow of blood trickle down his neck into the water.

He knelt there then, and again felt his shoulder, and this time it was as sore to his touch as the end of an exposed nerve. The pain of it shocked him into an awareness that his blood was steadily soaking his clothes, and that he must stop it. He tried to rip off his shirt and could not move enough without stirring the pain into something raging and sickening, and still kneeling, he beat his mind for some way to stop the bleeding.

He rose now, aware of his own unsteadiness and faintness, and tramped past Lea and the two horses to Lea's bedroll. Inside, as he expected, was a sack of grub. And in the sack was a smaller sack of flour. He plunged his hand into its cool whiteness and scooped up a handful and plastered it on the spot below the collarbone where the open mouth of his wound was seeping blood.

He looked about him then for a bandage, and then he thought of Red's bandage, clean and white across his nose. Picking up the sack of flour, he trudged back to Red, and now felt a weariness that stopped him twice with its leaden weight. Once beside Red, he knelt and rolled him over and ripped the bandage from his face, and then plastered great handfuls of flour on his wound. Much of it clung to the blood and checked its further flow, and when he was certain of this he plastered the bandage over the wound. Then he ripped Red's shirt from his back and stuffed it atop the bandage, so that it made a great thick bulk over his shoulder when his sodden shirt was buttoned again.

Now he sat down, his back to Red, and put his good arm on his knees and his head upon his arm, and when he closed his eyes, the whole world of dancing lights behind his lids seemed to spin and whirl. His shoulder ached now with a viciousness that he fought with a thin and wicked anger.

Behind the pain, he tried to think. The first job before him was to reach his horse. The second was to get aboard him, which seemed a monumental task in his mind now. The third was to get some attention for his hurt, and he thought immediately and unswervingly of Rose Leland.

He gathered the deep threads of his will in one assault that put him on his feet and sent him pitching out into the night, and it carried him to his horse, at whose feet he fell. He did not know how long he lay there, but he was wakened by his horse nosing his leg. When he moved, his whole body was afire, and he ground his teeth together and lunged to a sitting position. From there, he maneuvered his horse around and got hold of a stirrup and fought himself to his feet, leaning heavily against the saddle.

Now, when rest seemed to do no good, he plotted out his try and began it. It was easy to grab the horn, easy to put a foot in the stirrup. But his legs would not lift him. He tried once, and almost fell. The second time was fruitless, and he wondered, resting afterward, if he had not tried in his mind only, and not physically. He was finding it hard to remember things now that had happened only seconds before. His horse was restive, moving in a slow circle that seemed destined to push him over backwards.

Finally, when he felt his hands slipping from the horn, he knew that he must make it now or lie here until help came and it would not, he knew. He summoned up a kind of desperation that drove him up, knotting his weary legs with cramp, and finally pitched on his belly across the saddle. His arm rammed into the horn now, and the pain it roused made him cry out.

It was only this pain, driving him to a frenzy, that gave him strength to drag his leg over and slack exhausted into the saddle, beaten and sick and sweating. And it was in this condition that he turned his horse back onto the trail and settled down for what must come.

# CHAPTER XV

YOUNG Link Thoms was up before daylight and made a quick check of the brush corral where the half dozen horses were penned. Afterward, he had cold grub and tepid coffee, while squatted over the coals of last night's fire which still held a little heat. He wore a blanket thrown over his shoulders against the morning chill that lay heavy over the horse camp, and so fortified, he rolled his first cigarette of the morning and was content. His scout had turned out better than he'd hoped for, since six of the seven horses in Connie's string, which he had been ordered to bring in, were now here in the brush corral. The seventh—that golden bay Connie had never liked so well—was probably up in the salt meadows above the foothills, and he anticipated hell's own trouble in catching him. None of this had been exactly easy, Link reflected, and would have been impossible if he had not kept his eyes open these past weeks. For Connie's string, all except two, had been turned loose to summer grass in the Federals, and they liked their freedom.

He finished his smoke and pinched it out and threw it in the fire. Rolling his blankets, he cached them and the rest of his meager gear underneath a tree, and then went over to his horse, which was on picket.

At bare dawn he left camp, shivering a little in the chill morning and whistling, too, because it helped against loneliness. For Link Thoms was younger by far than any hand at D Bar, and he had not yet earned the right to call himself their equal. His apprenticeship was hard and he was cheerful about it because the events of the Bench never troubled him. And like all young men he had a dream. Some day, so the dream ran, Red Cates would have run enough cattle on the side to justify his own outfit, and he would pull out of D Bar. Ben would be old by that time, and he would confer with Connie before any move was made. And then one morning when Connie called the crew together for the day's work, she would give them their orders and then say, "By the way, boys, you'll get your orders from Link from now on."

It was just a dream, and sometimes young Link changed Connie's words about, or put the setting in a different place or different time, but Connie was always in it and she was always his boss. This morning, thinking of it, the dream was not perfect. It hadn't been for days now, ever since the afternoon he had hauled the Mexican woman and some of Connie's stuff over to 66. Bunkhouse talk, which he had already learned to discount, had it that Connie and Ben had quarreled. Nothing was perfect, Link knew, but he could not envision a catastrophe such as this. He had already made it right in his dream: Connie and her father had quarreled and Connie had moved out, but when a sickness laid Ben low, Connie came back to stay, and 66 was graded down to a line camp. It was always Connie and D Bar, because Link, with the straight unquestioning wisdom of his years, loved them both, and Connie especially.

He cut up through the lifting hill and took the trail into Hondo Canyon. Deep into it, the trail cut close to the side and began to lift. Link's black wanted to stop for a blow, but Link touched spurs to him and swore mildly, knowing to a nicety the difference between his horse's need and its sense of humor. The shelving trail rose and, presently, skirted the shoulder of rock on Link's right. He looked down into the dark, steep-sided canyon and saw on the far slope the faint gray shape of a jackrabbit humping awkwardly among the brush. The day was coming reluctantly, and Link looked back once to see if there was color in the sunrise, and saw there was not.

Where the trail achieved the level on top, Link left it and clung to the lip of the canyon, and was soon in timber. He rode into it, picking with a sure knowledge the trails that ribboned it, and finally came out in mid-morning to the open expanse of the salt meadows. These were a series of small parks that raised a salt grass all animals liked. Link rode through them, me-thodically examining the two springs in the middle park and a seep in the far one for horse tracks. Besides some deer and cattle tracks, there were the tracks of only one horse, and it unshod. The bay had shoes, and it was therefore evident to Link that he had guessed wrong in this instance. The bay had moved on up.

He sat there on his horse at the seep in a deep, a pro-found disgust, and knew what he would have to do. He couldn't leave the horses down below in the corral, waterless for another night. Since he had them, he might as well take them on in and come back for the bay.

Accordingly, he started back down the way he had come, grudging every minute of his misspent time. It was cool here in the timber, however, and he soon for-got his impatience and was content with the present.

He was almost down out of timber sometime in early afternoon when he heard the bawling of cattle. He reined up to listen, and judged the cattle were in herd and being driven. Both Bell and D Bar had cattle in the mountains now, but they would stay here for another month until the first snows. He rolled himself a ciga-rette, speculating idly on the identity of the cattle, and their bawling was moving slowly down the slope off to his left. And then, starting as a whisper and growing ever louder, was the rumble of the herd beginning to run. Link, cigarette halfway to his mouth, sat motion-less, wondering about that. You didn't run the tallow off cattle if you were driving them out to sell, he knew.

Now the sound was almost in front of him, hidden from sight by the timber, and a curiosity and uneasiness came to him. He halted an uncertain moment longer, and then put his horse around and cut over toward the edge of the timber. The rumble of the running cattle was almost dead ahead of him, and some urgency made him spur his horse and lift it into a dead run through the timber.

And then, as the timber began to thin out, Link, by lying low in the saddle and peering under the trees, saw the herd at last and they were at a dead run. And they were streaking for the trail down into Hondo Canyon, the yelling of the punchers hazing them on.

Link pulled over swiftly now and climbed a rise where the timber was sparse, and he had a look at the head of the trail, a deep uneasiness within him. That was dangerous.

Then he saw the herd, shaped like a rippling brindle wedge, pour onto the flat at a dead run, heading straight for the trail and hazed into it by a pair of punchers. On one side of them lay the rising shoulder of rock, on the other the canyon's edge. Link stood in his stirrups, involuntary protest in his face. The brown wedge kept driving into the narrowing head of the trail, and then Link saw it all happen. One side of the herd, as if sheared off, began to fall off sideways into the canyon and disappear from view. But the rest kept on, jamming into the narrowing trail, and the farther they got the more the wedge was narrowed by the cattle overside. They hit the trail now at full tilt, and the leaders tried to stop and were bowled over, and the pile-up on the trail began; the following cattle, flowing blindly around them, seemed to float off the edge and disappear below into the canyon.

It was all over in seconds, and only a scattering of cattle in the rear, brought to a halt by the heap of bawling downed cattle that choked the head of the trail, shied off and fought its way back. Two punchers came into sight now, and rode over to the edge of the canyon and held their nervous horses there long enough to look over.

Link Thoms knew the thin cold touch of fear, then. By instinct, he seemed to understand that he had seen something not meant for anyone to see. And yet, not knowing whose cattle these were or who the punchers were, the wanton cruelty of it enraged him. He pulled back into shelter that would screen him and tied his horse and set off at a run through the timber, dodging from tree to tree, trying to keep to cover, and the distant bawling of the hurt cattle rose in an insane chorus from the canyon's depths.

At last, clinging to the timber where it edged nearest the flat, Link came to the last trees, and now he crawled on his stomach up to a vantage place behind a tree and looked out. Some of the cattle, a pitiful handful, were in front of him, their heads turned toward the canyon listening uneasily to the din. They blocked his view and Link moved over, and then the two mounted punchers were in plain sight.

They were Tom Peebles and Bailey, and the remaining cattle were all freshly vented and branded Circle 66.

Peebles rolled a smoke without looking at Bailey, and only when he lighted it did his eyes lift to the Indian's face. It was sober, tired-looking, but then that was natural. Bill Schell had been in such a hurry to get this done while Nash was away that he'd ordered them to ride half the night, and at daylight they had started the drive from Relief.

The din of the agonized cattle made Peebles's hand shake, and he threw the match away, swearing savagely. "I wish they'd shut up!"

Bailey said, not looking at him, "That ain't right, Tom." The Indian in Bailey, the part of him which knew by instinct and teaching that the one crime against nature was to waste what you killed, rose in protest. He eyed the canyon darkly, knowing he would have to look into it again.

"They're her cattle, ain't they?" Peebles demanded.

Bailey nodded mutely.

"Then she can do anything with 'em she wants, can't she?"

Again Bailey nodded, and yet Peebles' words settled nothing. To kill something clean was all right; to maim it and leave it in agony was wrong, and they both knew that the cattle down there still alive had broken backs or legs or necks.

Peebles said suddenly, "Let's get out of here," and

put his horse over to the trail head, and Bailey followed quietly. They had to dismount here, and lead their skittish horses around and over the pile of down cattle. To get past the head of the trail and into it, Peebles had to shove one steer overside. He came back to get his horse, which Bailey held, and he was sweating and angry and he would not look at the breed. They led their horses past the last of the cattle, and then mounted and rode on down into the canyon. Three or four steers, stronger and luckier than the others in the van of the herd, were already down the trail, and at sight of the two riders they trotted away.

Peebles reined up on the canyon floor and waited for Bailey to draw alongside.

"You know the story, don't you?" Peebles demanded, and Bailey nodded.

"We'll go right to Crew, if he's there. She'll be in town too, she said. You let me talk."

Bailey only nodded glumly, not liking this.

# CHAPTER XVI

THEY buried Curley in the late afternoon in the sorry weed-grown cemetery below the town. A handful of the curious from the saloon hung back among the trees and watched, and Rose thought how strange it was that men who were not afraid of death were shy in its presence. There was Connie, straight and proud in her dull dark dress, and Bill Schell, whose eyes were a dangerous bright with liquor, and, oddly, Ben Dickason. There was Mrs. Parkinson, Doctor Parkinson's wife, and his deputy, here today. She was a broad jolly woman, a friend to the whole country, and the rusty black dress she always wore was appropriate today. There was nobody from Bell, where Curley had spent his best years.

After the ceremony a couple of the men under the trees filed out to fill in the grave, and the others turned back toward the gate.

Mrs. Parkinson came up to Rose and said in an outraged voice, "Wouldn't you think Frank Ivey might at least send a man? He worked Curley for ten years and he killed him. He'd shed a tear for a horse he did the same for."

"Not if you know Frank Ivey," Rose said.

Mrs. Parkinson nodded grimly and said, "If he ever gets sick I'll have Harvey poison him," and went on over to Connie.

Connie, Rose noticed, did not speak to her father, but she nodded a gracious good-by to Rose.

Ben Dickason fell in step beside her then and said, "That's a pretty dress, Rose. I think Connie envies it."

"Is it bad luck to wear a new one at a funeral?" Rose asked. "I don't care if it is." It was the dress made from Dave's present, and she had worn it out of some obscure desire to honor Curley. Nobody would understand that except Dave, and he was not here to see it.

Ben smiled gently at her question, and did not answer. The baked ground threw up the afternoon heat, and nothing, Rose thought, had ever looked shabbier than this cemetery.

Ben said suddenly, "Rose, I'd like to take care of the expense of this. All Curley's expenses. Could I?" He looked at Rose almost with pleading in his eyes.

"Why, he was a 66 hand," Rose said. "You might talk to Connie."

Ben did not answer. They had reached the gate, and Ben said, "Can I give you a lift back to town?" and indicated the paint-peeled buckboard and team tied under the cottonwoods.

"Thank you," Rose said.

Ben handed her in and got in himself and picked up the reins. But instead of turning back to town, he started out past the cemetery, saying, "This cuts into the south road down here, doesn't it?"

Rose, knowing Ben was troubled, said it did, and Ben idly studied the horses, the reins slack in his hand. He sighed once and murmured, "Poor Curley," and added presently, "I'm personally going to see that dog of a Lea hanged for this."

"I don't think you'll have to," Rose said quietly.

Ben looked at her steadily a moment and said, "Nash?" and when Rose nodded, he smiled grimly. "He'll take care of his own, that one."

"You didn't think he could once," Rose observed.

Ben grimaced wryly. "I've made a lot of mistakes, young lady. They say the older you get, the fewer you make. Who said it, is what I'd like to know?"

"Maybe they meant lasting mistakes," Rose said quietly. "I don't think you've made any, Ben."

"I have," Ben said grimly. "I've lost a daughter."

"And that's not lasting, either, once you talk to her."

"I've talked to her," Ben murmured glumly. "She says it's her turn to howl, and she don't need any help from me, thank you. She wants all her things moved out of D Bar—pictures, clothes, curtains, even the horses she rode when she was a kid that're pensioned off. Everything."

"You were pretty rough on her, Ben."

"I've admitted that."

"To her?"

"Yes." Ben settled slackly in the seat, and regarded the road ahead without any spirit in him.

Rose watched him with pity, and as she thought of Connie she was puzzled. Remembering Ben's genuine disgust with Curley's beating and his subsequent request that Connie be sent to see him, she wondered at Connie's indifference. Even if Dave had not told Connie to go see Ben, she had seen him anyway, and rebuffed him. It was a strange sort of heartlessness that Rose did not understand, and as they came to the forks and turned back toward town, Rose was silent and thoughtful.

Ben put her down at her door, and she thanked him. He murmured acknowledgement and then said with a faint embarrassment, "You ever see Connie, Rose?"

"Once in a while."

"Wonder if you'd tell her sometime I meant what I said. I don't want to fight her, I want to be friends."

"I'll tell her, Ben," Rose said. She watched Ben drive off, and knew an exasperation that was close to anger as she thought of Connie.

After the funeral, Bill Schell let Connie out of the buggy at the hotel, and Connie said, "I'll only be a minute, Bill."

She walked briskly downstreet and crossed the side street and turned into Bondurant's store. Once she was on the steps, hidden from Bill Schell's gaze, she slowed her pace and stopped. There was something so absurd in this, and faintly humiliating too. It was not too late to forget it. She could go in and ask for any of a dozen things and nobody would ever know what had been in her mind when she started. Or better yet, she could send away for it. And then a swelling of pride decided her, and she went in, turning toward the dry goods section of the store.

Martin Bondurant came up to her and greeted her, and Connie said levelly, "I want some dress goods, Mr. Bondurant."

Bondurant pulled up a small, high chair which was reserved for woman customers and seated Connie at the counter. Only when Connie looked over the bolts of rich goods stacked behind the counter did she again feel a faint contempt for herself.

Bondurant hauled down a dozen bolts, and Connie looked at them, feeling them with a faint excitement and pleasure. Bondurant did not try to sell her any certain cloth; he was wise enough to simply keep reaching down the bolts, content to let feminine nature take its course.

Finally Connie came to a rich, blue silk, and immediately her thought shuttled to Rose Leland. This was the same material as the dress Rose Leland had worn this afternoon, and it was, in a way, the cause of her being here now.

Connie said softly, "That's lovely," and Bondurant turned his head and looked at it, and smiled. "It is," he said, and then put both hands on the counter, and said smilingly, "A strange thing, Connie. A very seedy-looking puncher came in here a few days ago and bought most of that bolt. He asked me to trust him until he'd been paid."

Connie looked at the goods again, and asked in a voice she strained to make seem casual, "From what outfit?"

"Shipley's, I think," Bondurant said, and then, because he was a tactful man and did not want to embarrass Connie, he turned back to his business.

Connie's hand rested idly on the goods now. That was Dave, she thought; he had given the goods to Rose. Oddly, Connie was relieved now, and the reason gave her an obscure feeling of malice and comfort. A lot of questions she had asked herself were now answered. Rose had a free way with men, as witness her taking in of Curley and her friendship with Crew and Dave. They liked her because she gave them comfort, in what ways Connie didn't want to know. But a man who gave a girl that sort of present wasn't serious, and a girl who would take it was not the sort of girl to make him a wife. It was given in appreciation of favors granted. Connie had seen enough of men to know she must accept that part of them with toleration, if not liking. They went through that and then they were married and it was forgotten. Rose, therefore, was not a real foe.

Connie chose a gray-green silk, and while it was being wrapped she came to a decision. It was, she thought, the measure of her confidence, and after receiving the goods she went back to Bill Schell who was waiting in the buggy.

"Get some supper, Bill. I'll be some time," she said.

Now she crossed the street again and headed down it, and a couple of men loafing in front of the Special in the dusk touched their hats to her.

She rang the bell at Rose's place, and Rose opened the door, and greeted her pleasantly.

"Are you busy, Rose? I didn't pick a very good time," Connie said.

"I'll be glad for some work to do," Rose said, seeing the familiar bulk of her package and knowing what it held. "Come in, Connie."

Rose got a lamp, pulled the curtains, and then set about work fitting Connie, the while chatting pleasantly. Connie was gracious, too, and at mention of Dave she did not indicate that she knew his errand of last night. In the light of what she knew now, Connie saw that there was something professional in Rose's charm. The way Rose admired the goods and Connie's small perfect figure, and agreed with Connie on the style of the dress, making tactful suggestions, all seemed to lend substance to Connie's suspicion. She put on water for tea, and this, like everything Rose did, was done with such effortless, friendly casualness, that Connie suspected it. But there was another Rose, light and predatory and shabby and appealing to the gross side of men, Connie was sure.

As Rose, pins in her mouth, knelt to work on the skirt, Connie wondered why she had not noticed this before. Perhaps it was because she saw so little of women and scorned their gossip. Why, even Rose's beauty, though not common, was somehow too soft and full-blown, and she was almost without reserve.

Some time after dark, Rose brought in the tea and cakes and they had them as she worked. Rose, sitting back on her heels to rest a moment, said, "Your father brought me back from the funeral."

"I saw him," Connie said.

"He's not very happy, Connie."

"I hope not," Connie replied.

Rose looked up at her. "Why?"

"It wouldn't be fair if he was," Connie said flatly. "He doesn't deserve to be."

"But he's old."

"And I'm young. That's more important."

"Perhaps he's sorry he was so hasty," Rose murmured.

"Let him be," Connie said coldly. "Why should regret earn a person forgiveness. I've never understood that, and I don't believe it. You have to pay for what you do. If there's no punishment, then there's no crime in doing anything wrong, is there?"

"A man can punish himself, Connie. That's when it's real."

"Maybe," Connie said stubbornly, but she did not believe it, and Rose saw she did not, and went back to work.

Finished with that part of the fitting, she stood up and stretched, and said, "Want to rest a minute?"

"I'll help you with these," Connie said, indicating the tea things. She was putting them on the tray when the doorbell jangled so loudly it startled her. Rose handed Connie a wrapper and then went to the door, unlocked it and opened it slightly.

A man's voice said in the night, "Miss Dickason in there?"

"Yes."

"Crew wants her over at his office."

"I'll tell her," Rose said, and shut the door and turned to Connie, who had heard the man.

"That was Bailey," Connie said, puzzlement in her voice.

"Did Bill leave town?" Rose asked.

"No. He's here." Connie looked steadily at her. "Do you think he'll want Bill?"

"If he does, he'll have him," Rose said matter-of-factly.

Connie slipped out of the wrapper into her dress, and took a last look in the mirror before she turned to the door.

"Connie, don't argue with him," Rose said gently. "He's a fair man."

Connie smiled faintly, and she looked very cool and unexcited as she said, "No, I won't. It's like a game of chess, isn't it? You give away men to gain an advantage."

Rose nodded without speaking, and Connie stepped out. Rose walked slowly over to the dress, picked it up and stood motionless now, feeling an unaccountable depression. She had known in the back of her mind that Bill Schell would have to face this some time if he was guilty. Dave had warned her of that, and it was only right, since those were the conditions under which he took the job. But she liked Bill Schell and his happy-go-lucky cheerfulness, and could forgive him his instability and temper—except in this case. Dave and Connie were both right, of course, in submitting to Crew's judgment, but they did it for different reasons. Dave's reason was that it was simply a hard bargain understood by Bill from the first, and it was one in which sentiment and affection were purposely absent. Take orders, or take the consequences. Connie's was different, and she had expressed it perfectly when she said, "You give away men to gain an advantage." Hers was cold and calculated and heartless, like her treatment of Ben. She was right in principle, so wrong in method.

She roused herself and put the dress away, and now smiled wryly at herself. Maybe this was all for nothing; perhaps Crew had called Connie to tell her Bill was in the clear.

She gathered up the tea things and put them on the tray and took them back into the kitchen. She was at the sink when she heard the sound of a horse in the back yard, and she stood motionless a moment, sorting out the separate sounds of its slow tramp, the faint kick against the walk and its halting somewhere close to the house.

Rose took down the lamp and opened the back door and stepped out, and the eyes of a horse flashed green and iridescent as it turned its head toward her.

She held the lamp higher and saw the man in the saddle, and a terrible fear was in her as she stepped closer.

It was Dave. He was slumped over the neck of his horse, his bloody fingers laced almost inextricably in its mane.

Rose put the lamp down and ran to him, saying, "Dave, Dave."

He roused at the sound of her voice, turned his head in her direction, but did not raise it.

He whispered softly, "You'll have to help me down, Rose."

Rose took hold of his belt and pulled him gently toward her and whispered, "Let go, Dave. Let go!"

He seemed to collapse then, as if he had held out only until he reached her. He pitched sideways in the saddle, and Rose caught him and the weight of him beat her to the ground. She came to her knees beside him, and saw that his clothes were caked and stiff with dried blood, and a brighter spot started to spread its dampness on the shoulder where he had stuffed part of his shirt.

Rose pulled him to a sitting position and then said quietly, "You've got to help me, Dave," and he roused, the effort allowing her to haul him up by his good arm and duck under it. His weight was dead, and his dragging feet would have sent her to the ground if she had not staggered against the house for support.

She half dragged, half carried him through the

kitchen and into her bedroom, where she let him gently down on the bed. He fell heavily across it, his head
rapping the partition.

Rose ran out for the lamp and brought it in, and
put it on the table beside the bed, and looked at him.
His face was gray, made more so by the black dusty
wash of his beard stubble, and his face seemed shrunk-
en and strange.

She ripped the shirt from him, but when she came
to the shoulder, the blood had made flesh and cloth
one. She got warm water now, and patiently spent minutes soaking the cloth away from the skin, and when it
finally came away she saw the swollen, purple lip of
the wound under the solid ridge of the collarbone. A
trickle of blood oozed out of it now and she watched it
with a quiet despair.

She got clean cloths and covered it, and then pulled
Dave's boots off, and all the time he lay inert and
heavy, his breathing deep and slow.

With difficulty she tried to maneuver him lengthwise,
but the movement brought a sudden stiffening and a
groan from him, and his eyes opened. They were bright
and they studied her unsmilingly, and Rose said,
"Move around, Dave, so I can lift your feet."

He stared stupidly at her and she tugged at him
again, and she felt his muscles go iron hard in the
flinch against the pain. After that, he sighed and closed
his eyes, and she covered him.

Rose knelt now and picked up his bloody shirt.
From the shoulder of it something dropped to the floor,
and when she stooped to pick it up she looked at it
and her attention was held. She had seen too much of
this blood-soaked cloth in the last week not to know
that it was bandage. Where would Dave have got one
of Doctor Parkinson's bandages, with the trailing pig-
tail ties?

And then it came to her abruptly. This was the kind
of bandage Red Cates had worn across his nose.

Rose took it and the basin and went out to the
kitchen and slipped out the back door. She did not
know why she was doing this, but it seemed necessary

to her to get rid of Dave's horse. She led him into the woodshed and closed the door, and then started across the vacant lot at a run, bound for Jim Crew's office. She slowed to a walk immediately; nobody must know Dave was here, in case he was being followed.

Connie looked for Bailey to be waiting for her outside, but he had gone on ahead. *Which was just as well,* she thought; *it will make it appear more convincing.*

She cut angling across the street toward Crew's office and turned the corner and stepped inside.

Jim Crew was pacing the floor of the small room, and he turned to the door when Connie entered. His clothes were dusty and untidy, and he had a three-day growth of steel-gray beard that contrived to make him look years older. Bill Schell lounged in the doorway of the cell block and Tom Peebles and Bailey stood silently against the far wall.

"I got some bad news for you, Connie," Crew said slowly.

"So Bill was lying to us," Connie said, with a consummate cunning, and she looked reprovingly at Bill Schell.

"I couldn't find a thing against Bill. It ain't that." Crew nodded his head toward Tom and Bailey. "They claim Bell stampeded your whole herd off the rim of Hondo Canyon there at the head of the trail."

Connie turned slowly to Tom and Bailey, her lips parted slightly in feigned shock. "All of them?"

"Ten-fifteen left," Peebles said meagerly.

"How—What did they do?"

Peebles shifted his feet, but he was looking at her steadily as he began to speak. "We was just about down to the flat there at the head of the trail this noon. Ivey and his crew jumped us; come out of the timber shootin'. They split up, part of 'em taking the herd, part of 'em chasin' us. We couldn't fight 'em because they was too many, so we took to the timber. We circled back later, and they'd drove the cattle at a dead run, looked like, at the head of the trail. They jammed up in it and was crowded off the edge into the canyon."

Connie sank into the chair, her hands folded, and she stared down at them and did not speak.

"Who was in the gang?" Crew asked.

"I tell you, all I remember was Frank Ivey. Likely I couldn't remember him if he hadn't kept shoutin' 'Head 'em off. Head 'em off.' It all happened too quick."

"You seen some of 'em, didn't you?" Bill Schell insisted.

Peebles shook his head stubbornly. "I might of, only I ain't sure. And I ain't goin' to hang a man for doin' somethin' he might not of done."

Bill Schell's eyes glinted with a sardonic amusement at this. Peebles had the air of a man who would rather accept an injury than commit an injustice, and Bill asked, "What about you, Bailey?"

"I seen that paint horse of Abe Harmon's, but he wasn't ridin' it."

Crew said, "But you saw Frank?"

"Seen him and heard him."

Crew stood motionless a moment, and then came over to Connie.

"Well, Connie, Frank's gone too far this time. He's through."

Connie nodded and lifted her head, and then they all heard the rapid footsteps on the boardwalk, and Rose came through the door.

"Dave's at my place," Rose said. "He's hurt badly." She glanced over at Peebles. "Get Doctor Parkinson, will you, Tom, and do it quietly?"

Connie felt her heart almost stop, and then she moved swiftly toward the door.

"Walk, Connie," Rose said. "If he wants to hide, we can't give him away."

Some minutes later, when they were at Rose's, Doctor Parkinson came in, and Rose and Jim Crew moved out of the bedroom, leaving Connie with the doctor. Bill Schell sat in one of the kitchen chairs tilted back against the wall, and he watched Crew with an alert somber face.

Crew halted in the middle of the room and looked directly at Bill. "Where's Dave been?"

"He followed Virg Lea."

Rose went over to Dave's shirt lying on the table and picked up the blood-soaked bandage and held it in her hand and said, "Have you seen this before, Jim? It was on Dave's shoulder."

Bill came out of his chair quickly, and he and Crew looked at it. They both looked up to her at the same time, both shaking their heads in negation.

"Red Cates had that tied over his broken nose," Rose said.

Crew glanced at Bill Schell then, and Bill said softly, "So," and was silent a moment, and then he murmured, "Red never gave that to him, so he must of took it— and there's only one way he could take it."

Crew looked steadily at him for several seconds, and then remarked, "Red and Frank had the same idea."

Doctor Parkinson came to the door then and said, "I'll need you too, Rose."

Rose left them then, and Crew took a slow turn around the kitchen. He stopped in front of the mirror and rubbed a hand over his face, and the dry sound of his beard stubble bristling was plain in the quiet.

"Well?" Bill said challengingly.

Crew sighed and came across the room slowly, talking as he walked. "I'll go out and bring Frank in." He looked up at Bill, puzzlement in his pale eyes. "He's gone wild, Bill."

"He's been wild," Bill said flatly, angrily. "We been tellin' you."

Crew nodded tiredly and said, "Send Connie home with Tom and Bailey and keep her there. You stay here until I bring Frank in. Don't go out and don't leave Dave, because Ivey may get to him before I get to Ivey."

"Who you takin'?" Bill asked.

Crew's jaw thrust out faintly. "Nobody," he said, and walked over to the door and went out.

# CHAPTER XVII

His restlessness had built up until it was unbearable, and Frank Ivey had been on the prowl now since daylight. Three days had passed, and Red had not returned, and Crew was gone. The sum of these had driven Frank to the saddle, for his patience, never strong, was worn thin and ragged by waiting. A hundred times yesterday after he had sent Jack Bender on Red's trail, he had been tempted to saddle up and himself ride over to the water hole in the Breaks, and he had questioned Jess Moore, Lea's companion on the ride, almost half that many times. Something had happened to Red, something had gone wrong.

In early morning Frank came on to 66 and watched the house from a distance. It was too far for him to see much, and he dare not go closer, but if he only could see Dave Nash, he would know what had happened out there in the Breaks. He pulled away and rode aimlessly for a while and then picked up the road to D Bar. Maybe Red had reported to Ben, although he knew that was unlikely. The day was just beginning, and he might as well call there and check.

The thought no sooner struck him than he lifted his horse into a lope, and only minutes later reined him into a walk, remembering patience. He was a solid figure in the saddle, and he handled his horse with a sharp ruthlessness this morning.

He crossed American Creek, presently, and it put

him in mind of Connie's boast. She had claimed all this land that he had passed over this morning, but now there was little prospect of her getting it. For when Crew's scout in the Federals turned up Bill Schell's guilt, which was certain, he would not even bother to serve Connie an ultimatum. It would be the excuse he had waited for so patiently; he would first get Nash and then sweep Connie clear off the Bench. The thought pleased him, and yet there was that quiet torment behind it which had been there lately whenever he thought of Connie. Would this, when it was accomplished, break her pride and her stubbornness, or must he go on, winning again and again, until she gave in to him? He had sustained himself for so long on the belief that it would that he would tolerate no doubt now, and yet it was there, riding him constantly.

He left the willow-bordered creek and bottomlands and saw far ahead a bunch of horses being driven toward him along the road. As they approached and moved off onto the grass, Frank saw it was young Link Thoms who was driving them, and he reined up.

Link came up alongside and said gravely, "Hello, Frank," and Frank nodded casually.

"Red at your place, Link?" he asked.

"Wasn't last night," Link said. "I ain't been around much, though."

Frank wasn't surprised much at this information. He looked idly over the horses and saw they were Connie's and he asked, "Where you drivin' them, Link?"

"Sixty-six."

Frank smiled faintly and said, "Waste of time," and waved carelessly and went on. He had no stomach for talking to Ben Dickason now; he didn't care enough about Ben to argue with him or listen to him, and he pulled off the road, turning back toward Bell.

At midday he entered the mouth of Bell's canyon, and the hand who was stationed as guard here broke out of the foothills and cut over to him.

Frank headed toward him, and they met off the road, and his man said, "Crew went in a little while ago."

"Ah," Frank said with satisfaction. "All right." He touched spurs to his horse now and rode on and, coming into his place, saw Crew's horse tied under the cottonwoods.

As Frank approached, he saw Crew rise from his seat in the office doorway, and he felt a solid satisfaction at seeing him. Crew wouldn't have stopped on his way down from Relief unless he brought favorable news.

Frank stepped out of the saddle and said cordially, "You look thirsty, Jim," and Crew didn't answer him, only leaned against the log wall, his chill eyes regarding Frank carefully as he tied his horse. Frank, getting no answer, looked over his shoulder at Crew, and saw the hostility in his glance.

Frank came slowly toward him and halted in front of him, and Crew didn't move. "What's the matter, Jim?" Frank asked carefully.

"I took a ride over to Hondo Canyon this mornin'," Crew said.

Frank regarded him blankly, and when he saw Crew expected an answer he said, "What's over there?"

Crew shook his head and said, "Comin' in with me, Frank?"

"All right," Frank said in a puzzled voice. "Look, what about Bill Schell?"

"He's in the clear," Crew said, and shoved away from the building and tramped toward his horse. He halted then and looked back at Frank. "Comin'?"

"Wait a minute," Frank said flatly. "I want to know what you did."

Crew said meagerly, "I said I couldn't find anything against Bill. Are you comin', Frank?"

The deceptive quietness in Crew's question seemed to filter through Frank's anger now, and he studied Crew with a wrathful intentness before he walked toward him. "Comin' where?" he asked softly.

"Jail."

Frank just stared at him a long moment, and Crew said thinly, "I'm too old to bluff, Frank."

"Why would I go to jail?" Frank asked slowly.

Crew said with bare patience, "When you stampede a herd of someone else's cattle off rim-rock into a two-hundred-foot canyon, Frank, you go to jail."

"No," Frank said flatly, and then the full surge of his anger hit him. He came closer to Crew and said in blazing anger, "What in the name of God are you trying to tell me? Say it!"

"You and your crew jumped Peebles and Bailey bringin' down Connie's herd. It was right at the head of the trail out of Hondo Canyon and you drove the boys off and run the herd over the rim-rock." He paused. "I'm takin' you in, Frank."

Frank said with utter calmness, "You're a liar, Crew."

Jim Crew's face altered a little into a wintry hardness. "If you think I'm lyin' when I say I'll take you in, I'm not."

"I wasn't off this place yesterday," Frank said thickly.

"I saw the cattle."

Frank wheeled and walked past Crew and said, "Come down here," and he tramped over to the bunkhouse. The four or five hands who had been working close to the ranch had finished their midday meal and were sitting around the bunkhouse steps, smoking and yarning.

At the approach of Frank and Crew, they fell silent, and at sight of the expression on Frank's face, two of them rose from the steps.

Frank halted and asked them, "Where was I yesterday, boys?"

Nobody answered for a few seconds, and then Jess Moore said, "Right here."

Somebody else said, "I seen you in the afternoon here, Frank," but Frank had already turned to face Crew. He said again, "I wasn't off the place."

"You'll get a chance to prove that in front of a jury, Frank," Crew said tonelessly. "Now, come along."

"No," Frank said.

Crew looked at him carefully and Frank said roughly, "Get out of here, Crew."

Crew silently looked over the Bell crew, and without looking at him they broke slowly, so they were on three sides of him. Somebody said softly, "You give the word, Frank," and his words summed up Bell's fear of Jim Crew.

Crew's glance shuttled back to Frank, and he said, "I'll tell you once more. Come along." There was something utterly implacable, utterly fearless in the way Crew spoke.

Frank didn't answer. Jim's hand started to move, and Frank said with a rising inflection to his voice, "Don't do it, Jim."

Crew's hand hesitated the briefest part of a second in its journey and then it streaked toward the gun at his hip. From between two of the Bell hands there was a shot, and Crew's thin body was driven back a step. Frank's gun came up then and he shot twice, fast, and Crew was already falling when the second shot hit and turned him around so that he fell face down, his head away from them. He made one savage exertion and his gun came out, and Frank moved over and put a foot on Crew's wrist. Crew tugged once, and then gave up and sighed deeply, the last of his breath whistling faintly.

Ivey raised his glance now and looked at each man with a curious deliberation, and then he said calmly, "Go, round up the boys. We'll settle this now."

Connie was hanging curtains in the window of the big room when she saw Link Thoms come in with the horses. Both Bailey and Tom helped him haze the bunch through the corral gate and on into the horse pasture. Connie watched them absently through the window, and it brought unwelcome memories. There was the little *grulla* mare she had when her father taught her to rope years ago; and there too was the sorrel Frank had given her two years back, and which, out of the beginning of her defiance, she had never ridden. Behind her, she could hear Josefa scrubbing the floor, and silently she went back to work. There was something blessedly narcotic about the work of cleaning up the place and making it livable, putting her own things about that her father had sent over. For Connie was tasting fear, and if she stopped to think it grew into something ugly and monstrous that she could not fight. It was the first time in her life she had been afraid for somebody else, and now she was. The image of

Dave lying there in Rose's bed, gray and hurt and out of his senses, crawled into her mind and made her sick with fear. For she would no longer deceive herself after seeing Dave last night; she wanted him well more than she had ever wanted revenge or an outfit of her own or power. There was an irony to all that had happened, and it did not escape Connie this morning. Her gamble had won Jim Crew over to 66, and insured the eventual defeat of Frank Ivey, for Crew would be implacable now he had climbed off the fence. He would arrest Frank, but that seemed unimportant now.

Josefa interrupted her thoughts. "It is more better if we scrub it again," she observed.

"Just so it's clean, Josefa," Connie murmured absently.

She stood back to look at the hang of the curtain and saw young Link Thoms riding toward the house. Stepping outside to the porch, she waved and called, "Hello, Link."

He rode up and dismounted, grinning shyly and worshipfully and touching his hat. "I couldn't catch Monte, Connie. I'll bring him over later."

"Fine, Link. Want some coffee?"

"No, thank you," Link said. He hesitated a moment, looked back at the corral, where Bailey and Tom were, and then said in a low voice, "Reckon I could talk to you private?"

A faint amusement touched Connie as she observed his conspiratorial air, and she said, "Certainly."

She went on down the porch through the mess hall and out into the kitchen, and Link followed her. She went to the table and leaned against its edge and said, "What is it, Link?"

Link was fumbling with his hat, but his eyes were as sober as only those of a troubled fifteen-year-old can get. "You know about what happened up in Hondo Canyon?" Link asked.

Connie said carefully, "Yes, Link. I know. But how do you?"

"I seen it," Link said.

Connie's breathing seemed to stop, and she repeated softly, "You saw it?"

"Tom Peebles and Bailey drove them cattle off the rim!" Link said with a fierce solemnity. "They done it a-purpose. I seen 'em do it—your cattle!"

"You—must be mistaken, Link."

"No ma'am," Link said flatly. "Your men, and they drove your cattle off, killed 'em!"

Connie rose slowly and put her back to him. This was the end of her well-laid plans, ruined by the presence of a gawky, half-grown boy who did not yet realize the importance of what he had seen. A wild panic seized Connie, then, and she knew that some way, somehow, she must close Link's mouth. She must threaten him, or drive him out of the country, or bribe him, or intimidate him—anything to close his mouth. She had the men to do it, men who would do anything for her. And then she knew none of this would work; nothing short of killing Link Thoms would close his mouth against his will, and that she would not do. She walked slowly around the table and saw Link watching her with a dumb adoration that was never absent from his eyes.

Connie stopped abruptly, still watching him, and the seed of an idea was in her mind now. As it grew, she smiled faintly, knowing the answer was here and had always been here. Link was hers, body and soul, and always had been. Since the day she had persuaded her father to take him in, a half-starved, dirty thirteen-year-old who had run away from the beatings of a drunken father, he had worshiped her with that unquestioning faith. She had been kind to him, and now she was going to ask payment.

"Sit down, Link," she said quietly.

He sank into the chair and laid his hat on the table, and he never ceased watching her.

Connie sat on the edge of the table, and looked down at him beside her. "Link, I don't know how much you know of what's been going on here. Between me and Walt Shipley and Dad and Frank Ivey. You know some of it, don't you?"

"A little," Link said, already embarrassed.

"Did you know that Dad has been trying to force me to marry Frank Ivey when I didn't want to? Did you know that was why Frank drove Walt away?"

"No, ma'am," Link said slowly. His tone indicated he was impressed.

"I left home, Link, because I couldn't stand that bullying. I didn't want to marry Frank Ivey and I didn't want Dad's help. I wanted a life of my own. You can see why, can't you?"

"Yes'm," Link said. He felt a faint embarrassment that he was included in a revelation so intimate, and yet he was proud too. He felt a little like a yard dog would feel if invited to lie on the hearth rug—shy, happy, fiercely protective and with a fathomless gratitude.

And Connie knew it. She smiled sweetly, and said sadly, "Dad and Frank have fought me, Link, with every weapon they had. Until Dad finally quit, when Frank's men killed Curley Fanstock."

Link only nodded, a welling anger making him inarticulate. Connie was filling out the blanks in the bunkhouse gossip, giving them life and substance and tragedy and bravery.

Connie slipped down now and walked around the table, and Link followed her with his sober gaze. Connie stopped beside him then and put both hands on the table and said, "I've got to destroy Frank Ivey, or he'll destroy me, Link. And if I have to fight as dirty as he fights, I will."

Link nodded mutely and Connie took her hands off the table and spread them in a simple, innocent gesture. "That's when you caught me, Link. I was fighting dirty."

Link was staring at her with sober, breathless concentration, and Connie said unashamedly, "I had Tom and Bailey drive those cattle off into the canyon, Link. They rode in and told Sheriff Crew that Bell did it. Crew will arrest Frank and jail him, I hope, and he'll never trouble me again."

Link took that without a murmur, turning it over in his mind.

Connie said softly, "I lied to Crew because I had to lie, because I had to get a man out of the way who was a killer." She hesitated and then asked gently, "Did I do wrong, Link?"

"No," Link said slowly. "No. No, you didn't, Connie. He had it comin' to him."

"You're a good friend," Connie said quietly. "You know something nobody else must ever know. Nobody, ever. You see," she added, smiling faintly, "you have my happiness in your hands, Link."

Link blushed deeply and came to his feet, and at that moment he gladly would have died for her. And, because nothing half so wonderful had ever happened to him in his drab and simple life, he did not know how to pledge his word and his trust and his honor. He said, "Sure, Connie, you're my friend," knowing his words were inadequate and wishing miserably that they were not.

Connie knew this instinctively and she put a hand on his and squeezed it and said, "Thank you, Link. I trust you, and I always will."

Link tramped blindly from the room, and Connie made no move to follow him. A faint, crawling shame touched her for a moment, and was gone, drowned in her quiet exultation. She was safe, she knew; torture by fire would never drag her secret from Link. She thought of him now with liking and pity, and both were touched with contempt. Three of the men who knew this secret were so deeply involved in it that they would never talk of it, and the other, Link, was hers. Someday, she thought wistfully, when all this was over she could tell it to Dave, and he would laugh with her and call her sly. But he would admire her, Connie knew.

# CHAPTER XVIII

ROSE came out of a deep exhausted sleep to feel Bill Schell shaking her gently, and she opened her eyes.

"He's awake," Bill said, "and he's hungry." He grinned swiftly, and Rose was somehow encouraged by that. Bill's grin was the barometer of his mood.

She rose from the sofa and asked quietly, "Has Crew come back from Bell yet?"

"No."

They looked at each other in silence, each knowing what the other was thinking. As long as Crew was gone, Ivey was loose and Dave was in danger.

Rose went over to the stove and found Bill already had a fire going. Looking out the window she was surprised to see the shadows pulled in under the trees below the noon sun. She washed her face and the cold water drove away the last drowsiness from her all-night vigil. She picked up the hair brush and immediately put it down, too impatient for primping now, and went into the bedroom.

Dave turned his eyes from Bill to her, and his smile was slow and oddly uncertain, so that Rose fought down a swift pity.

Last night she had taken a shirt for him from the dozen she was making Martin Hawthorne at the bank, and its immaculate white broadcloth in contrast made Dave's beard growth seem a solid black against his pale face.

"66 will pay you rent on this room, Rose," Dave said.

Rose smiled. "What do you want to eat?"

"A cigarette," Dave said.

Bill pulled out his sack of tobacco dust and quickly rolled a smoke, and Dave looked at Rose a full and troubled moment. "How bad am I hurt? I feel broke in two."

"A bullet passed clear through you," Rose said. "Bad enough I'd say."

Bill said, "Whose was it?"

"Red Cates'. He was waitin' for me at Virg's camp."

"We found his bandage. He didn't give it to you, did he?"

"No, he didn't give it to me," Dave said. "Neither did Virg." He took the lighted cigarette from Bill, who was grinning faintly at this information, and dragged the smoke deep into his lungs. Again he looked at Rose, who was watching him soberly.

"Were you followed?" she asked.

"I don't think so," Dave said, and he looked at Rose with a humorous quirk to his mouth before he put his cigarette to his lips again.

"The only place Red could have come from is Bell," Dave said musingly. "I'll get an answer to that one from Frank, too."

"And sooner than you expect," Rose said.

Dave looked at her, puzzlement in his face.

"Bell stampeded Connie's herd off the rim-rock into Hondo Canyon yesterday. Jim Crew has gone out to get Frank."

Dave was silent a long while, staring at the ceiling. Then he turned his head and smiled at Rose, and she knew this news held a deep significance for him. It was the first solid move toward eventual victory for 66. Rose had watched him play for this with a care and cunning that came hard to a man of his temperament. He had been cautious when his instinct was to be reckless; he had been iron-hard in the punishment of mistakes, and he was a tolerant man; he had been cool where others would have been angry. He was like a man coming into a high-stake poker game with a few

white chips, who must husband them timidly and add
craftily to them until he sees the chance for the kill. It
had paid out now, Rose knew; Dave had bided his
time waiting for Frank's first misstep which would bring
Crew over to 66.

Dave looked at Bill now. "Then I was wrong about
you, Bill."

Bill shrugged. "It's under the bridge, kid. But you
came close to makin' me mad."

The two of them smiled at each other, and Rose
went out to fix Dave's breakfast. The nightmare she
had lived through last night was over, but Rose did not
deceive herself. Dave was sick and hurt, and the punishment he had taken had exhausted him. Still, in the
background of her mind, where it had been since she
first saw Dave by lamplight last night in the back yard,
was the thought of Frank Ivey. If Frank knew Dave
was hurt, he would not be sitting at Bell waiting for
Jim Crew to get him; he would be hunting Dave. Jim
Crew, with that gray wisdom of his, understood this
too, and was doing his best to insure against it. If Crew
missed Ivey, then no place was secure, and Dave could
not move to hide.

Rose fixed Dave a breakfast of oatmeal and eggs and
biscuits and coffee, and took it in to him on a tray. Bill
offered to help him to a sitting position, but Dave refused his aid, and sat up unassisted. His face, Rose
noticed, paled a little further with the effort, and beads
of sweat stood out damply on his forehead. He wolfed
the first half of his breakfast and then gradually
seemed to lose interest in it, and as he drank his coffee Rose noticed the brightness of fever coming back
into his eyes. Afterwards, she changed the dressing on
his shoulder, and before she finished he was asleep in a
deep, sick exhaustion.

Back in the kitchen, Bill was at the window, watching the livery and the street beyond. He was whistling
thinly, tunelessly, and Rose knew he was worried. He
turned to her suddenly and said in a low, worried voice,
"Why ain't Crew back, Rose?"

She couldn't answer him, and he started his restless
pacing, stopping occasionally at the window. Dave's

deep breathing came to them, now, and Bill stopped to listen and shook his head worriedly.

Rose went out to the shed to look at the horses, for Bill's was here now, too. They, too, were restive with hunger, and she knew that tonight she would have to contrive some way to get some feed for them without arousing suspicion.

She went back into the house and found Bill at the table staring boredly at some old newspapers. She patted his shoulder as she passed him on her way into the front room. There was Connie's dress to be done, and she laid it out and began to work on it, thinking then of Connie. Last night, in the sheriff's office, she had surprised Connie into disclosing something she would never have admitted in words—her reaction to the news of Dave's injury. Rose kept thinking of that. It was the action, Rose knew, of a woman in love. It was instinctive and naked and utterly without Connie's cold reason guiding it, and it told Rose volumes. It explained, among other things, the reason for this new dress, and Rose smiled wisely and tolerantly. Women were the same, really. Hadn't she herself looked forward with a womanly pride to the time she would walk out in front of Dave wearing her new blue dress? Hadn't she planned a mocking little curtsy that would bring his slow smile and fill his eyes with an admiration of her? She had, just as Connie doubtless had.

Rose sat motionless now, thinking of this, trying to see ahead. She loved Dave, and had, since that evening he had come to her with his present. One moment she was thinking of him as a big, silent man with ugly memories that he could not shake, and a few moments later all that was changed by the simple gesture of his gift. Rose didn't look beyond that, only she knew he was a man she could live out her life with and make happy and complete. And Connie had seen it, too, only Rose knew they had not seen the same things. Connie had seen strength to make her stronger and further the ambition in her, a man so strong he did not need Frank Ivey's arrogance, a man she could give in to without humility. And Rose saw shrewdly that Connie's weapons were potent and undeniable. She had fought brave-

ly against the shabby bullying of her father and Frank
Ivey, and her courage was a real thing that any man
might admire. But somewhere along the way she had
become as cold and heartless as the man she hated,
and it was this Rose knew was wrong. It was something
a man might not see until it was too late, but it was
also something he must find out for himself.

Rose put it out of her mind, and fell to work. She
was absorbed in it when she heard Bill Schell's footsteps and looked up to see him in the doorway.

"Ivey just come in," Bill announced.

Rose came to her feet and hurried to the window and
saw a group of horsemen whom she recognized as the
Bell crew dismounting in front of the Special. Their
horses were lathered with sweat.

"Was Crew with them?"

"No."

She and Bill looked at each other wordlessly, and
Rose turned again to watch Bell. This time she glanced
at the sheriff's office on the corner. There was no activity there; none of the Bell hands paid it any attention.

Bill said quietly, "Somethin's happened, Rose."

"What could?"

"I dunno," Bill said slowly. "Ivey's there. Jim could
have followed that bunch if he was blind. He's had
time."

The Bell crew all moved in to the Special, and Rose
went back to her work. Bill stayed at the window,
waiting with the alert patience of an Indian, and Rose
found herself watching him for any sign of Bell's movement. Frantically, now, she cast back in her mind to
last night. She had hidden Dave's horse, and she had
gone to the sheriff's office unobserved. She had even
contrived, she was sure, to keep the exit of all of them
from Crew's office a casual thing that would not arouse
curiosity. Peebles swore he was not seen on his way to
Doctor Parkinson's office, and the doctor was also certain his call had gone unnoticed. There was nothing to
excite Frank Ivey's curiosity about this place, except
the memory of Rose being a friend of 66 and Curley

Fanstock. Only, if Frank Ivey was thorough enough, her name would occur to him sooner or later. Which meant they would have to get Dave out, get him safe where Frank Ivey could not kill him like a cornered animal.

The time ribboned on into late afternoon and the Bell crew still stayed on at the Special. Only, something had happened. There was other movement on the street, and all of it centered in the Special. Once a boy ran, shouting, into the livery barn, and Joe Lilly came out and went into the saloon.

Presently, Bill turned his head and said, "Mrs. Parkinson is headed this way."

Rose moved to the window and watched the doctor's wife approach. Mrs. Parkinson, in her black dress and dowdy hat, spoke to the men in front of the Special. It was she who did the only nursing Signal knew, turning her home into a hospital, when necessary, and everyone knew and liked her. Her walk was leisurely, and she stopped to talk to a boy who was cutting across the vacant lot. She broke away from him finally, and came on, and then they lost sight of her. Rose and Bill both looked at the door, listening intently, and they heard her footsteps pause. Then the bell jangled with a loudness that made Rose jump.

She moved swiftly to the door and opened it, and Mrs. Parkinson stepped in. Her round, florid face was grave as she nodded to them and then closed the door herself.

"Frank Ivey killed Jim Crew this morning," she announced.

Rose glanced at Bill and saw the stunned look in his eyes. "Killed?" Bill echoed. Crew, somehow, had seemed immortal to them all.

"Crew tried to arrest him for that cattle killing, and Frank wouldn't go. Jim pulled on him, Ivey says, and he shot him."

A fleeting pain crossed Bill Schell's face, and he made an involuntary gesture of protest that died immediately.

Mrs. Parkinson said in a businesslike voice, "Harvey sent me over, because he didn't dare come himself. Ivey doesn't know Dave Nash was shot, but he'll tear the country wide open to find him." She paused. "He says you'll have to move Dave, Bill, before Ivey thinks of this place."

"With that crew campin' on our doorstep?" Bill said miserably.

"After dark."

"If he'll wait that long," Bill observed bitterly, moving to the window.

Rose and Mrs. Parkinson looked soberly at each other and Mrs. Parkinson said in a low, passionate voice, "Frank Ivey is a dog. He isn't fit to kiss Jim Crew's boots."

Rose said, "I must tell Dave," and went into the bedroom.

Dave was awake, and his eyes were still bright with fever as he looked at Rose. "I heard," he said. "Hand me my gun."

Rose lifted out his gun from the belt hanging on the wall and gave it to him, and he said grimly, "Rose, if they come here, I want you to promise me one thing."

"What?"

"That you'll get out."

"I won't promise it," Rose said shortly, and she moved toward the curtain to go out.

Then Bill Schell's voice came to them. "Oh-oh. Here he comes."

Rose went out swiftly and saw Bill Schell's head turned toward her, and his face was hard and sullen. Beyond, she saw Frank Ivey and Jess Moore, dwarfed by Frank's solid bulk, passing the livery.

"Rose, go out the back way. Now," Bill said.

"Wait," Rose said flatly. "There's another way, Bill. It's a chance." She turned to Mrs. Parkinson. "Will you help?"

"Certainly, girl," the doctor's wife said calmly.

"Then go in Dave's room and take off your dress and don't let them in there. . . . Bill, you go in too and hide. Now go!"

Mrs. Parkinson rose and went into the room, and Rose pulled Bill away from the window. He was hesitant, not liking this, and she shook him impatiently. "Hurry, Bill. It's Dave's only chance."

Bill's gun was hanging from his hand at his side as he walked into the bedroom too, pulling the curtain closed behind him.

In the tiny bedroom, Mrs. Parkinson took a look at the two men and said, "I'm too old to be very modest, young men." She peeled her black dress off over her head, and stood there defiantly in her petticoat.

Bill Schell's smile was quick and gentle and he said, "You're a lady, ma'am."

In the other room, Rose looked around frantically for any trace of Bill's presence, and saw a cold cigarette butt lying on the window. She picked it up and stuffed it in her pocket as the bell jangled imperiously. Scooping up some pins and putting them in her mouth, Rose picked up her shears and went to the door and opened it.

Frank Ivey and Jess Moore stood there, hats off, and nodded. Rose's surprise seemed genuine as she took the pins from her mouth before she spoke. "Hello, Frank. Hello, Jess."

"You alone, Rose?" Frank asked.

"Why no," Rose said, a feigned puzzlement in her voice. "I'm fitting a dress on Mrs. Parkinson." Frank looked steadily at her for so long she knew she must speak. "This is mysterious. What's the matter with you, Frank?"

"I'm looking for Dave Nash," Frank said grimly. There was a kind of terrible calmness in him that frightened Rose.

Rose's voice was cold with dislike. "I haven't seen him, and I wouldn't tell you if I had."

"I'll take a look," Frank said heavily. "Stand away, Rose."

Rose stood defiantly just long enough, and then she stepped aside and said bitterly, "I can't stop you."

Frank and Jess Moore stepped into the room. They looked around it and Frank said, "What's back there?"

"My bedroom, a closet, my kitchen."

Frank drew his gun and said, "Come on, Jess," and started toward the corridor.

At that moment Mrs. Parkinson started out of the bedroom in her petticoat. When she saw the two men, she shrieked and dived back into the bedroom.

"You're such a gentleman, Frank," Rose said quietly, bitterly.

Frank went doggedly into the corridor and Mrs. Parkinson stuck her head through the curtains, holding them tightly around her neck.

"Frank Ivey, what in the name of sin are you doing in this house?" she said angrily.

"Excuse me," Frank said heavily and tramped back into the kitchen, Jess Moore, his glance on the floor, following him. Rose followed Jess.

Frank looked around the kitchen carefully, and he saw nothing except the homely litter of a place well-lived in.

"Would you mind telling me why you're doing this?" Rose asked.

"I told you," Frank said idly. He came back past her and paused in the corridor. Mrs. Parkinson, her hair a little awry, glared at him.

"What's in there?" Frank said, using his gun to point into the bedroom.

"I am, you fool," Mrs. Parkinson said tartly. "I am also undressed."

"I want to look," Frank said. His face was flushing a dark red with embarrassment.

Mrs. Parkinson said in a voice trembling with rage. "You come in here, young man, and I'll have Harvey beat you within an inch of your life! There are limits to what even you can do, Frank Ivey. Now get out of here!"

Frank hesitated a long second, and then turned on his heel and threw open the door to the closet. It was a large closet hung with Rose's clothes.

"Maybe you'd like me to shake out my dresses," Rose said, from beside him.

Frank walked in, looked around, moved some dresses and then came out in the corridor again.

"All right, Jess. Let's go."

He walked out into the front room and paused again, as if reluctant to go before he found some evidence of Dave's presence. Connie's dress lay on the table. Frank poked it with his gun, lifted it and looked at it incuriously, and then, without another word, tramped out the door, Jess Moore following him.

# CHAPTER XIX

Back at the Special, Frank tramped moodily up to the bar, and Burch, without being asked, shoved a bottle and a glass toward him. Burch leaned his soft white arms on the bar and said, "You might try the sheriff's office. He'd pull an Injun trick like that."

"Don't talk like a damn fool," Frank said with an ominous anger. He poured himself a drink and tossed it off, and stood there looking blankly and angrily at the glass a moment. Then he wheeled and regarded his crew scattered about the room, some playing cards, some watching.

"Jess, go over and check Crew's office," he ordered.

A soft, pleased smile touched Burch's pasty face; his advice was valued. He said wisely: "He'll turn up. He ain't the kind to run."

Jess Moore and another man passed on their way to the sheriff's office.

Somebody from the tables called. "Let's get some lamps goin', Burch. We can't see in the dark," and Burch moved off to accommodate him.

Twilight was creeping into the saloon, and night would soon be here, and still he was inactive, Frank thought savagely. He had a man watching 66, he had a man watching the Ridge camp, and he sent a man to scout Relief. But, most important, he did not want to move until he heard from Bender, who was scouting the Breaks. Maybe—just maybe—Red had done the

job. A vast and passionate anger rode Frank. He knew
now that just one man stood between him and complete victory over Connie, and that man was Dave Nash.
He would hunt him down and kill him if it took every
man in his crew a year to do it. Nash had failed on his
boldest bid for grass. He had sacrificed Connie's cattle
in one daring risk to pull Jim Crew over to 66. For
Frank never doubted that Dave Nash was behind that
stampede. And now, because of Nash, Jim Crew lay
dead in Bell's wagon shed.

Frank thought of that with a feeling of thankfulness.
Crew, he could admit to himself now, had been a
bogyman. He hadn't been afraid of Crew, or of his
reputation with a gun, but he had been willing to
sacrifice much for Crew's help just as Connie had.
All that seemed foolish now, and only increased his
impatience of the moment. Crew had gone down with
the fearless stupidity of his kind, and he had gone
down in the wrong. It was this that gave Frank a
wicked satisfaction. It had given him the right to walk
into the Special and announce calmly he had shot Crew
when Crew, trying to frame him, had pulled a gun
first. It gave him the right to invite any man to investi-
gate his guilt in the killing of Connie's herd; but, most
important of all, it gave him the right to smash Connie,
and no man alive could blame him. Only Dave Nash
and, incidentally, Bill Schell remained to be taken care
of. After that, he was the power on the Bench. Connie
was finished and Ben Dickason was fading. He, Frank
Ivey, was the Bench.

He poured another drink and downed it and looked
outside to find it dark. He shoved the bottle away from
him in disgust. The liquor wasn't touching him. He
fired up a cigar and saw in the bar mirror the entrance
of Martin Bondurant.

Bondurant came up to the bar and Burch moved over
to him and took his order. Bondurant, as a man always
does, should have looked around to greet his friends,
but he did not. He studied his hands, folded on the bar.
Slowly, it came to Ivey that Bondurant was avoiding
speaking to him, and it touched off an angry malice in
him.

"Evenin,' Martin," he said.

Bondurant looked at him and nodded coolly, and looked away and Frank moved over to him.

"Remember me, Martin?" he asked with a heavy attempt at humor. "I'm Frank Ivey."

Bondurant looked coolly at him and said, "Yes, I remember you. Don't come in my store again, Frank."

Frank stared at him, bewilderment and wrath mounting in his eyes. Bondurant took his drink and downed it, and then turned to Frank and said quietly, "He was too good a man to go that way, Frank. A lot of us think so."

He turned and walked out, and Frank looked blankly at Burch. "Did you hear that?"

Burch smiled softly. "Give 'em time to get used to it."

Frank went back to his bottle and had another drink, but a new kind of anger was prodding him, and behind this was a complete bewilderment. Didn't they believe his story about Crew? Did they think he had really killed Connie's cattle, and then cut down on Crew when he came to make the arrest? Slowly, a feeling of outrage took hold of him, and just as slowly passed, leaving a hatred now fed by his arrogance. Let them think what they wanted. He was in the right, his conscience was clear. He despised them all, the whole town, and always had.

He went over to one of the tables and said, "I'm goin' to eat," and wheeled and went out.

The dining room at the hotel held only a few diners, and Frank noticed they all seemed occupied with talk or with their food as he passed on the way to his table. Alice, the girl who usually served him, did not come near him tonight. A new girl served him, and Frank ate in angry silence.

When he was finished, he was alone in the room. Nobody, not even a waitress, remained. He drew out a cigar and studied it. His arrogance would not let him hurry, and yet he felt this deep within him, and his whole being was outraged. He did not expect affection from people, but he did demand respect. He had defended himself as any free man has a right to, and no-

body believed him. Dave Nash, Frank thought wickedly, would pay this score in full. The whole west was
not big enough to hide Nash from him after tonight.

He paid his score and rose and went out through the
lobby and took a chair at the corner of the veranda,
and the soft darkness of it somehow helped his patience. His cigar was smoked half down when Rose
Leland crossed the side street and mounted the steps of
the hotel, a package under her arm. Frank looked at
her and she looked at him, and neither of them spoke,
and she went inside. Frank heard her in low conver-
sation with Bice, the clerk, and presently she came out
without the package. She did not look at him, but
went on down the street toward her place.

Frank rose then and went up to the desk and asked
flatly of old Bice, "What did she want?"

Bice knew, too. Frank could see it in his face, weak,
disapproving, and it only made him the more stubborn.
When Bice did not answer, Frank put both hands on
the desk and said quietly, "I asked you a question,"
and his eyes, baleful and bright, held a flat warning.

"She wanted to know if anybody was takin' the
stage. She's got a dress for the agent's wife she wanted
dropped off."

Frank considered that a moment, and could read
nothing suspicious into it. He wheeled and went out to
his chair on the porch again, and sat down to wait for
Bender and news of Red and Nash.

Dave heard the front door open and close, and he
looked toward the curtain in the doorway of his dark
room. Bill Schell's cigarette glowed in the dark beside
him, and Dave listened again. The ringing in his head
from the fever might have deceived him, and he
listened for Rose's footsteps. Suddenly the curtain
parted and Rose stepped into the room, which had been
kept dark against the prowling of any curious Bell
hand.

"Sitting up?" Rose asked. "How do you feel?"

"Good," Dave said. "What did you find?"

"Nobody's taking the stage from here." She hesitated,
and when she spoke her voice was grave. "Frank Ivey

was on the veranda. I don't know about this, Bill."

"We got to, Rose," Bill Schell answered in a discouraged voice. "Dave couldn't last a mile on a horse."

"Suppose Frank looks."

"Then that's that," Dave said. He was glad for the darkness, because it hid the sweat on his forehead and the shaking which he could not stop.

"It's close to time," Bill remarked. "Try your legs, kid."

Dave came unsteadily to his feet. The pain in his shoulder and all down his side was hot and searing as he moved, and he held his breath, steadying himself against the bed, until it died. His left arm was dead, useless.

"It's all right," he said, and was immediately sorry he had spoken. There was a quaver in his voice that he could not control.

The sound of Bill's cigarette being tossed into the saucer came to him, and then Bill moved up beside him and put a hand under his arm. Three cool drops of sweat channeled down his back, and the ringing in his ears was loud and steady, and he was suddenly so cold he shook.

He moved slowly out into the corridor and Rose went past him and into the kitchen. She knelt by the cabinet and pulled out his hat where she had hidden it, and she came back to him, holding it out. Dave took it and put it on, and looked at her, and the image of her was not quite steady. He beat his mind for something to say to her, some way to express his gratitude, and he could not find it in this fever. His brain seemed sick, slowed to a pace where it could only register his dogged determination to keep his knees from buckling.

He only said, "So long, Rose," and she did not answer him, and he turned into the front room and was guided across it by Bill Schell. Bill left him then and went outside and presently came back and said, "All right, kid."

He felt Rose's hand on his arm, and then he was out on the walk. Immediately, Bill guided him across the dark stretch of the vacant lot, and Dave breathed deeply of the cool night air. He began to shake again, and he wanted more than anything in the world to lie down, but Bill's insistent hand guided him on until they were against the wall of the livery.

"Lean against that," Bill whispered.

Dave did, his head hung on his chest, breathing deeply and steadily against a nausea that was rising within him. If he only weren't so weak, he thought angrily. His side and shoulder throbbed savagely with every beat of his heart, and he concentrated now on keeping his knees from folding. He turned his head and saw Bill standing at the corner of the building, looking upstreet.

He closed his eyes and waited for what seemed hours. Bright points of light came and faded behind his lids, and he speculated with a terrible concentration on this. He could hold his mind to nothing, however. There were absurd, heartbreaking memories of Ruth and the baby that came to him, and before he could feel sad they had vanished and he was thinking of Ivey. And then of Connie and Rose, and he remembered stupidly he wanted to say something to Rose. But his mind would not hold that either, and he stood there and shook with a rising delirium. He was roused by Bill shaking him so roughly that his side came awake with pain.

"This is it, kid. You understand it, don't you?"

"What?" Dave whispered stupidly, and Bill's soft, despairing cursing came to him as in a dream.

"Listen," Bill said fiercely. "Harry will duck into the Special for a drink. Joe will unhook and take the teams back and bring the fresh ones out. In between, you get in the stage. Don't talk, just sit there."

Dave nodded stupidly, unhearing, and came erect with a lurch, and Bill guided him toward the corner of the building. He heard the stage now making its turn and pulling up in front of the livery archway.

He heard Joe Lilly's murmured greeting and he heard Harry say distinctly, "Take a look at that off wheel horse, Joe. He's lamin' up."

Bill paused at the corner and peered off at the stage, and through the wait Dave could hear the jangle of harness chain and the soft swearing of Joe Lilly, and then the clatter of the horses' feet on the plank runway. Each sound was loud, and somehow seemed important, though he did not know why.

Bill said, "Now," and pushed gently, and Dave began to walk and he stumbled. Bill caught him, and he was swearing softly, bitterly. He guided Dave around the rear of the stage and opened the door and then said, "Step up, step up," in a whisper filled with despair.

Dave gathered all his strength and felt Bill place his foot on the step and he lunged up and lost his balance and grabbed weakly for the door brace. He missed it and fell and remembered to fall on his right side, and he hit the floor of the stage with a crash that sent the pain racking through him, rousing him to its bitter message. The door was shut.

*This won't work,* he remembered thinking, and he fumbled at his hip and got his gun. He lay there, his face in the dirt of the floor boards, and presently he twisted his head and looked to see if there was anyone with him. There wasn't, and he lay there sweating, not trying to move, waiting for the pain to subside.

He heard the fresh horses hooked up and presently Harry came out of the Special. He and Joe Lilly discussed the shooting of Crew in grave undertones, and then the stage creaked and gently tilted as Harry stepped up. It started with a lurch that drowned out Harry's solemn swearing and it trundled along and then halted again, and Dave wondered why.

"What you got, Bice?" Harry called then, and Dave knew they were at the hotel.

A voice said, "Drop this off for Mrs. Gentry, Harry."

Then Harry's voice came again, and Dave, through the pain, caught the subtle change in tone. "Oh, hello, Frank."

"Meet anybody comin' through the Breaks, Harry?"

"Old man Wharton, is all. Why?"

"Never mind."

There was a pause, and then the crack of Harry's whip, and the stage lumbered off.

Somewhere on the grade all sound ribboned off, and Dave slept. Sometime later he roused and tried to remember where he was and he could not even hold the memory in his fevered brain. He was awake a long time, then, and the pain now was something alive and close and overwhelming. His face was ground into the floor boards and each lurch of the stage on the road across the flats sent a fresh flood of the pain. He knew he could not stand this, then, and in the strength of desperation he shoved himself to his knees, and groped drunkenly for the seat and found it.

For a while he let his head rest on its thin cushions, and the immediate pain ebbed slowly, and the relief was so blessed he slept. He was awakened only moments later by a shock of agony that made him cry out. The swing of the stage had thrown his slack weight against the side of the stage. He buried his face in the cushion, then, biting its rough duck cover until the wave of agony had passed. His shoulder was freshly wet, and he knew the wound had reopened. Now, a panic was driving him. He must get onto the seat and lie down. Nothing had ever seemed so important as getting onto the seat, and he knelt there, wet with sweat, summoning the stubborn courage to accomplish it. He tried once and the lurch of the stage flung him back. On the second attempt he rode with the swing of the stage and his head crashed into the back of the seat. But he turned his body and felt the seat under him, and then he let himself down on his back with his free hand, and was asleep then in seconds.

He dozed fitfully, but it was never real sleep. The fever in his brain made a bitter nonsense of his waking moments, so that he could call back none of what had passed, nor where he was going and how he had got here. Once, from the slow steady pull of the stage, he knew they were climbing, and he suddenly remembered the grade out of Signal and knew despair, then. He could not live this out if he stayed here much longer.

Sometime, hours later, he came out of a dream to hear voices, and he was aware the stage had stopped.

He lay there, and heard the door opened, and somebody come in.

"You all right, kid?"

It was Bill Schell, and Dave stared at him stupidly

and licked his lips so he could speak. Bill turned and said sharply, "Give me a hand here, Harry."

They lifted him out, hurting him, of course, and laid him against a sloping bank, and Bill Schell struck a match.

Dave squinted against the light and answered Bill's question then. "All right," he whispered.

"I'd of took it easier if I'd knowed, Bill," Harry said earnestly.

"I couldn't risk Lilly," Bill said. "I been tryin' to catch you all night."

They were silent a moment, and then Harry said in a low voice, "You can't move him, Bill."

"I got to." Dave felt Bill's hand pinching his cheek and he opened his eyes. "All right," he said again.

"Kid, I'm goin' to tie you on a horse. Can you do it?"

Dave couldn't answer, and Bill moaned a little in despair, and swore with a dark and bitter vehemence. "Help me, Harry," he said, rising.

They got Dave on a horse, hurting him again, and now he had one memory; it was his ride back from the Breaks. He grabbed the mane of his horse with his free hand, and Bill tied his legs together under the belly of his horse.

Harry said, "Where you takin' him?"

"You're a friend of mine, Harry, but not that good a friend," Bill said. "One more thing, too."

"What?"

"If Frank Ivey ever hears of this, Harry, I'm goin' to kill you. Damn dead, too."

"He won't," Harry said. "I don't love the man."

"I said dead," Bill reiterated.

They moved away, and presently Dave felt his horse walking, and again he slipped off into the nightmare of fever. Of that night, he later remembered nothing at all beyond being placed on a horse. He was aware that time had passed only when Bill took him off the horse, which hurt savagely. It was daylight and then it was suddenly dark again, and he felt solid ground under his back.

Bill's face, weary and sober, came into focus in the halflight of where he lay.

"Want to eat?" Bill said.

Dave shook his head and Bill's swift grin crossed his face. "You can sleep, kid."

He must have looked puzzled, because Bill said, "It's an old mine above Relief, kid. You're all right."

He must have thought so, because he slept.

# CHAPTER XX

THE wagonload of her things arrived at 66 in early morning, and Connie, as the wagon approached, saw an outrider with it whom she identified as her father.

It drew into the yard and the team was halted by the porch under the warm sun. Connie, leaning against one of the porch posts, said, "Morning, Pop."

"Morning, Connie." Ben gestured toward the wagon. "Still want this stuff?" he asked mildly.

The aching uncertainty she had gone through yesterday when no word of Dave had come to her, and the sleeplessness of last night had both combined to put Connie's nerves on edge. There was a hardness in her voice as she said, "I do. I told you I did."

Ben said, "Unload it, Fred," to the hand driving the wagon, and then he shuttled his puzzled glance toward Connie. "A house is all right. What do you do for cattle, though?"

"Jim Crew will take care of that," Connie said. . . . "Put it on the porch, Fred."

She noticed both her father and Fred Lindstrom looking strangely at her, and Ben said, "You ain't heard, then? Jim Crew is dead."

"No," Connie said quickly.

"Frank got him when Jim went to arrest him."

For a long stunning moment, Connie did not move, and then an overwhelming feeling of guilt flooded over her. She turned and put her face in her hands as if to hide, and Ben dismounted and hurried onto the porch to her. The agony of that brief moment was sharp and terrible to Connie, and when she felt her father's arms about her she clutched the lapels of his coat tightly, shivering uncontrollably.

"I thought you knew," Ben said gently.

Then the panic started, slow and insidious and ugly, and her body was rigid against her father's. Nobody ever, ever must know, she thought wildly. It was a fear, gray and monstrous, that held her now. She had killed Jim Crew, and nobody must ever know. She made a violent effort to stop her shaking, but she would not look up at her father. He stroked her hair as he had done when she was a child, and slowly, then, a kind of reason came back to her, and she sighed shudderingly. It came to her then that this was the ultimate test of her strength; this was what she must fight for with all the cold cunning she could bring to bear. She straightened up after long minutes of gathering her courage, and pulled away from her father, and dabbed her eyes with her handkerchief. Ben said gravely, "Frank has gone crazy mad."

"He'll pay," Connie said dully. "He'll pay."

"How?" A note of pleading crept into Ben's voice now. "Connie, you're not safe from him here. Take my word for it."

Connie turned and walked into the living room, and Ben tramped in after her. She went down in the nearest chair and stared dully at the floor, trying to beat her mind into action, and Ben watched her gravely.

"He was camped in town last night with his crew, looking for Nash. He thinks——"

"Did he find him?" Connie asked swiftly.

"No. Nobody knows where he is. Frank thinks he stampeded your cattle and saddled Bell with the blame. Where is he?"

"I don't know," Connie whispered, and then she cried in wild protest, "Oh, Pop. Let me alone. Let me alone!"

Ben stepped out onto the porch and Connie sat there alone feeling only a kind of numb despair. Slowly, then, she tried to separate her torments. There was Dave, sick

and hurt, and Frank Ivey in town looking for him.
There was nothing she could do except hope blindly
that Bill and Rose could keep him hidden, could nurse
him and save him for her. She had to believe that, or
she would go crazy.

And then, the other thing, the thin dismal fear came
back again, and her mind wrestled with it cunningly.
She thought *There are only four of them that know.
Peebles and Bailey and Bill Schell and Link Thoms. The
first two won't tell because they're guilty with me. Link
Thoms is mine. It's Bill Schell I can't be sure of.* She
thought of Bill Schell then with a searching pessimism.
He was Dave's closest friend, and wouldn't he, seeing
the sorry mess she had made of this, tell Dave of her
guilt in Crew's death? Bill was impulsive and strange,
and he could not be trusted. Yet if he told Dave of her
scheming, she was lost, and she did not want to live if
Dave learned her share in this.

She listened now to her father and Fred unloading
the wagon, and she speculated desperately on a way to
stop Bill. And then it came to her with a suddenness
that brought her to her feet. Of course! She had a hold
on Bill, the same kind of hold he had on her. For she
was sure of his guilt in Ed Burma's death, and she
would buy his silence with her knowledge. She must
find Bill and Dave. She would nurse Dave herself, show
him her love, and she would seal Bill Schell's lips forever.

She turned now and ran out onto the porch, and saw
her father and Fred Lindstrom both standing by the
wagon, facing the far end of the house, listening. Then
the sound of swift-running horses came to her, and
within seconds three horsemen rode around the end of
the house at a dead run on their way to the corrals.
Connie came up by Ben, and at that moment Frank
Ivey and Jess Moore rounded the end of the house and
Jess, too, cut toward the corrals. Frank, seeing them,
yanked his horse around and came up to the porch.

He said to Fred Lindstrom, "You stay set," and then
looked over at Ben and Connie.

His heavy face, shadowed by the Stetson he wore

squarely on his head, was cold and expressionless, and his glance raked Connie harshly and clung to her.

Ben said warningly, "Be careful around here, Frank."

Ivy laid his glance on Lindstrom and said, "Don't unload," and then he kicked his near foot from the stirrup and put a heavy hand on the saddle horn.

"Your man Nash made a mistake, Connie," Frank said heavily. "You got him here?"

"No."

"I'll look."

Now from the barn, Moore and the other two Bell hands were driving Peebles and Bailey, both afoot and both with hands high over their heads, toward the house.

They halted by Frank, and Ivey said, "Two of you search the house," and Moore and another man dismounted and went around Connie and Ben into the house.

Frank looked again at Connie. "You're pullin' out of here, Connie. I'll wait for you to go."

"No, I'm not," Connie said quickly.

Frank didn't even answer, only turned his head to regard Peebles and Bailey. "You two are finished on the Bench. Get out today."

Connie said now, looking squarely at Peebles, "Maybe he's right, Tom. He's killed Jim Crew, so you can't appeal to law."

Peebles eyed her searchingly, and she knew he understood her. It was all the warning she could give them that her orders, which they had carried out, had resulted in the death of Jim Crew. Peebles licked his lips and said, "Now?" and looked at Frank, and Frank said flatly, "Now. Saddle up a horse for Connie."

Peebles and Bailey, their guards following them, tramped back to the corral, and now Ivey turned again to Connie.

"Your man Nash killed Cates, all right. Trouble was, Red hit him too."

"Red Cates?" Ben said, with a rising inflection.

Frank didn't even look at Ben, but watched Connie.

"I'll get him, Connie. Doc lied for him and Rose Leland lied for him, and he got out of Signal. But I'll get him. There aren't"—he ceased talking, and looking at Connie's face now he said—"So you knew he was there."

Connie didn't answer him. She knew the relief that was flooding over her had shown in her face for Frank to see. Frank said slowly, "Worried, Connie?" Still she did not speak, and Frank said, "There aren't many places a hurt man can hide from me. I'll find him."

Moore and his companion, Josefa following them, stepped out onto the porch, and Jess said, "He ain't here."

"I didn't think so," Frank remarked, and he looked at Josefa. "Get in the wagon," he said to her, and she climbed off the steps and went over and got into the wagon.

Now Peebles and Bailey, with the two Bell hands, rode up, leading Connie's horse.

Frank said to her, "Get on your horse, Connie."

"No."

"I'm burning the place."

Connie knew then she couldn't fight him. He was out to destroy 66 while he could, and she had no weapons with which to defend herself.

Ben said mildly, "Frank, this is all goin' to catch up with you. Don't do it."

"Get on your horse, Connie," Frank repeated, ignoring Ben. "Don't go to the Ridge camp, either. I've got that."

Connie went out to the horse Peebles was holding. She put out her hand and he took it awkwardly and she said, "Thank you, Tom. If I were you I'd ride as far away from here as a horse would take me."

A faint smile touched Peebles' lips. He understood her, and said dryly, "I aim to."

She shook hands with Bailey then, and was handed into the saddle.

Lindstrom, with Josefa beside him, turned the wagon around, and Ben mounted his horse. Connie put her horse beside her father's and was riding out when Frank called, "Connie!"

She halted and he rode up beside her, while Ben went on.

Frank looked at her with a kind of hunger in his bold eyes, and he said quietly, "What's the use, Connie? It's still not too late to stop this."

Connie didn't even answer him. She moved her horse on and caught up with her father. They rode in silence a ways, and Connie was aware that Ben was watching her. Ben said then, "Well, Frank's done what I couldn't, Connie. He's brought you home."

Connie reined up and looked at her father. "You're wrong there, Pop. I'm not going home."

She pulled her horse around and cut off north and Ben called, "Connie! Connie! Where are you going?"

Connie didn't answer him. She was headed for town to find out from Rose where Bill Schell and Dave were hiding. When she crossed the Ridge she turned to look back at 66, hidden behind the low hills. A lazy column of brown smoke was lifting into the still morning as 66 burned.


Rose left Bondurant's with her small package of groceries and turned toward home, and as she passed the Special she experienced again that small glow of pleasure that had been with her all day. Dave had got out safely. She knew that, because this morning Frank Ivey had made a second search of her house, evidence in itself that he had not found Dave. There was a flaw in her feeling, of course, for Dave was still sick and hurt. But somewhere deep within her Rose had a faith that he would be all right. He was well hidden, and time would work for him, and Frank Ivey did not know where to look for him.

She passed Lilly's and cut across the lot, and discovered now that she was dead tired, and she did not care. Halfway across the lot, she heard her name called, and turned and saw Connie Dickason running toward her. Connie wore an apron over her house dress, and she was breathless as she halted in front of Rose.

"Rose, you've got to tell me where Bill and Dave are," Connie said, and her voice was both sharp and angry.

"Of course I will," Rose said slowly. "Is anything wrong?"

Something in the gentleness of her reply must have shamed Connie, for the color crept into her cheeks. She brushed a wisp of hair off her forehead and said in a low voice, "I'm sorry, Rose. I'm almost crazy with worry, I guess."

"Come along," Rose said, and took her arm.

Connie said, with a burst of bitterness, "I was burned out today, Rose. Frank paid me a visit."

She told Rose of what had passed at 66, and her words were angry and sharp with passion, and as Rose opened the door and let Connie in ahead of her, she felt a sudden and inexplicable weariness with Connie. What did 66 matter, except that it had almost got Dave killed, and had brought torment to all of them? She was suddenly aware that Connie had ceased talking long ago, and she looked over and saw Connie standing in the middle of the floor, her eyes bright with a suppressed indignation.

"I guess I'm tired, Connie," Rose said apologetically. "I wasn't listening."

"That's hardly it," Connie answered. "It doesn't matter to you, that's all."

Rose looked at her curiously, and said with blunt honesty, "That your place was burned? No, I don't suppose it does."

"It was my home," Connie said coldly. "Everything I——"

A vast impatience seemed to unfold in Rose, and she cut in on Connie's words. "It wasn't your home, Connie. Walt Shipley left it to you. It was something you could spend like money if it would beat Frank Ivey."

She was sorry she had said it as soon as she had finished, but in a way she wasn't either. She saw the momentary surprise in Connie's face that soon gave way to a look of anger.

"You don't like me, do you, Rose?" Connie asked then.

Rose drew a deep breath, and she knew she had a

grip on her temper now. She wasn't going to argue with Connie, and yet she wasn't going to give in.

"That doesn't matter, either," Rose said slowly. "What does is that it's time someone looked at reality, Connie."

"Let's look at it, then."

Rose debated a moment, and then a kind of resignation came to her. She'd tried to help Connie, she would not any more. She said calmly, "All right. I used to pity you, Connie. You got a rough deal from Ben and Frank, and nobody could blame you protesting. But your protest has cost the lives of too many men, and it will cost more. Is it worth it?"

"Isn't it?"

"Not if Frank gets Dave."

"Now we're talking your kind of reality," Connie said, with an open malice.

Calmly, Rose nodded. "He's the only thing that counts to me."

"And I happen to feel the same way about him."

"Not the same, Connie. You happen to want him, along with revenge, and power."

The cool accusation, spoken without any passion, brought a light of recklessness to Connie's eyes. She said wickedly, "You've told him that, I suppose."

"I've never told him anything about you."

"Since you want him, too, I'm surprised at that."

Rose smiled faintly. "You don't tell a man about any woman, Connie. He has to find out for himself."

Connie said wickedly, "I don't know so much about getting men, Rose. I've never had your practice."

Rose felt a swift anger then, and she said, "Then I'll tell you how *not* to get one, Connie. You don't let him break himself on your greed and ambition."

Connie said slowly, "Maybe I do. We'll see." She looked hotly at Rose, and then said, "I suppose you won't tell me now where he and Bill are?"

"Why, yes," Rose said slowly. "They were going to hole up in the old St. Louis mine above Relief."

"Thank you," Connie said, and turned to the door.

"Wait, Connie," Rose said.

Connie turned belligerently to face her, but Rose spoke without anger and with a deep seriousness. "You love Dave, you say. Then remember this! Frank Ivey will watch you. The only way he can get to Dave is to follow someone who goes to him."

"Are you trying to frighten me out of seeing him?"

"You love him," Rose said quietly. "It's up to you."

She and Connie regarded each other a silent moment, and Connie turned and went out.

# CHAPTER XXI

DAVE'S fever broke in the evening. He woke from sleep to find himself alone, and for many minutes he looked about him in the half-light of the drift, trying to orient himself. The telltale pick and drill marks on the sides of the drift told him he was in a mine. Behind him, far back in the bowels of the mountain, he could hear the constant drip of water. He saw the canteen then, and gingerly sat up and reached for it. Holding it between his knees, he took the cap off and drank deeply time and again. Afterward, he was glad to lie down, for the movement exhausted him. He was tired to the bone, drained of strength by the fever, but he felt clean and tired and faintly sleepy. His back was still wet from the sweat not yet dried, and his clothes seemed stiff with it.

After minutes of labor with his good hand, he contrived a cigarette from the sack of tobacco dust by the canteen, and after lighting it, he set about puzzling as to how he had got here. Bill Schell had brought him, he knew, but he wondered how. And where this place was.

The sudden whinnying of a horse back in the drift startled him momentarily. He supposed then that Bill had hidden their horses back near the water, and he wished Bill would return.

The cool wind rushing constantly past him on its way out the drift mouth was chilling, and he pulled the blankets about him. Slowly, now, he experimented with his arm. It was stiff and almost impossible to move, but the throb was gone, and the ache returned only when he moved it. The cigarette made him hungry, but he wisely did not get up to hunt food. His mind kept returning, with a faint wonder, to his escape.

Slowly, then, as night came down and the cave grew utterly black, he thought of what was past. He remembered the visit of Frank Ivey to Rose's place after the doctor's wife had told them of the shooting of Jim Crew. He let his mind linger on that, feeling a sadness that was deep and lonely, a feeling he knew Rose would understand. For Jim Crew had been a friendless man, and had died a friendless man's death; yet in his tired, taciturn way, he had been generous and just. He thought then of Rose, and of the magnificent courage of her as she brazened out Ivey's visit, and he felt with a humbleness the depth of his debt to her. He wondered then if Ivey would punish her when he learned of it, and he speculated as to what Ivey would dare to do now that Crew was out of the way. It was Connie who would suffer at his hands, and it galled him to think that he had failed her when she needed him most. The thought left an aching bitterness within him, but he was wise enough to know that part of it was pride.

He brooded on this, and, presently, he slept. He came awake later to find Bill Schell squatting over a fire at the foot of the blankets, and when Dave moved, Bill looked at him. His swift grin came, as Dave knew it would, and Bill stepped over to him.

"You take a lot of killin'," Bill drawled. "How are you, kid?"

"Hungry as hell."

Bill laughed then, and said, "I'll put the kettle on and go back and feed the horses." He pointed to a burlap bag leaning against the wall. "I had to wait for dark to raid George's feed bin."

"Where are we?" Dave asked.

Bill told him. The St. Louis mine, he said, had been abandoned a dozen years, and, scarcely remembered, lay in a brush-choked canyon in the high timber above

Relief. Bill went on back to feed the horses and presently returned and started the meal.

He told Dave of his exit from Signal, and Dave quietly wondered at his luck. His greatest luck, of course, was Rose; she had nursed him and doctored him, protected him from Ivey and helped him out of Signal. It seemed strange to him that two women, Rose and Connie, had been his deepest friends here, and as he watched Bill preparing the food he said, "Rose's grub?"

"Everything is hers," Bill said gently, and he smiled faintly. "Some day Rose's man is goin' to make her quit takin' care of strays, and she won't know what to do."

"Has she got a man?" Dave asked curiously.

Bill shook his head. "She can take me right off the Christmas tree any time, but she knows I'm a joker. Nobody fools Rose much."

Dave didn't know why, but Bill's words gave him an odd satisfaction. Bill had spoken with a wry humor, but Dave knew that beneath it was a dead seriousness. Rose wouldn't have him, and the strange part of it was that Bill knew she was right. There was something too lightweight in him, and Rose knew it.

Bill served out the supper, then, of steaks and coffee and a loaf of bread. Dave propped himself against the wall, and wolfed down the food in silence. He was tired, now, and he longed to lie down again.

Afterward, Bill dragged a couple of logs from the mouth of the tunnel and put their ends over the fire, and then sank wearily on his heels and drew out his tobacco. His dark face, smeared with its beard stubble, looked lean and fined down and tired, but there was the same bold recklessness in his eyes as he regarded Dave.

"Took a look-see over the Bench, this mornin'. Saw smoke from beyond the Ridge. I think it was 66."

"Burned?"

Bill nodded somberly, and Dave studied his cigarette. They were both quiet for long minutes, thinking of this, and then Bill moved restlessly and asked, "Well, kid, where are we now?"

"How do you figure it?" Dave asked slowly.

Bill dragged in smoke from his cigarette and threw the butt into the fire with a careful deliberation, and said quietly: "Connie's licked. Frank got her cattle, he broke up her crew, he's burned her out, he's killed Jim Crew." Bill sighed and said softly, "That curley wolf," and it was like a curse.

Dave said thoughtfully, "What pushed him over?" When Bill glanced up at him in puzzlement, Dave said, "I mean, what made him cut loose his dogs? He was playin' for Crew, same as we were."

"He's got a wild streak," Bill said.

"No," Dave said, with quiet insistence. "The things don't fit. All of a sudden, he decides to kill Connie's herd. He knew that would bring Crew down on him. If he wanted to kill Crew, there was easier ways."

"But he could get both the cattle and Jim that way."

Dave came back stubbornly to his first question. "But what decided him?"

Bill shrugged, and watched Dave carefully, and his eyes were sober and veiled with secret thoughts. "It don't matter, kid," he observed. "He did it, that's all. And we're licked, I say."

"No," Dave said slowly. "We're not."

Bill shook his head in disbelief, but he was watching him curiously as Dave stared into the fire.

"There's one load in a gun between Connie and what she wants," Dave declared. "That's the load that gets Ivey." He looked across at Bill now, and spoke deliberately, as if he were thinking this through as he talked. "Nobody loves Ivey, Bill. They're just afraid of him. Get him, and his crew will scatter. Any jury will pay back Connie out of Bell cattle. She can build a new headquarters out of Bell money." He repeated, "Just one load."

Bill shook his head. "Not my load, kid. I've seen Ivey work." A hard anger came into his face now. "I saw him get a man, once. He don't give up. He'll hunt you into the brush and then he'll hunt the brush. At first, it's easy. You dodge him and you laugh at him, but he keeps comin'. And pretty soon you get jumpy, and you think you got to move—and you do. You don't sleep, and everywhere you hit for grub one of his crew is waitin'. And all the time he's behind you, and when he ain't you think he is. And then, when you figure you'd rather let him have you than go on, he's got you where he wants you. You're tight and you're edgy, and he comes after you like a butcher." Bill shook his head. "I've seen it. Give me four-five men, and I'll corner him and take him. But alone, no. I'll drift."

Dave said nothing, and Bill looked over at him and said, "When you can walk out of here, kid, it's over the hill for me."

"All right, Bill," Dave said quietly. "Let's get some sleep."

Bill noticed the dead weariness in Dave's face, but he wanted to settle this, to clear up some things. "You better come along, kid," he said.

"I'll stick."

Bill shook his head. "I don't get it. What is it—Connie?"

Dave looked up swiftly, frowning, and he considered this and finally said, "I don't know," and looked back at the fire. When he looked up again he surprised a pity in Bill Schell's eyes, and then it was swiftly gone. He was too tired to puzzle out a reason for it.

Bill grinned and rose. "I got shot at for kissin' a girl once, but Connie will get you killed just workin' for her," he observed dryly. "You better sleep on it, kid."

"I'll sleep, but not on that, Bill. I'll stay here."

# CHAPTER XXII

TOWN was an unaccustomed treat for Link Thoms, but this afternoon, as he came off the grade into the main street, he felt only a small stirring of pleasure. He had his pay in his pocket, and ordinarily his routine included a visit with Joe Lilly, some pleasant hours spent in Corbett's saddle shop on the other side of the lumber yard, and a visit with Jim Crew, with maybe a swim down below town with a couple of friends his own age.

Today, however, Link was in town on a different sort of business. He passed the sheriff's office and regarded it with a quiet misery, mingled with uneasiness. Jim Crew was dead, and Link knew why.

He glanced ahead at Lilly's, and he knew suddenly he did not want to hear Joe's gossip or even face him, for Link felt a depression now that he couldn't shake. It had started with a hand from D Bar returning from Signal with the news that Frank Ivey had killed Jim Crew when Crew tried to arrest him for destroying Connie's herd.

That scared Link. He knew then that he was possessed of a secret a hundred times more important than it had been two days before. All day yesterday he had shunned the crew, because he knew the anxiety he felt must show on his face. And all day, too, he had waited for some word from Connie or her crew indicating their faith in him and that they were sharing the burden of this secret with him.

And nothing happened until Fred Lindstrom returned from 66 and told the story of Ivey's visit. But what Link listened for and remembered was Fred's description of Connie as she received the news of Crew's death. The image of her turning away and burying her hands in her face, as if from a blow, tore at Link's heart. He knew Connie would feel a terrible guilt, and that she would need a friend. And, because he loved her with the unreasoning vehemence of his years, he had come to comfort her.

He dismounted in front of Bondurant's and crossed the street, a leggy youngster in patched and faded work clothes whose troubled face was a banner for his feelings. Lindstrom had told of Connie's riding off to town, and Link decided to try the hotel first.

The clerk told him the number of Connie's room, and Link, yanking off his hat, took the stairs two at a time and halted breathlessly in front of her door. He raised his hand to knock, and then hesitated. What was he going to say to comfort her? What could he say except that he would die before anyone could drag her secret from him?

He knocked softly then, and, ashamed of his timidity, immediately knocked louder.

The door opened presently, and there was Connie in front of him. Small, neat, smiling her welcome with no sadness in it. Link was tongue-tied and did not speak, and Connie, laughing, reached out for his arm and pulled him into the room. "You're shy, Link. Come inside." She shut the door behind him and said, "I'm glad you came."

"I thought," Link began, and he fumbled for words, standing there watching her. "A—a lot's happened," he finished lamely.

Connie said soberly, "Yes, quite a lot," and took his hat and put it on the table. She sat down on the sofa and Link sank into a stiff-backed chair, and he watched Connie closely. He didn't know how he had expected her to receive him—maybe in tears, maybe frightened of what she had done, maybe desolated by grief and the terrible loneliness of guilt. But she was none of these; she was just Connie—pretty and gracious and kind. And strange, Link thought. She seemed almost as if she had not yet heard that Jim Crew was dead.

Connie said gravely, "I only heard about Jim Crew this morning, Link. I—I don't know what to say."

Link didn't either, but he would not have said this. He said only, "He was a good man."

Connie looked at him levelly. "I'm to blame, Link," she said quietly.

To Link, she spoke all the necessary words, and yet she was just speaking them, not feeling them. He nodded, still watching her with an intentness that made Connie uncomfortable.

"What shall I do?" Connie asked then.

Link looked down at his hands and shook his head. "I been figurin'," he murmured slowly. "You admit it, Connie, and who's it goin' to help? Frank Ivey."

"Do you think he deserves help?"

"No."

"Do you think I should admit it, Link?"

"No."

"Neither do I," Connie said gravely. "I made a mistake, and I'm sorry for it, Link, But you can't look back."

Link thought, *But you can be sick at heart for a wrong you've done. You can take a little time out from living to look back, too, because that hurts you enough to make you live better.* He said nothing, and Connie rose and went to the window and looked out.

She said slowly, "Jim Crew was my friend, Link."

"I know."

"Frank Ivey didn't have to kill him. Frank did it because he knew he could, because he knew Jim would turn against him in the long run."

"Yes'm," Link said. But Frank wouldn't have killed him if it hadn't been for the blame put falsely on him, Link knew.

Connie turned around to look at him. "Then am I wrong, Link, in trying to square Jim's death by beating Frank?"

Link said slowly, "He's got to be beat." About it squaring Jim's death, he would say nothing, because he knew it wouldn't.

"Then I'll go on fighting him, Link. I'm not beaten yet. And some day when I can I'll try to repay you for your help."

Link stood up and Connie handed him his hat and smiled and shook hands with him. Link went out, shutting the door behind him, and walked slowly toward the head of the stairs, where he halted. He had come to comfort Connie, and she did not need him.

Something had happened in that room, and he would never know exactly what. But he didn't love Connie any more. He would help her and fight for her until he died, because she had been good to him and he paid his debts. Only, he did not love her any more. He accepted this quietly, without any feeling at all, and put on his hat and went slowly down the stairs.

Connie, from her room window, watched Link get his horse and ride past the hotel on his way to the grade, and then she went over to the bed and lay down. She thought narrowly of Link, then, and knew something had changed him. It was almost as if he'd ceased being a boy now and was suddenly a man. That was natural and inevitable; he had seen ugly things and was a part of them, and they had changed him. But that look of dumb adoration she was so used to was not there when he left. She sat up, then, thinking of this. Link couldn't blame her too bitterly, for she had acknowledged her mistake, and he had pledged his secrecy. And then she smiled faintly at herself. It didn't matter. The main thing was, Link was still loyal.

She lay down again, summoning patience to wait for dark. It was all working out. Tom and Bailey were gone, Link was still her friend. Tomorrow she would make sure of Bill Schell, and she would see Dave again. For Connie was going to ignore Rose's advice. She was going to Dave.

# CHAPTER XXIII

BILL SCHELL came awake with the instant alertness of an animal. He rolled out of his blankets, which were spread just inside the tunnel, came erect, and listened to the night sounds, trying to select from them the one that had roused him. It came presently—the sound of a horse walking. Bill listened intently; a stray horse feeling is easily distinguishable in the sounds it makes from a ridden horse, and Bill listened for the broken rhythm of its walk. This horse, he soon knew, was being ridden.

He looked at the stars and saw it was not long until daylight, and now a kind of cold fatalism was on him. Somebody was scouting up here, which meant their time here was up. He holstered his gun, which he had kept in the blankets beside him, and pulled on his boots. From back in the drift he could hear Dave's faint deep breathing. He rose now and listened for the horse, and caught its sound again down canyon.

The old mine mouth was at almost the level of the bottom of the canyon. Its heap of tailings had been hauled across the canyon and scattered, so they did not mark the mouth of the diggings. The log mine buildings, long since rotted and tumbled down, lay up canyon a ways. A tangle of brush and scrub oak neatly covered the tunnel head, and now Bill, moving with a swift stealth, came out from them and circled silently up canyon toward the buildings, where, if trouble came, he would not draw attention to Dave's hiding place.

He moved into the deep shadows of the old bunkhouse and listened, and now the sound of the horse approaching was distinct. He drew his gun and backed up against the wall, and his nerves were tight and fine-drawn.

Presently, from the darkness down canyon, the figure of a horse and rider loomed out of the night and paused in the tall rank grass in front of the shack. The horse nickered uneasily, and Bill grinned wickedly into the night. The horse sensed he was there, and if the rider also didn't, he was a fool. Bill held his gun loosely and turned his head to listen down canyon. This was almost too easy, too simple. Whoever it was out there some thirty feet away was, if alone, caught fair. He could hear no other sounds, and now his attention, cool and wicked, settled on the horseman.

Bill knelt noiselessly and fumbled for a rock and found it, and tossed it soundlessly across the canyon. The noise of its landing spooked the horse, which danced swiftly away from the sound of the rock and immediately in front of Bill.

Bill lifted his gun, and now a new noise stopped him. It was the swish of cloth, and for a brief second he was puzzled, and then he knew this was a woman. He said softly, "Rose?"

"Bill, Bill," Connie said in a frightened voice.

Bill stepped out toward her, saying angrily, "Why didn't you sing out, Connie?"

"I wasn't sure where I was," Connie said.

Bill came up to the horse and took its bridle and said roughly, "What are you doin' here, Connie?"

"I came to see Dave."

"Were you followed?"

"But it's night. How could I be?"

Bill said in savage disgust, "Ah, hell," and the censure in it was sharp as a whiplash.

"What have I done?" Connie asked.

"Nothin'—I hope," Bill said bitterly. "Didn't Rose tell you you'd likely be watched?"

"But I had to see Dave."

"See him dead?" Bill gibed.

Connie's voice turned sharp then, and she said, "Don't talk to me that way, Bill. I won't take it."

"All right," Bill said wearily. "Get down. It's already done."

Bill handed her down, and Connie smoothed out her skirt and murmured, "How is he, Bill?"

"Weak as a kitten," Bill answered grimly. "Three-four more days of lyin' around and he'd be right enough to ride out of here."

The implied criticism flicked Connie's temper, and again she said with anger, "What was I supposed to do, not knowing if he was dead or alive?"

"The same thing Rose is doin'," Bill retorted. "Wait."

Connie sighed. "All right, Bill. Only I wasn't followed. I was careful."

Bill said nothing now, and Connie asked in a low voice, "Does he know about the stampede?"

"Not from me."

Connie put her hand on Bill's arm. "Oh, help me, Bill! I'm trying to make up for that any way I can."

Bill asked oddly, "Think you can, Connie?"

"No," Connie said quietly. "I'm not proud of it, and I won't have him know it, Bill. I feel about it the way you must feel about killing Ed Burma."

Bill was silent a long while, and then he said, "You're guessin', Connie. You don't know."

"I know," Connie said calmly. "That's my secret, Bill, the way the stampede is yours."

Bill said dryly, "That sounds like a deal."

"It was meant to."

Bill smiled into the darkness and said wryly, "You're tougher than a boot, Connie."

"No, I just know what I want."

"Dave?"

"Yes."

"Peace be with you," Bill said dryly. "With him, too. I'll keep your damned secret. Now come along."

At the head of the tunnel Bill said, "I'm goin' to take a look around, Connie. Better get the fire goin' now, so it will be burned out by daylight."

Connie murmured something, and went through the

brush into the tunnel head, and Bill heard Dave's startled exclamation as he wakened, followed by Connie's answer.

He tramped down canyon now, walking as silently as an Indian in the night. There was a feeling of uneasiness with him now that he could not entirely still. Connie had been a fool to try this, and unless her luck was fantastic, she had been followed. Some Bell hand was bound to pick up her trail; Ivey was not fool enough to let her go unwatched. He wondered bitterly, then, how much time they had. Dave was still too weak to travel.

Bill thought of Connie then, and smiled faintly. A kind of simple tolerance graced Bill Schell's dealings with everyone, so that he wasn't severely critical of Connie even now. She had made a mistake, and she sensed this mistake, if it became known, might rob her of the man she wanted. That was natural enough, and Bill, who had made his mistakes, too, didn't blame her for that. Only, it was shabby. Dave Nash deserved better than that from Connie, just as he deserved better than the glib lie about Ed Burma's death from him. There was a strange kind of integrity in Bill that made him see this, and it explained why he had stuck by Dave until now. He was, in an obscure way he himself didn't realize, trying to atone for that mistake. Connie, though, was not, and Bill did not like it.

The inky blackness of night was lifting a little now, and in the east the stars began to fade. Bill came to the canyon mouth, and waited there, listening for anyone on Connie's back trail. Satisfied, he turned back now, and then the sound came to him. It was a gunshot.

It was downslope a couple of miles, and Bill stood there, rooted, listening to its echo battering up through the timber, a cold misery stirring in him. And now he heard the answering shot far to the north.

This was it, he knew. They'd picked up Connie somewhere, trailed her long enough to learn she was not going to Relief, and now they were gathering.

He turned back up the canyon at a jog trot, a deep disgust and anger riding him. Connie had risked them all on a selfish whim, and she'd lost. She would lose Dave, too, unless they were lucky.

He arrived at the tunnel and found Dave, blankets wrapped about him, sitting up. He took a careful, searching look at Dave, seeing his pallor and the listlessness of his movements, and he cursed silently.

Connie was kneeling by the fire over a pan of steaks, and Bill said, "Get some food in you while I saddle up. Ivey's after us."

Connie whirled and came to her feet, and Bill glared at her with a cold malice and said, "Happy now?" and brushed past her toward the horses.

Dave said, "How close?"

"Couple of miles down," Bill said. "He's callin' together his bunch. But we better be out of here before daylight."

He didn't wait for Dave to answer, but went on back to the horses. Saddling up, he thought narrowly of this, and knew a dismal feeling of impotence. Dave wasn't in shape to dodge anybody. They'd wear him down in a day, and then it would be over. In some way he must pull them off Dave, must give Dave time to get out of here.

He led the horses out into the chill morning, and then came back into the drift. Meat and coffee were waiting for him; he took the coffee and looked up at Dave, and saw the tough, taciturn cast of his face.

Bill said, "I feel mean enough to hit anybody that argues with me. I'm boss." He looked at Connie and saw the fear, ugly and sick, in her eyes, and his glance shuttled to Dave. "You're takin' Connie's horse, Dave. Connie and me are headin' out of here together, cuttin' up toward the pass. You're headin' south, just as fast as you can ride."

"You'll run into them," Dave said.

"We'll split before we do. Connie won't get in on it. And I ain't worried about myself. I never saw the man yet that could get through these hills fast enough to catch me."

Dave didn't answer, and Bill went on in his harsh voice. "I figure when Ivey sees two pair of tracks, neither one of 'em Connie's horse, he'll figure it's you and me lightin' out. Those are the ones he'll follow."

Dave said flatly, "I won't do it, Bill."

"What other way is there? I tell you, he can't get me, and he don't want Connie. And I can pull him off you for a day. What other way is there?" he repeated.

Dave couldn't answer. Bill stood up and threw his coffee grounds in the fire and dropped his cup. "No time to argue, kid. Just do it my way for once."

He walked around to Dave and helped him to his feet. It was frightening to Bill, knowing what lay ahead, to see the big man's weakness. He could feel Dave shake, and he saw the sweat on his forehead which his battered Stetson could not hide in the fore-light. More than that, he saw the implacable stubborn-ness in Dave's eyes, and knew Dave had no illusions about this either.

They walked out to the horses, which were standing in the first graying light of true dawn. Dave's left arm hung straight and useless at his side, and his bandaged shoulder bulked a little under his coat. Connie was frightened too, and she turned away to Dave's horse as Bill and Dave halted beside her own.

Dave looked at the horse and then at Bill, and said with a grim humor, "If I ever get on him, I'll have to stay."

Bill laced his fingers together and Dave put his boot in them, and Bill hoisted. There was no strength in Dave, Bill saw then. He had to fight to take his weight up, and he fell heavily into the saddle as his breath whistled thinly through his teeth. He sat there a mo-ment, eyes closed, and Bill swiftly rolled a cigarette and handed it to him and lighted it for him.

They looked at each other in the half-light, then, and Dave said quietly, "Keep her out of it, Bill. Whatever happens, keep her out of it."

Bill said impatiently, "I'm goin' to run away from her, I tell you. Hell, I'm headin' out of the country and drawin' Ivey with me."

Dave put out his hand and murmured, "Luck."

Bill took it and grinned, and Connie rode up be-side them then.

Bill said dryly, "Connie, I want you to hear this, too." He looked up at Dave. "Me and George braced Burma, Dave. I got him cold. I ain't sorry, either."

Dave nodded and said slowly, "I figured you did."

Bill grinned, and looked over at Connie in the half-light, and there was a contempt for her in his eyes which she did not see, but felt. He would keep her secret, his words seemed to say, but he would not be blackmailed into keeping it. And to prove it, he was telling his own guilt.

He said dryly, "Ready, Connie," and went over to his horse.

Connie looked at Dave then and said bitterly, "I never do anything right, do I?"

"Nobody does, except Ivey," Dave observed.

"But look what I've done," Connie said miserably. "I came up to help you, and now I've put the whole pack of them on your trail."

Dave said gently, "It'd have to come some time, Connie. What I'll remember is that you came."

"Remember when, Dave—when you're out of the country?"

"You want me to go?" Dave asked.

"I want you well. I'll wait, Dave. I'll wait forever, if you say you'll be back."

"I promise that, Connie," Dave murmured gently.

At the mouth of the canyon they parted in silence in the bare light of dawn, Dave going south, Bill and Connie north.

# CHAPTER XXIV

DAVE clung to the trails, working south in the timber, and he rode steadily without any attempt to cover his trail. But before midmorning, he knew he could not keep this up. There was nothing wrong with him except he was weak as water, and more than anything in the world he wanted to pick a spot in the sun and lie down and sleep for a week. He seemed to be sunk in a gray apathy that increased hourly, and he believed he knew its cause. It went against the pride in him to skulk out of this country like a kicked dog. Connie's plans were wrecked and Jim Crew was dead, and Bill Schell was on the dodge and Rose's courage had bought him only a brief rest before a beaten escape.

He came to a meadow in the timber and crossed it, feeling the sun on his back, and suddenly he knew running wouldn't settle anything now. If Bill was buying him time to escape, then he could use that time to go back. And then he knew with a sick certainty that he could not do it. His body would not do it. It would fail him, as it was failing him now, and he would have to swallow his pride and husband his strength until he was out of reach of Frank Ivey. But he would come back, just as he promised Connie.

At the far end of the meadow he put his horse up a sharp, almost bald ridge among the timber, and the climb seemed to needle muscles he had not used, and the ache in his shoulder started again. He reined up on the ridge, and considered now. The only way left him was to the south. If he kept to these trails, riding steadily, he could work across the Federals where they leveled off far beyond the Bench, and he could pick up food and a change of horses at the south end of the reservation. That was what he must do.

His glance dragged across the tops of the trees and raked the meadow, and he knew he was looking at this for the last time. And then abruptly, he came awake. A lone horseman at a comfortable jog was following his trail across the deep grass of the meadow.

A hard awareness shocked him into action now, and the morning sun suddenly took on a sharp brightness to him as he put his horse hurriedly over the ridge and now into the deep timber, breaking away from the trail. He thought about the man behind him, wondering if he had seen him. He doubted it; there was something about the leisurely, open way he was following him that indicated he thought this was Connie ahead of him. Ivey had probably given strict orders for her to be watched, but not molested.

He concentrated now on covering his trail, but he went at it with a kind of fatalism he himself was aware of. To do a job of covering a trail, he must pick the rough spots, and he knew bleakly that he couldn't do it well. He was certain of this when, in midday, he put his horse down a sharp bank into a rocky wash. As his horse, stiff-legged, slid down the bank, Dave gripped the saddle with his knees and could not hold. He went over the horn and threw his good arm around his horse's neck to save himself from falling. In the wash, he spoke soothingly to the horse, and then worked his way back into the saddle, and now he knew a gray despair. If his horse hadn't been thoroughly gentled, he would have been pitched off. Likewise, if he were driven into any kind of a run for safety, he couldn't stick in the saddle. He faced this quietly, as he worked on down the wash. There was one thing left to do, and that was pick a spot for a stand, and get this over with.

He regarded the banks of the wash carefully now, feeling his shirt wet with a sweat that was not from the midday sun. He rounded a bend in the wash and picked out a spot to his right where a brush-tangled coulee came into the wash, and paused to study it and then the screening timber that came down almost to the lip of the bank. That would do.

He rode on down the wash some hundred feet, and looked back. It was a straight stretch here which was what he wanted too. He dismounted heavily and tied his horse to a root, without any attempt to hide him, and then retraced his steps to the coulee.

Once there, he walked up it, fighting his way through the tangle of brush, pausing often to rest, and then he cut over into the stand of pine. Here he sat down, gently hauling his arm around so that it lay comfortable on his lap. He drew his gun and put it beside him, and then sat down to listen and watch. The drowsy hum of the summer afternoon, rank with the scent of the pines, seemed to isolate him now, and he picked out the individual sounds.

He had a wait of perhaps a half hour, and then he heard the unmistakable ring of a horse's shoe on the stones of the wash. He gripped his gun now and came to his knees, and the sound came closer, and presently Jess Moore's slight figure, hunched in the saddle, came into sight around the bend in the wash.

He was looking ahead of him, and he suddenly yanked his horse up with an abruptness that almost made the horse rear.

He had seen Connie's horse tied down the stream bed. Dave knew what was coming next. Moore turned his head to study the banks of the wash, the other side first. And then his glance shuttled to the side Dave was in, traveling slowly. He had his gun in his hand by now. At last his glance passed Dave, and then came back to him, and for a brief second the two of them looked at each other.

Dave said, "Here I am, Jess."

Moore's gun was already lifting, and its roar shattered the afternoon stillness. At the same time, Moore had wheeled his horse, and as Dave sighted he saw the horse cross his sights, and it was too late to stop.

He fired, and the horse went down heavily, and Moore sailed over his head and was lost to sight behind the bend of the wash.

Dave came to his feet now and crashed down into the coulee, and fought his way through the brush on the other side, and came out on the lip of the bank hoping to cut Moore off.

Suddenly the bank underneath him gave way, and he leaped back, but too late. The whole overhanging shelf, eaten away by floods, caved, and he fell heavily, pitched forward on his face into the rough stream bed.

The shock of his landing was simultaneous with Moore's shot, which was close enough to deafen him. Dave rolled over, heedless of his shoulder, and came to his knees, facing around. He leaned unconsciously on his left arm, and it gave way, and as he fell he saw Moore, hugging the steep bank, shoot again. Dave fell on his side now, his gun straight out ahead, and now he lifted it and shot twice.

His second shot caught Jess in the side, slamming him up against the bank so hard that a small avalanche of dirt started falling, and then its thin sound was lost as Moore fell heavily on his face.

Dave came to his knees now, and the old aching throb was back in his shoulder. He reached his hand inside his coat and found he could not get it inside for the gun he was holding, and he holstered it.

Then, still kneeling, his breath held tight against the pain, he reached in and felt the bandage wet again. He drew his hand out and stared at the thin smear of scarlet on it, and then he heard the shots. They came from below, very faint in the still afternoon. They were shots in answer to his and Moore's.

A kind of dread came to him then. He had traded Jess Moore for another man, who would be warned and would call more help. The urgency now was something bright and sharp, and he stumbled to his feet and skirted Jess's horse and went down the wash as fast as he could walk.

It took him a good two minutes to get on his horse. He achieved it by pulling his body across the saddle and then, regardless of pain, working his leg across and pushing himself straight.

Afterward, he pulled out of the wash and cut directly back toward the mountains, in the opposite direction from which the shots had come. It didn't matter that he didn't want to go that way; time enough after dark to sift down through his pursuers and shake them. For he knew with a calm certainty that he could stick this out today, but not tomorrow, and that he was going back to make the day count.

When they came to the pass road, Bill Schell pulled up short of it and waited for Connie to come alongside. When she did, he pointed to it and said, "There it is, Connie. Get in the middle of it and ride slow and head for Signal. You'll get picked up in an hour."

"Where are you going?" Connie asked.

Bill shrugged and looked at her and said, "I'll work on ahead."

"Why don't you head for the reservation?"

Bill smiled wryly. "This road is the first thing they'd bottle up." He pulled his horse out of the way, and made a mocking gesture for her to precede him.

"Wait, Bill," Connie said. Her blue-green eyes were wide and sober, and she looked at Bill searchingly. "You don't like anything about me, do you?"

"You're all right," Bill murmured, with a kind of rafish humor in his eyes. "You're like a horse or a dog or a man or any other woman. Once I understand you, you're all right."

"I'm going to win out in this, Bill."

"By marryin' Frank?"

"No. I'll win out. And when I do, I want you to come back and work for me."

"No thanks," Bill murmured.

"Why not? We understand each other."

Bill grinned and impatiently shook his head. "Too well, Connie. So long." He looked briefly at her. "When they stop you, tell them you were ridin' with me—not Dave. They won't believe you."

He moved out to the road and studied it briefly,

and then touched spurs to his horse and crossed it quickly. Afterward, not particularly careful about his trail, he struck up toward the boulder fields and the peaks. He rode steadily, and his face, as the day wore on, grew more grim with his thoughts. When, in mid-day, he heard signal shots behind him, he did not even look around. For Bill Schell was having a look at himself, and he did not like what he saw. This whole thing from the start had been something of which he was not proud. He had taken Dave's offer because he was a too good hater. He thought he saw a chance to get even with Bell and Frank Ivey, and still have his vengeance recorded as legal.

Well, it hadn't turned out that way. He'd managed to circumvent the only three honest people concerned in this—Dave Nash and Jim Crew and Rose Leland. He had helped to kill Jim Crew, with Connie's aid, and Dave had only a thin chance of getting away with this. The whole thing was sour in his soul, and he thought of Connie now with a gray distaste. She was like Ivey, really. She was one of the breed who would get power and then abuse it, and die rich and honored. A kind of humorous irony in this appealed to part of Bill's nature, but to the other it stirred a deep disgust and self loathing. Why hadn't he come right out and told Dave that Connie was a sharper, out for him and out for anything else she could get her greedy little hands on? She wasn't worth a hair of Dave's head —but then, she wouldn't get a hair of his head, either.

For Bill was no fool, and he knew that Connie would stumble and Dave would see her for what she really was. And once he saw, he would see Rose also for what she was. Bill thought of that without much bitterness. He'd lost Rose before he had ever tried to win her, but she was there for a better man, and Dave Nash was the better man. And Rose loved him, Bill knew. All this being so, the important thing now was to save him for Rose.

Time, then, was the essence. Within the hour now, Ivey would flush him into whatever Bell hand had been sent to hold the trail around Granite Peak. They would close in on him and get him, and before midafternoon

Ivey would know he'd been following Bill Schell instead of Dave Nash and turn back for Dave. Bill thought then, *But suppose I don't even try for the Granite trail? Suppose I pull them on up into the boulder fields where they'll know they got me and hole up at dark for the shoot-out? It'll be morning before Ivey knows who he followed, and that means twelve hours more for Dave.* Bill chewed at this idea until, later in the day, he came to the faint trail he knew lifted up and around Granite Peak. He halted and looked at it a brief moment, and then shook his head, as if answering a question he had put to himself. He went on, but not on the trail; he was headed for the boulder fields.

He rode steadily all afternoon and at dusk he came to timber line, and kept on into the boulder fields until, at dark, he found a canyon whose only exit was its entrance. He did not bother to make camp, but turned his horse loose and picked a spot among the strewn boulders that gave him a little shelter from the bitter wind. He took all his shells out and laid them at his feet, and then rolled a smoke and waited.

It wasn't yet dark when the first rider tentatively poked his nose into the canyon. Bill shot at him, and the rider disappeared, and Bill heard him shouting. There were some more shots, and then answering shots, and Bill smiled thinly. The pack was gathering.

Sometime after dark, when the wind had died down, he rose to stretch, and there was a flat report of a rifle shot on the rim behind him. The bullet hit a boulder close to him and richocheted off into the night, and he ducked down.

And then Bill heard Frank Ivey's voice. "Nash, come out of there or we'll come in after you!"

Bill grinned delightedly, and he was only sorry he could not answer. He did the best he could and shot in the direction of Ivey's voice.

After that, Bill watched it take shape, and it was as thorough as Frank Ivey could make it. There were men around the rim of the canyon, and two or three inside it. It was cold and still, and his every movement seemed to register sharply in the night, bringing a shot at him. It would have been, Bill decided around midnight, an exciting game if the finish were not so obvious. Twice, he gathered up his remaining shells and moved to a different boulder, and once his movement was detected. He had to lie face down behind the cold rock and let them shoot in his direction because he had miscalculated in the dark and had no shelter.

He was cold now, and hungry too. A smoke would have been worth its weight in solid gold, but he did not dare strike a match. He kept moving stealthily to new boulders, but somehow the new ones always seemed colder than the last. The Bell crew wasn't moving much; they had him, and they could wait until daylight.

Along in early morning, he was shaking with the cold. This rock behind which he was crouching now seemed made of ice. He swore between chattering teeth, and picked up his gun and moved softly away in the darkness, heading back for his original rock. He moved slowly, noiselessly, stooping low so that his dark figure would not stand out among the gray granite boulders as he crossed the end of the canyon floor.

He saw his original rock, tall and almost white, and he slipped into its shelter. He squatted on his heels and put his hands under his armpits, because he was miserably cold. He felt the gun barrel touch his back, and his body was tensed and already moving when the thing hit him. It didn't hurt; that was the last thing he remembered.

The match flared and went out, and Frank Ivey cursed. The second match he cupped in his cold hands and knelt and put its guttering flame on the body at his feet.

When he saw who it was lying there, he let the match blow out and stood motionless a second.

Then he kicked the body savagely and walked away, calling angrily to the two men who were running toward him. "Wrong man! Saddle up!"

# CHAPTER XXV

THE house at D Bar was dark when Dave rode in, but there was a lamp burning dimly at one end of the bunkhouse. He put his weary horse down there, waiting for a dog to raise the night with his bedlam. But oddly enough, he crossed the yard and pulled up in front of the bunkhouse without raising anything.

And now the problem became more complicated. He did not think he could dismount without falling, but it had to be risked. He leaned his chest on the horn and brought his leg over and tried to lower himself gently with his one good arm. It did not have the strength and he fell heavily into his horse, which snorted and wheeled away. He clung to his mane, however, and stood there a moment, head hanging, trying to get to his feet.

He was aroused by a voice saying curiously, "What's this?" and he looked up to see Ben Dickason standing in the doorway, fully dressed, his eyes heavy with recent sleep. The lamp behind Ben laid its light upon Dave as, squinting against it, he looked up and said, in a voice drugged with weariness, "I've got to have a fresh horse, Ben."

Ben Dickason stepped out and halted briefly in front of him, and then turned and went to the bunkhouse door and called sharply, "Link! Link Thoms!" There was a wait, and then Dave heard Ben say, "Get this man a horse, Son. Better make it my black. And hurry it up." Ben came back to Dave now and said matter-of-factly, "Come inside and wait."

Dave tramped in behind him and sank into the barrel chair against the wall, tilted his head back, and closed his eyes. Ben regarded him with a look in which anger and compassion were oddly mixed, and in his eyes was quiet shock. Dave's wound had opened again and had bled through his coat. It had bled down his arm, too, so that his hand was caked with dried blood. His dark beard stubble was matted with blood and dirt, and his face above it was gray, his eyes sunken deep in their wells and stained almost a black underneath. He seemed a man on the thin edge of collapse.

Ben said, "You awake?" and when Dave opened his eyes Ben asked: "How far behind you are they?"

"Enough for this."

"That's Connie's horse out there, ain't it?"

"She was with us when they moved in on us."

Ben said swiftly, "Was she in on a fight?"

Dave shook his head in weary negation, too tired to explain, and the two men regarded each other in wretched silence. Dave said then, "Get her back here, Ben, where you can watch over her."

Ben didn't smile. "I've tried. She won't come. She hates my lights and liver."

Dave looked at him stupidly, as if he did not understand, and Ben said, "I've asked twice, begged her. I don't think I want her now."

Dave still didn't understand, but he saw Ben didn't want to talk about it.

Ben said, "So now what do you do?"

"Clear out of here, if I can make it."

Ben said, "You'll need grub. I'll have it before your horse is here."

He went out and Dave sat there, trying to puzzle out Ben's words about Connie through his leaden stupor. He went to sleep in seconds.

It seemed to him he came back from a long distance to feel somebody hitting his face, and he opened his eyes. There was some youngster, wide-eyed with alarm, standing in front of him. He had seen him before, but couldn't call his name.

"You went to sleep," Link Thoms said. "I couldn't wake you."

The urgency was here again, and Dave said, "Help me up," and he put out his hand and was pulled to his feet.

"Your horse is outside," Link said.

Dave walked toward the door, weaving drunkenly, his left arm dangling like some useless appendage, and Link followed him.

Outside, Link boosted him on his horse, and heard the low sigh of pain as Dave settled into the saddle.

Link handed him his reins then, and said quietly, matter-of-factly, "You don't need to worry about me, Nash. I'll keep my mouth shut."

"It don't matter now," Dave said wearily. There wouldn't be any hiding the fact that Ben had given him a horse.

Young Link said slowly then, "But what'll Connie do if they find out?"

Dave turned those words over in his mind, and they did not make sense, and he said thickly, "You'll have to make it plainer, son."

"What'll they do if they find out Connie ordered the stampede? They'll blame her for what happened to Crew."

Slowly, this sifted into Dave's mind, and he looked sharply at Link. He was awake now, his mind working. "Connie ordered what stampede?"

"Oh, Lord," Link said angrily. "Don't try to act like I don't know. I saw it happen. Ain't Connie told you I did?"

"No."

"Well, I did," Link said. "I was watchin' from the timber when Peebles and Bailey done it. I've talked to Connie. I promised her I wouldn't talk." He paused, puzzled. "But now you say it don't matter."

Dave leaned over and said slowly, "You saw Bailey and Peebles stampede those cattle?"

"Yes, I know what Connie and you planned. Don't treat me like I was nine years old!"

"And what did we?" Dave asked slowly.

"You aimed to blame Ivey for the stampede and pull

Crew in on your side. Well, you couldn't tell Ivey would kill him. It was hard luck. I'm not blamin' you and I won't tell anybody!" Link's voice was shrill with protest, and now he repeated, "But now you say it don't matter if they know. Who do I believe, you or Connie?"

"Connie told you to keep it quiet, did she?"

"Yes. In town. Yesterday."

Dave heard Ben Dickason returning and he said quietly, "You keep it quiet. Who are you?"

"Link Thoms."

Ben came up then with a flour sack partially filled with grub. He tied it around the horn of Dave's saddle, and then said, "You better not waste any more time."

"No," Dave said. "Thanks, Ben. I'll be back."

Neither Ben nor Link spoke, and Dave rode off into the night. He crossed the bridge and was soon on the road across the flats, and he sat slack in his saddle, beating his weary mind into accepting this.

He believed Link Thoms, and because he did he must accept the fact that Connie had ordered the stampede of her own cattle while he was away. It was designed, Link said, to put blame on Ivey and pull Crew over to 66. Yes, Connie would know how important that was, for hadn't he dinned it into her time and again? So she had made her treacherous bid for Jim Crew's help behind his back, and when it turned to disaster she had kept it from him. And Link Thoms, supposing it was a plan everyone at 66 shared, had in all innocence given it away tonight.

The whole sordid history of his time here now lay before him, and he felt a sick shame. From the start it had been wrong, cursed by ill luck and destined for disaster. He had made the mistake of thinking he must have riff-raff to beat riff-raff, of believing with a hard-headed pride that he could control his men. He had had doubts and Crew himself had expressed his pessimism. Rose, too, had not believed, though she had never said so. He saw now where he had made his mistake. When Bill Schell blandly protested his innocence in the killing of Ed Burma, Dave's instinct had been to doubt him. Instead of backing away then, he had bulled it through—to this end; that Connie, as shifty as Bill or Peebles or Bailey, had betrayed him and caused the death of Jim Crew. He had stuck against his own instincts, because of pity for her, and she had used him as shamelessly as she had used Walt Shipley.

He saw Connie now as he had not seen her before, and the seeing was something deep and shameful. Without her sweetness to hide behind, she was cold and scheming and ambitious as Frank Ivey. They were alike, really. Ivey had climbed to power on the necks of lesser men, and held it by ruthlessness. Connie was bidding for his power by the same method and, once she had it, would be just as ruthless. And he had been one of those men, just as Crew and Curley and Bill Schell had been.

He wondered then if Rose had seen this in Connie, and he knew she had. But she would never tell him, just as Bill would never tell him. Bill had held his silence out of some fundamental tolerance for the weaknesses he himself shared. Rose had held hers, because she knew a man must learn these things in his own way. She had had the wisdom to understand him, and now he knew why, when night overtook him in the mountains and he turned downward again, he was going to see Rose. He had planned, with a sick determination, to see her and to tell her that he was beaten, that his best was not enough, hoping desperately that she would understand. He knew now that he would see her still, but that he was not beaten. Not yet. Link Thoms had made the difference.

He came down the grade into Signal and found the town dark, except for the lights of the Special. Lilly's night lantern was burning and Rose's place was dark. For a moment he had an overwhelming desire to see Rose, and he knew he could not. From here on in, his hand was a lone one.

He glanced around him now, and his gaze fell on the dark office of Jim Crew. He looked at it curiously a moment, and then put his horse along the tie rail and rode him in behind the jail. There, in the weeds behind it, he dismounted. This time he fell, and he lay there a moment, fighting sleep. Afterward, he struggled to his feet and secured his horse, took the sack of grub, and then came out onto the boardwalk and tramped slowly up to the door of the office.

His hunch was right. The door was unlocked. He went inside and bolted the door behind him, and then crossed to the wall which held the gun rack. He took down a carbine and laid it on the floor, and then sank to his knees and lay down gingerly. He was asleep almost immediately, the food and the rifle at his head.

The bright sun of early afternoon reflected on the buildings across the street wakened him. He lay there a moment, feeling the ache in his face pressed against the floor boards, and then he pushed himself to his knees. His shoulder was stiff, and he could still not move his left arm, and he pulled himself against the wall under the window and sat there until the drug of sleep washed out of him. He saw the flour sack of food, and hauled it over and fumbled it open with his good hand. Cold meat and a piece of crushed pie were inside, and he ate them hungrily, trying to work some feeling into his left arm as he ate.

He was thirsty now, but he saw nothing in the room to satisfy it, and he forgot it. He crawled across the room, away from the window, and then stood up and looked across at the Special.

There were a half dozen Bell horses, mud and sweat dried on their flanks, tied there, and he surmised that Ivey had returned for food and drink after yesterday's fruitless chase. He was studying them for Ivey's horse when suddenly his attention narrowed, and then settled on a gray. He looked long, and then his lips thinned out imperceptibly.

The gray belonged to Bill Schell. Its presence here told a story that took little reading. They had got Bill. He thought of that for gray and dismal minutes, his back braced slackly against the wall, his eyes vacant and musing on the street. Bill had kept his word to the bitter end; he had pulled Ivey away to let Dave escape and he died doing it. It was his way of atoning for the misery he had created, Dave knew. In life, Bill had been impulsive and unreliable and weak; in death he had been steady, and dogged and strong with a selfless man's courage. He had been a friend.

And thinking this, Dave's attention roused again. He came erect, and moved toward the window. Across the street Rose was passing the Special. The sun touched her golden hair with fire under her small hat, and the sight wrenched at his heart. She was wearing a blue dress—his blue dress—and he thought then he had never seen a finer sight. He felt his spirit lift as he watched her hungrily. She, too, as she walked down the boardwalk, was looking over the horses. And then she stopped, staring at the gray horse too. She paused for only a moment, reading the story there, and then walked on, and Dave shook his head in obscure and angry protest.

A couple of men came out of the Special then and halted on the walk and turned toward the saloon. Three more men came out, and among them Dave saw the blocky black-clothed figure of Frank Ivey. The four men gathered about Ivey for a moment, and Dave saw his slow, incisive gestures as he gave his orders. Then the group split, and now Dave pulled the gun from the holster at his side and looked at it.

He raised his glance again through the window, moving toward the door, and then he halted. The four men were seeking their horses, but Ivey remained standing. He shouted something to them, and they pulled out and headed toward the grade, their horses in a tired walk.

Dave saw Rose come out of Bondurant's now and turn toward home. She passed Ivey without looking at him, and Ivey regarded her back a long moment, and then turned upstreet toward the hotel, walking solidly and slowly. He crossed the side street, and Dave opened the door and looked out. The Bell hands were just past the hotel, and Frank mounted the hotel steps and went in.

Dave waited in the doorway for many minutes, his patience edging him. A gunshot too soon now would call the Bell hands back into town, and he wanted Ivey alone. He waited, watching the hotel, smelling the warm dust of the street and the faint ammoniac smell of manure around the watering trough by the cotton-wood near by.

He was standing thus in the doorway minutes later when Ivey came out of the hotel and down the steps. He glanced about him, as a man will entering upon a street, and then his glance touched the sheriff's office. He walked on, stepping off the boardwalk, his glance still on the office, and then he halted abruptly in the middle of the cross street.

Dave knew Frank had seen and recognized him, and he stepped out onto the walk and ducked under the tie rail, heading toward the middle of the street.

Ivey, without speech or waiting, came toward him, and as he walked he brushed back the tail of his coat and pulled out his gun. And then, as if some overpow-ering impatience was driving him toward this moment, he started to run toward Dave, who stopped.

Ivey, running heavily, lifted his gun and shot, and only then did he seem to realize that this was not sense. He halted, and Dave's gun came up once and steadied and he fired. Ivey sat down abruptly, jarringly, and a surprised look came into his face, and he lifted his gun far past its natural arc and clubbed it down, and fired again, and dust geysered up at Dave's feet.

Dave stood utterly motionless then, his gun half lifted, and when he saw Ivey's gun lifting a third time, he leveled and fired swiftly, mercilessly, and was al-ready walking forward as Ivey fell over on his back.

Dave stopped then; Ivey rolled over on his face, and shoved himself to his knees, and with a massive and dogged strength came to his feet and turned slowly. He was bleeding at the mouth now, and his black eyes were terrible with death, and again his gun started to lift.

Dave watched it narrowly, and it came as high as Ivey's hip, but its barrel was down slanting, and then Dave's glance raised to Ivey's face. Ivey's head sank deep on his chest and he pitched to his knees and then full out, flat on his face, and his hat rolled off into the road and the dust roiled slowly around him.

Dave went over to him and stood looking at him, and now he was aware of people running toward him. He felt a strong hand on his arm, and he turned to find Connie, her face buried in his sleeve, shaking with fright.

Martin Bondurant turned Frank over and then let him fall back and looked up at Dave and shrugged. He was smiling, and the combination struck Dave as odd, and then he heard Connie say, "Oh, Dave, thank God!" And then, swift on the heel of it, "You're hurt again," and she tugged at his arm.

Docilely now, Dave fell in beside her, and they went up the hotel steps and through the lobby and up to her room. She went in first and tried to guide him to a chair, and he spoke then.

"I'm all right, Connie."

Connie was still trembling, and she turned away from him a moment, putting her hand to her forehead. "I—I can't stop shaking," she said.

Dave looked at the gun he still held in his hand, and then rammed it in his waistband, and said quietly, "It's all over, Connie, and you got what you wanted."

Something in his tone of voice, in the gray contempt of it, made Connie turn to look at him, and for a silent and terrible minute they regarded each other, and Connie said finally, "So you know?"

Dave nodded and started for the door and Connie ran past him and put her back to the door. "Wait, Dave. Wait before you judge me. Just wait a little is all I ask."

Dave halted, and he watched Connie's back straighten, and the cool desperation mount in her eyes.

"Would it make any difference to you if you knew I was sorry, bitterly sorry?"

"Difference?" Dave murmured.

"Oh, look at us!" Connie said desperately. "Don't you see what we've won, Dave? It's happiness and freedom and the way we want to live!"

"Why do you include me, Connie?"

"But 66 will be as much yours as mine! We're partners. We can get back our cattle and our ranch in the courts. Dad won't fight us. We've got something big and fine, and what does it matter now, except we've got it."

"But you'll have all that alone, Connie," Dave said gently.

"I don't want it alone!" Connie said desperately. Her eyes were bright and imploring and humble, and Dave felt a hardness coiling within him.

"So you don't want it alone, Connie," he observed. "Then I guess that squares everything. You don't want it alone."

He moved toward the door and Connie stepped out of the way and Dave opened the door. "Good-by, Connie. Good luck."

Connie's face was contained now, hard and beautiful and appealing. Only the eyes showed her misery as she said steadily, "I don't always win, you see. Good-by, Dave."

He stepped out and went downstairs and into the street, turning down it. A crowd was gathered around Ivey, still in the street. Bondurant broke away from it and came up to Dave. "A few of us are riding out to Bell tonight. I think we'll scatter that crew in short order."

Dave nodded and went on down past the Special, and when he got to Rose's place, he turned in. He did not ring the bell, simply walked in.

She had been sitting in a chair against the wall, and now, seeing him, she came slowly to her feet. The despair and sadness still lingered in her face, and only her pride covered it.

Dave closed the door behind him and looked long and hungrily at her, and then his face altered gently, and he said, "That's a beautiful dress, Rose."

She looked down at her skirt, her face stiff with uncertainty, and said, "It is, isn't it?"

"Would it do for a wedding dress?" Dave asked.

For one brief second Rose looked at him, and the light came into her face and her dark eyes, and Dave held out his arm. She was against him, then, clinging tight to him, her body warm against him.

## ABOUT THE AUTHOR

LUKE SHORT, whose real name was Frederick D. Glidden, was born in Illinois in 1907 and died in 1975. He wrote nearly fifty books about the West and was a winner of the special Western Heritage Trustee Award. Before devoting himself to writing westerns, he was a trapper in the Canadian Subarctic, worked as an assistant to an archeologist and was a newsman. Luke Short believed an author could write best about the places he knows most intimately, so he usually located his westerns on familiar ground. He lived with his wife in Aspen, Colorado.